Too Good to Hang

a&b

Too Good to Hang

A Bradecote
and Catchpoll Mystery

SARAH HAWKSWOOD

Allison & Busby Limited
11 Wardour Mews
London W1F 8AN
allisonandbusby.com

First published in Great Britain by Allison & Busby in 2023.

A CIP catalogue record for this book is available from
the British Library.

10 9 8 7 6 5 4 3 2 1

ISBN 978-0-7490-2943-2

Typeset in 11.5/16.5 pt Sabon LT Pro by
Allison & Busby Ltd.

FSC
www.fsc.org
MIX
Paper | Supporting
responsible forestry
FSC® C171272

Printed and bound by
CPI Group (UK) Ltd, Croydon, CR0 4YY

For H. J. B.

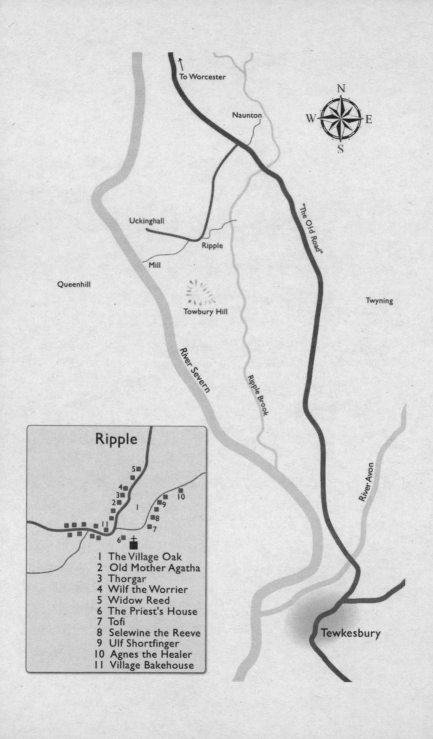

To Worcester

Naunton

N
W   E
S

Uckinghall

Ripple

Mill

"The Old Road"

Queenhill

Towbury Hill

Twyning

River Severn

Ripple Brook

River Avon

Ripple

5
4
3
2
1
10
9
8
7
11
6

1 The Village Oak
2 Old Mother Agatha
3 Thorgar
4 Wilf the Worrier
5 Widow Reed
6 The Priest's House
7 Tofi
8 Selewine the Reeve
9 Ulf Shortfinger
10 Agnes the Healer
11 Village Bakehouse

Tewkesbury

Chapter One

Ten days after Lady Day, April 1145

Spring, everyone agreed, had come a little early this year, and the plough-team had made very good progress in the Great Field. Easter would be late in April, and it was thought that nearly all the spring sowing would be complete by Holy Week. Overnight, however, there had been a storm, with howling winds and lashing rain, and that rain had persisted until noon, nature chastising the eagerness of man to claw the rich earth with blades of iron and bury his hopes of the harvest within the gashes. It had now eased off, but the unfurling leaves of the big oak, vivid in their fresh verdancy, wept sporadic 'tears' upon the scene playing out beneath them. A blackbird sang its sweet and melodious song into the ozone freshness, a song whose beauty belonged to a different world from the angry voices of the crowd that had gathered about one young man. Thorgar would normally have given thanks to Heaven for that song, appreciating God's creation, but right now he was breathing fast, and his desperate gaze passed over the crowd gathered about him rather than to the skies. He was confused, frightened and bruised from being dragged roughly from the church. He saw the blood lust in the eyes of many and, in some, a relief that what had been done would be paid for and the incident closed swiftly. Perhaps the priest could have held them in check, but Father Edmund was dead, a crumpled heap with lids not yet closed over unseeing eyes that outstared the living; that stare, the angry villagers surmised, was accusing.

'I found him, that is all. I saw the blood on his face and knelt to see if there was any slight breath to 'im, but there was none.' Thorgar's voice had urgency. He held up his hands in a futile plea for mercy, or at least a delay for consideration. The gesture looked as if he had just released a dove from his hold, for he could not spread them wide now that his wrists were bound. 'That was when Widow Reed saw me, and made the same mistake you all do now. It was not me.'

'But I saw you, heard you, Thorgar, this mornin', at the door of the priest's house. You was right angry.' A raven-haired young woman spoke up. 'I never seen you that angry afore, not ever. You raised your voice to Father Edmund, you did. Deny it not.'

'It – I-I was surprised, that is all.'

'About what?' It was Selewine the Reeve who asked the question.

'I had given 'im something to keep for me, and he would not give it back.'

'So you went and killed 'im. Was you checkin' that he was dead, or searchin' the body for what he kept back?' Selewine glowered at the young man, his face grim.

'I did not kill him. I went to Tewkesbury and on my return went to tell him I had been wrong.'

'What cause could you have to be there? 'Tis not a market

day.' A pock-faced man, with a resemblance to the reeve that shouted his kinship without need of words, came straight back at him.

'I went to the Abbey and came to speak with Father Edmund when I returned. I found him as I said. If Widow Reed had not raised the cry, I would have done so.' The bound man tried to catch the eye of others who might see good sense, but every man dropped their gaze as his found theirs.

'You says that to save your neck, but no good will it do you. The Law is clear, brother. If you will not act you are not worthy of your position as reeve.' The pock-faced man turned to Selewine, and the look between them was not fraternal love.

'I knows my duty, Tofi. Caught in the act you 'ave been, Thorgar, with the blood of Father Edmund upon you, and hang you must. None will swear oaths for you.' This was an assertion, almost a threat to any who might think of it.

'I simply found the body. You would see me hang because I said you nay, Selewine, that is all.'

'Nay to what?' The Widow Reed enquired, curious.

'He wants to marry Osgyth, and I said no.' Thorgar spoke with a sudden hint of hope. They would see reason, yes?

'Marry her? What foolishness is that?' the reeve's brother scoffed.

'But it is true.' A young woman, scarcely out of girlhood, let go of the hand of a weeping woman with a shawl pulled tight around her and three small children about her, and stepped forward. 'I did not want to marry him, what with Mother as she is. And besides, he is older than Father when he died.' She glared at the reeve. 'I will never marry you, upon my good oath.'

This divided the men between those nearest Selewine's age, who felt their manhoods insulted, and the younger men who quite saw how a maid would far prefer their looks and virility. There was muttering by both groups.

'I say again I had no cause to kill Father Edmund,' cried Thorgar.

'You says that, but 'e lies in the nave, dead,' came a voice, and the ripple of sound became one, and it was agreeing.

'Look, it was not my hand that killed him. I swear my oath upon my hope of Heaven.'

'Little hope you have of goin' to Heaven, killin' a priest in his own church,' a sharp-faced man snarled.

'Eternally damned, that is what 'e will be.' That was a woman's voice.

Thorgar's small flame of hope was snuffed out.

'Go home, Mother, Osgyth. I promise you I did no wrong. I am *unscyldig*.' He tried to keep the tremor from his voice, and his eyes pleaded with them to obey. Osgyth opened her mouth to remonstrate, and he repeated his command and vow of innocence.

Tears ran down her cheeks, and she held his gaze for a moment. Her mother set a trembling hand upon her arm, and the pair, with the frightened children clasping their skirts, turned and made their way back through the throng, which drew back as though they carried contagion. Once clear of them, Osgyth turned back one last time, and cried out to her brother and to the crowd.

'I will see justice done, Thorgar, upon my oath.'

'Stay a bit longer and you can see it now, right enough,' came a man's voice, and another laughed without mirth.

'Go. It is best,' murmured an older woman at the back of the crowd and now near to Osgyth, and there was at least compassion in her tone.

Thorgar begged for a priest to be called, but was met with a refusal. They would not wait for Father Ambrosius to be fetched from across the river, and the Severn was running too high for him to come this day.

'Father Edmund's death is not upon my soul. My death will be upon yours.' The tremor was in Thorgar's voice now. 'I am *unscyldig*.'

His pleas of innocence did not prevent a noose being placed about his neck, the rope cast over the oak bough, and Thorgar the Ploughman, son of Alvar who was ploughman before him, being hauled up and hanged.

Osgyth wetted her dry lips with the tip of her tongue. It had seemed so clear and simple when she had set off, in the predawn half-light, filled with righteous determination and no small degree of desperation. It had taken her all morning to cover the nigh on dozen miles northward to Worcester from Ripple, and she had been very aware that she was a maid walking alone, and at risk from the travellers upon the road from Worcester to Gloucester who might take advantage. She was tired, stressed, her feet were blistered, and now she was unsure of herself. Everything was too big and noisy and imposing. She had never been anywhere bigger than Tewkesbury, and certainly never seen a castle. She stood in front of its open gates, which she felt would crash closed behind her if she entered, and offered up a little prayer to the Holy Virgin to give her courage. Tears pricked her eyes, and she felt suddenly as if the burden not just of carrying out her promise to Thorgar, but of grief at his loss, crushed her so that she might fall to the ground.

'What is it, girl?' A woman's voice, half challenge and half-sympathetic enquiry, caught her unawares.

Osygth turned to the woman with a besom who had appeared at her shoulder, and whom Osgyth would call old.

'I have come all the way from Ripple, mistress, to seek justice, and now I am here, my heart fails me a little. None will listen in a place like that.' She nodded at the castle gateway. 'I asked at the priory about the lord Bishop as our overlord, not knowing where he lives, and then them at 'is palace told me he were north at Hartlebury, and I cannot get there and back to Mother this day. I thought to ask for the lord Sheriff, but . . .'

'Well, they will not hear you at all if you stays out here.' The voice was brisk, but then mellowed. 'And you go in at the gatehouse and ask for Serjeant Catchpoll, who will hear you, aye, and listen also, whether the lord Sheriff does or not. If he asks how you know of him, tell him there's bream goin' in the pot tonight. He'll understand then.' Mistress Catchpoll pushed Osgyth towards the gateway.

'Speak slow, and think first,' Catchpoll held up a hand, his voice calm. The girl who had been brought to him at first flooded him with words, though she did not need to give Mistress Catchpoll's message.

'My brother was hanged yesterday for a killin' he did not do, and the last thing I promised 'im was justice.' Osgyth tried to slow down.

'Very sisterly, but it tells me little. Where did this 'appen, who is he meant to have killed, and why do you think 'im innocent?'

'I knows it. He said it, and he would not lie.'

'Child, faced with a rope's end, most men would lie, and no blame to 'em for tryin'.' Catchpoll had heard such professions many times.

'No, no. He did not do it. I come from Ripple.'

'That's the lord Bishop's holding?'

'Aye, and it is our priest, Father Edmund, as is dead, yesterday, after noon.'

'So what 'appened?'

'I was bringing in turnip from the clamp when Alsi Longshanks came running to the house, yellin' that Father Edmund were dead and that my brother Thorgar killed him. He said they found 'im by the body with his hands all bloodied, and they was goin' to hang Thorgar from the Village Oak.'

'So it was a knife that did for the priest?'

'No, no, he was beaten and Thorgar found 'im, and then Widow Reed found 'im, Thorgar that is, and cried murder.'

'He was not seen actually beating the priest then?' Catchpoll wanted detail.

'No, but it did not stop him bein' hanged for it. He swore he was *unscyldig*, but Master Reeve and his brother said he was guilty, and had to be hanged and so they . . . they hanged 'im. They said it was the law, and they had to do it. They buried 'im without a priest and up by the Old Road, not in consecrated ground, Serjeant, and 'tis all wrong.' Osgyth began to weep, in part from relief that she had told her tale to someone in authority.

'That may be, or mayhap it ain't, but you wait here. Better still, go out the gate and over to the door next to the cooper's with the barrel outside, knock and tell my wife I says for you to wait with her. Whether your brother did it or not, there has been a killing, and of the lord Bishop's appointed priest at that, and it would be worth me comin' to see how things stand, if the lord Sheriff agrees.' Catchpoll did not say 'allows'. 'Go and rest your feet, and I will see what is to be done. Off you go.' With which he turned and headed across the bailey.

'I don't see as it makes much odds, Catchpoll. The man is dead, or rather both are dead and buried, and it is likely that this Thorgar was guilty anyway. It looks very like it.' William de Beauchamp had turned his attention from a letter being read to him by his clerk, and listened to Catchpoll's recounting of the situation.

'It looks it, aye, my lord, but I would feel the happier just checkin'. Also, if the lord Bishop asks you about his dead priest, you can tell him it was looked into.'

'True enough, though I prefer to keep away from Bishop Simon. He always manages to sound so disappointed about whatever I do, and prattles on about charity.'

Catchpoll hid a smile. William de Beauchamp was not a charitable man, in thought or deed.

'If you says as I can, my lord, we will go to Ripple today, and report back to you tomorrow. I doubts it will take long.'

'Fair enough, Catchpoll. But not just you and Walkelin. If we are to make a show of this, in case of Bishop Simon asking questions, I want my undersheriff to accompany you, since the dead man was the priest.' De Beauchamp gave a wry smile. 'Prising Underserjeant Walkelin from his new wife will make you popular with him.'

'Bein' sheriff's serjeant isn't about bein' popular, with anyone, my lord.'

'Except perhaps, me, Catchpoll?'

'If I happens to bask in your pleasure, my lord, rare as it is, that pleases me no end.' Catchpoll's face did not betray him by a single muscle, and de Beauchamp raised a sceptical eyebrow, then smiled. 'I will ready a horse and warn the wife. I doubts the fish she went to buy for this evenin' will keep beyond the morrow so it would be nice if all we has to do is confirm the right man was strung up.' Catchpoll sniffed, made obeisance, and left William de Beauchamp to the monotone of the clerk. He also sent a man-at arms to bring the underserjeant from the quayside, whence he had been sent to sort out a dispute.

Walkelin did not know whether to feel worried or important when the man at arms tracked him down, and returned at speed, arriving a little breathless and with the hint of a furrow between his brows, though he looked happy otherwise.

'You sent for me, Serjeant.' It was both question and statement in one, somehow indicating obedience to an order as a subordinate, yet hinting at something closer to equality. Walkelin also knew that if he asked it as a pure question, the answer he would get would be pithy, since of course Serjeant Catchpoll had sent for him.

'Aye, just could not bear to be without that grinnin' face o' yours any longer today.' Catchpoll's expression was of mock relief, but the tone was bantering. It was, thought Walkelin, far better than being told not to ask fool-headed questions. 'We is off to Ripple, 'bout as far south as we can go in the shire, to find out if a murderer has been hanged already or an innocent man taken, by chance or evil intent, for another's crime. You sorted out the problem between the two shipmen?'

'I did that, Serjeant. They was happy to see sense.'

'Never tell me they did because you threatened to take a spike and put a hole in both their boats? With the witless grin you goes around with these days, you could not "persuade" anyone. Troubles me, it does, for in all else you is becomin' a good serjeant, but . . .' Catchpoll sucked his teeth with a hiss.

'I did not threaten them, Serjeant. I just said as you would come and put a spike through both their boats, and mayhap someone's foot if they did not come to an agreement.' Walkelin's smile broadened into just the grin Catchpoll had bemoaned. 'Worked a treat, it did.'

Catchpoll was divided between pride that his reputation was such that even two men who plied the Severn, but never stopped long in Worcester, feared his retribution second-hand, and concern that Walkelin needed to be developing a reputation of his own, and not as everyone's cheerful and friendly face of the Law.

''Tis all very well and good, Young Walkelin, but you needs folk to do things 'acos of you, not me. If'n I's said it the once, then I's said it an hundred times; it is important that you can make folk think the better of doin' bad things for fear of upsettin' "the Serjeant", rather than us chasin' about after them when they has gone and committed a crime and faces worse than even what they thinks we could mete out.' Catchpoll shook his head. 'Gettin' wed has made it worse. You go about lookin' as happy as a rat in a granary, or rather as a man as has forgotten that night is for sleep, and 'alf of Worcester would like to put their fist in your face just out of plain jealousy.'

'I can't help bein' happy, Serjeant.' Walkelin blushed.

'No, but you can help lookin' like it.'

'And I doesn't like people bein' afeared of me.'

'You will live the longer if they do, and some of 'em also. Think of it as part of the duty, lad.' Catchpoll sniffed. 'Anyways, you won't be enjoyin' a sleepless night tonight unless the reeve of Ripple snores loud and long. Let your mother and that Welsh armful o' yours know you are away, and be back afore the bell for Sext. I wants you to ride first to Bradecote and fetch the lord Undersheriff, since the killin' took place on a manor of the lord Bishop of Worcester and the lord Sheriff has some reason of 'is own to want to keep Bishop Simon sweet at present. Catch me up on the Old Road to Tewkesbury as soon as you can. I will be goin' slower, for I will have the hanged man's sister up behind me, but we should be there afore it darkens.'

Hugh Bradecote made no comment upon Walkelin's demeanour, though he did ask why the Underserjeant had not abandoned his habitual mount, since Snægl had always been a cause of complaint from Walkelin.

'I would have thought you would have selected a more willing and er, less bear-coated, horse now you are established as the lord Sheriff's Underserjeant.'

'I know, my lord. I had intended to take another, but the beast gave me this long look, sort of sad and reproachful and . . .'

'Catchpoll will tell you you are too soft, Walkelin, and I think you will regret it before we are halfway to Ripple.'

'Oh, I was regrettin' it afore I even reached Bradecote, my lord.' Walkelin smiled.

'And what exactly takes us to Ripple? What do we know?'

Walkelin explained, and Hugh Bradecote sought out his lady with the hopeful expectation of returning home very soon.

Christina looked up from feeding the babe at her breast and smiled beatifically.

'We shall await your return, my lord, anxious only that you do so in good health. However, you must remember that you promised Gilbert that you would sit him up before you on your horse and ride three times about the bailey because he was a good boy this morning. Might I suggest that you do so before your departure, for I fear that otherwise I may be driven to distraction by his asking when you will be back.'

'I think that much delay will not be detrimental.' He bent and kissed her cheek, fondly, and she made a purring sound of appreciation.

It was thus only after Walkelin had seen his superior ride very slowly about his bailey with the infant Gilbert astride the big grey's withers and clasped tightly by his sire, that the two sheriff's men cantered out and headed towards the road that linked Worcester to Gloucester.

Catchpoll's reception from his wife was resigned rather than aggrieved. When he suggested the girl Osgyth sit up behind him on his horse, it occasioned no more than a womanly warning to her that if she was not used to it, sitting upon a horse would have her stiff of rump come next morning.

'And if you comes not back by sunset tomorrow, Catchpoll,

that fish is all mine.' With which admonition Mistress Catchpoll sent them upon their way.

He rode at a sedate pace, not wanting Osgyth to either fall off or grip him so tightly that she was snuggled up behind him. She was perhaps fifteen or sixteen, and Catchpoll knew it would be unseemly. If he could still enjoy the visual charms of a good-looking woman, it was always those twice Osgyth's age. He was old enough to be her oldfather, and it was certain that is how she regarded him.

After a while she began to speak, at first to cover the discomfort of silence. He let her talk, asking only the occasional question about the events of the day before, drawing from her the details without her dwelling upon them, and aware she might give him something of relevance to how things stood in Ripple, not just about yesterday's deaths.

'Selewine, the lord Bishop's reeve, is not a bad man, I suppose, not as a reeve. He just takes the position very serious, perhaps a bit too much, sometimes. Very full of "The Reeve of Ripple" as though t'were "King of England", if you understands me. He knows his tasks and responsibilities, but is a right dunghill cock for crowin'. It makes 'im think he is not just the most important man in Ripple, but the best catch as an 'usband.' Catchpoll could almost feel Osgyth's blush. 'He has buried two wives – the second he lost last summer to a fever. The other evening he came to Thorgar, as man of the house, and asked to speak privily with 'im. Turns out he had his eye on me for 'is next wife!' She sounded suitably surprised in a shocked and horrified way.

'Some would take that as a compliment,' suggested Catchpoll, to see what it would elicit.

'Some might, but not me, not ever,' Osgyth responded in a low and determined growl. 'Besides, Mother cannot keep the home and the little ones, her being stricken some years back, and not able to move her right arm. It is sort of curled up to her bosom and stuck there. Until Thorgar weds . . .' She gasped, and stifled a sob. 'How can I keep us all? Baldred is two years short of the tithing, and not a big lad, and the twins has but eight years come midsummer. They cannot do more 'n lead the oxen, at best, not guide the plough, and Thorgar and Father afore 'im was the ploughman in Ripple. We may well starve. I cannot dig and weed our strips and keep the home with but three young boys to aid me.'

Privately, Catchpoll thought there was a fair chance that a man, less old and off-putting to a girl than the unlamented reeve, might solve the family situation, but he said nothing of it.

'How old was Thorgar?'

'Only twenty years he had, and him not deserving to die. There were two more between Thorgar and me, but they died young.'

'Of an age to be thinking of maids, then.'

'Oh, I think he thought of them, but mayhap he was not quite sure which one.' Osgyth sighed. 'Not that Mildred, who is the fairest maid in the village, did not make it plain she wanted to be his choice. Always makin' eyes at 'im, she were, and givin' 'im such smiles as only a wife should give a husband, to my way of thinkin'. Even more than she did to all the other young men.'

Catchpoll could not see Osgyth's face, but could tell from her tone that she wore an expression of outraged virtue. Then he frowned at her next words.

'I wonders why she spoke up against Thorgar.'

'What did she say?'

There was a pause, and he felt Osgyth tense.

'What did she say, girl?' Catchpoll's voice dropped. It was not threatening but brooked no refusal to give up the information.

'She – she said as she had seen Thorgar very angry with Father Edmund early in the day, afore 'e went to Tewkesbury.'

'You mean the priest went there afore 'e were killed?'

'No, no. Thorgar it was as went.'

'Why did Thorgar go to Tewkesbury that mornin'?'

'I does not know, other than it rained hard overnight and was still rainin' well past dawn and the ground was too wet to plough or to sow where Thorgar 'ad finished, so he was free to go. Everyone did things indoors. In the forenoon I mended my brother Baldred's cotte where a bramble had broke a thread and ripped it.'

Catchpoll now had quite a list of Ripple villagers he would like to speak with directly, and matters he would like to mull over with both Walkelin and the lord Bradecote.

He did not have too long to wait, for the sound of horses loping along at a gentle canter made Osgyth turn her head in concern, as though she was about to be attacked by desperate outlaws. Who else, in her mind, would travel so fast and be catching them up? She was not much relieved when Bradecote's big, steel grey horse drew close enough for her to see the quality of the rider. Osgyth had never encountered anyone more important than the village reeve and priest until today, and had found it traumatic enough speaking with a haughty clerk at the lord Bishop's residence by the cathedral and then Serjeant Catchpoll. When Catchpoll introduced the rider as the lord Undersheriff of the shire she very nearly fell backwards off the croup of Catchpoll's horse as she attempted a sort of crumpling motion that indicated an obeisance. Bradecote found it hard not to laugh, and although he controlled himself well, his eyes danced.

'How are the knees, Serjeant Catchpoll?' Bradecote thought the question a suitable greeting.

'Holdin' me up as sturdily as ever, my lord, though I prefer to let Walkelin do the runnin' around Worcester. They doesn't bend as well as they once did, but then I 'ave made 'em bend a lot all these long years, so I mustn't grumble.'

Since grumbling about his stiff knees was something Catchpoll did upon a very regular basis, this did not make the humorous light in the undersheriff's eyes dim one bit, but it did so with his next question.

'So, we are looking into the death of the priest of Ripple, for which a' – he paused for a fraction of a moment, catching the tensing in the girl on the horse – 'price has been paid?'

'Aye, my lord, we are.' Catchpoll was not going to discuss his thoughts in front of the girl Osgyth, and instead told a somewhat rambling tale of a recent domestic killing in Worcester, which had not needed the lord Undersheriff to be called from his manor. Bradecote caught the look that told him anything on the current death would need to wait.

Chapter Two

It was mid-afternoon when the three horses turned off the well-used road to Gloucester, which was known as the Old Road, since it still showed, in its straightness and in hints of a cobbled surface, its Roman origin. They turned off it and along the gently descending trackway that led into Ripple, a village whose most fertile fields lay beside the waters of the Severn. Osgyth sniffed and caught a tearful breath as they passed a narrow strip of fresh-turned earth near where the track left the road. It was about the length of a tall man and a noose had been pinned into the earth with withy pegs. Beyond, sheep grazed the common and a man with a crook stood watchful over the remaining heavily pregnant ewes and many lambs at foot. A bulging bag was slung across his shoulder, which would have stones for his sling to keep crow, fox and raven from the vulnerable arrivals. The man spared but one glance at the strangers, and returned to his vigilance.

Catchpoll suggested that Osgyth dismount before they entered the village, and return to her mother, who would be worried about her absence. In reality he needed the time to relay what he had discovered to his companions. He also wanted them to arrive 'having heard of the death of the priest by violence', and thereby have all wondering how they had learnt of it so fast. It meant they would have an added advantage and authority over them. It was always good, he felt, to give the impression that the lord Sheriff's officers knew things by almost mystic powers, since most folk then doubted they could hide things.

'The reeve, Selewine, will be of interest to us, my lord, because his voice calling for a hangin' would be the most listened to, if these folk are as most in small villages, and "sheep" who leave big decisions to others.' Catchpoll, a man of Worcester through and through, always felt that townsfolk were more independent and less biddable than those who toiled in the fields, year in, year out. Walkelin, equally urban, would have agreed with him, but Hugh Bradecote, who had known the peasants of his manor all his life, saw this view as biased. 'What is more, he had a reason, mayhap, to think that Thorgar, the man whose neck felt the noose, stood in 'is way.' Catchpoll went on to explain what Osgyth had told of Selewine's marriage offer and rejection, and the failure of Thorgar to persuade his fellow villagers of his innocence.

'So we know that Thorgar was found by the corpse, and accusation of murder was made. I take it we do not know exactly how the priest died?' Bradecote was frowning.

'It is said, my lord, the priest were beaten bad, and that blood were upon 'is face and on Thorgar. If they hasn't buried the priest, and who would there be to do so, then we shall find that out soon enough. Since everyone is likely to be in the fields, we might visit the church first, nice and quiet like, and see both the body and where the priest died. That will give us truth when questions might get answers that is either plain false or just guessin'.'

'Agreed, Catchpoll. The "answers" you get from dead bodies never fail to be important.'

They were now reaching where the track broadened in what might loosely be called the centre of the village. A great oak stood there, freshly in leaf, and it looked as though the dwellings had given it space as water parts about a rock in the bed of a tumbling stream. The church was no more than fifty paces away. They tied the reins of their mounts to the church gate. It was a large church for a small village, though the parish took in hamlets some miles distant, and even across the river. Its decoration and weathered stonework showed it to pre-date the death of The Confessor, and it appeared that Bishop Simon was disbursing silver upon repairs to some part. The side walls of the north porticus were propped and a temporary structure, somewhere between a tent and a lean-to, roofed in oilcloth, was set against the church's north wall, halfway down the outside of the nave. The sound of an adze biting into wood came from within. Bradecote raised a questioning eyebrow and looked at Catchpoll. If there was work being done to the church, it was odd that the killer had risked discovery by a workman.

It was a cold afternoon, and both ends of the lean-to were draped with pieces of oilcloth that had too many holes to be used for a roof. Catchpoll stepped forward and drew one aside.

'Well, there's a surprise. I had not heard as you was away

from Worcester, Pryderi.'

A florid-faced man turned, his adze half raised. He did not look especially pleased to see Serjeant Catchpoll, but nor did he look worried.

'Well, see, we has been in Ripple this last eight days, me and young Gwydion 'ere, working for the lord Bishop, who knows a good man with the wood.'

'And doesn't know how often you lie senseless from the ale.' Catchpoll sighed. 'At least here you is less likely to be robbed of your pennies when you cannot keep awake.'

'You'll be 'ere about the priest, then.' Pryderi did not want to discuss his unfortunate weakness for drink.

'Aye, and since you are workin' on the church and is all set up out 'ere, the lord Undersheriff,' Catchpoll indicated Bradecote with his hand, 'and me too, would like to know what your ears and eyes told you.' He did not specifically include Walkelin, but the underserjeant did not take umbrage at that.

'Nothing. Nothing at all.' The words were swift, distancing the man from the deed.

'That seems unlikely.' Bradecote frowned, and the carpenter made haste to explain.

'I was ill yesterday. Never left my bed, and we are lodged with the reeve's brother, it being so cold of a sudden. We had hoped to sleep 'ere, but the weather turned the day we arrived, it did, and so we 'ave walls and a roof about us.'

'And Tofi's wife cooks a fine pottage.' The lad Gwydion, just at the point where the chest had broadened and the voice dropped, added his mite.

'So you was ale-sodden again. Mystifies me, it does, how

you keeps all your fingers, let alone work.' Catchpoll shook his head.

'It was not *tad*'s fault, Serjeant Catchpoll. Tofi kept refilling the beaker and saying "just a little more" until both of them could not stand. His wife spoke harsh words over him as she dragged him to their bed – Tofi, that is. I had to help her.' Gwydion, used to his father's failing, still defended him.

'But did you not work yesterday, lad?' Catchpoll looked at Gwydion.

'I did. There were pegs to make for the joints.'

'Yet you too can tell us nothing, despite being here?' The undersheriff folded his arms.

'No, my lord. Leastways, only for the forenoon. I saw Father Edmund come to say Sext, and leave afterwards.' Gwydion coloured a little, his face adopting more of his father's hue. 'He . . . he said the lord Bishop was paying for a craftsman, not an apprentice, and if there was another day without *tad* at his bench, he would make sure the lord Bishop heard of it. I finished the pegs just after that and, well, I did not want to ruin the wood with a badly made joint, so I stopped and went for a walk.'

'Went for a walk?' Pryderi looked at his son as if mad. 'Why?'

'I . . .' The lad looked at his feet and shuffled them.

'Why, Gwydion *bach*?' the father repeated.

'Tofi's daughter dared me to go up the hill yonder, where the old banks and ditches are among the trees. She said there were *ysbrydion* there, the spirits of warriors from many generations before the village even existed, and when they gets to tithing age, all the village boys go up there alone to prove their manhood.'

He pointed to the wooded hill just beyond the village, where an Iron Age hill fort slept beneath its patchwork coverlet of ash, oak, holly and birch.

'Pretty, is she?' enquired Catchpoll, with a wry smile. The boy blushed more furiously. 'So when did you return from this brave feat?'

'When all the excitement was over, and they had hanged the man who did it. I just saw them take him down from the oak, that is all.' Gwydion clearly felt he had missed something far more exciting than a potential encounter with a ghost.

'And the work is delayed today, look you, since it would be unseemly to be working, hammering in pegs and climbing the ladders, with a priest's corpse before the altar, and a priest dead by violence at that.' Pryderi sounded as if Father Edmund had sought his own demise just to be inconvenient. 'They cannot get the other priest back across the river, or leastways not until tomorrow now.'

'The other priest? What other priest?' Catchpoll looked genuinely taken aback, which was rare.

'Why, this is a large parish, with some parts lying on the other side of Severn, and has had two priests for generations. Father Ambrosius, the other priest, had to go across to a woman who was long in travail, and was feared might die. That is what I 'eard, but it might not be that exactly. Anyways, he is away, and so it will be the morrow when we can get back to finishing our repairs to the porticus roof trusses.'

Bradecote thought there was nothing much to be gathered further from the treewright and his son, and glanced at Catchpoll, who gave a small nod.

'We will let you get on with what you can out 'ere, then, and see where the killin' took place.' Catchpoll did not add that they would be inspecting the body also.

'*Diolch yn fawr.*'

'Hmm.' Catchpoll understood the thanks, but did not appreciate them in Welsh.

The sheriff's men entered the church by the west door, their eyes adjusting to the lower level of light within, genuflected and crossed themselves, and walked up the nave, with Catchpoll to the fore, casting his gaze over every flagstone for some indication of where the attack itself took place. It was just before they reached the chancel arch that he raised a hand to halt his companions, and, with a grumble, crouched down towards one side.

'Been cleaned, o'course, but that is what tells us the place. Not often a church floor is scrubbed not swept, and especially not just one bit of it. Too clean is this, and you can see there is traces of mud t'other side, from the feet of the *treowwyrhta* Pryderi and his lad as they brings things in and out.'

Walkelin, with the ease of youth, also squatted down, and looked very hard where Catchpoll was now pointing.

'Missed a bit here, Serjeant, in the crack between two flagstones. That's dark, and dried blood, yes?'

'Your eyes is better 'n mine, so I will not doubt it.'

'But this we would discover anyway, when we speak with the reeve and those who dragged Thorgar from the church. At this stage the body is far more important, even if,' Bradecote conceded, 'we then find it was not he who killed the priest.'

29

'True enough, my lord, but it is good to know things before we is told, and very bad to be taken by surprise, as we was to hear there is more than one priest to this parish.' This clearly rankled with Catchpoll.

'In Worcester you might have reason to grumble but here, in a place we do not know, our ignorance is no shame upon us. And' – the undersheriff added with a small smile – 'we will sound very knowledgeable to the villagers when we ask about Father Ambrosius.'

'There is that.' Catchpoll looked visibly cheered. 'You are right, my lord, and the dead will likely be of far more use to us than a cleaned floor.'

They approached the shrouded corpse, laid upon boarded trestles before the altar, and Catchpoll uncovered the head, carefully drawing back the cloth. They looked into the face of Father Edmund, pinched and waxy in death, and were surprised for a second time that day, but this time by the degree of violence meted out to the priest. It was the face of a man of fewer than thirty years, at best guess, with chestnut hair ringing the tonsure, high cheekbones and what had been a straight, sharp nose, though it had clearly been broken before death and was freshly misaligned. Bradecote found himself thinking of a fox. Any blood upon the face had been cleaned away, but it was obvious that he had been badly beaten, for purple-blue bruises discoloured cheek and jaw. The stiffness of death was easing, and Catchpoll found no difficulty in parting the lips, naturally thin but puffed and split from a blow, revealing a missing lower tooth at the front, the gum raw and damaged.

'Someone really did not like you, Father. I wonder why?' Catchpoll mused.

'Who would do something like this to a priest?' Walkelin was shocked, not at the physical damage, but the idea of such a thing.

'Someone who felt they had a very good reason, and I imagine who lost their temper when they confronted him.' Bradecote was frowning. This was, to his mind, something that had been done in the red mist of anger.

'Which makes us ask what that reason could be, even afore we asks who.' Catchpoll was now uncovering the rest of the body.

'But who should not be hard. No woman could do that, and the man that did will bear the marks upon 'is hands for sure.' Walkelin sounded confident.

'Ah, but look harder and you will see them bruises are not many of 'em from knuckles. Think of all the fights you have broken up in Worcester, Young Walkelin, and the faces of them as gets the worst of it. The broken lip and missing tooth, well them was a fist, quite possibly, but for the rest, no. Our angry man, and yes, it feels all wrong to have been a woman, felled him with that first blow, I should think, and then gave him a good kickin', if you look at the marks on the body and arms as well. I think the arms was raised in defence of the face for a bit, but the attack continued even after all resistance ended. The face shows that.'

'I suppose he stopped when Father Edmund was dead,' decided Bradecote.

'Ah.' Catchpoll, studying the contusions upon the body

more closely, pulled a face. 'Now that makes things even more interestin'. You see there, my lord? It was neither fist nor foot that actually killed 'im.' He pointed to a puncture mark between the ribs.

'It makes no sense to beat a man to this degree and then stab him. And the beating was not after death, for that makes even less sense. So this means that we may have two people who wanted their priest dead, and on the same day. The second one came in, saw him senseless upon the floor and stabbed him.' Bradecote looked puzzled and rubbed his chin, thoughtfully.

'It would certainly give a good reason for the man who did the beatin' to think that they were the killer, even if they did not stab him, and who is to say that the injuries within might not have killed him anyways, even without the stab wound.' Catchpoll was also frowning.

'Which means we have one soul who knows they did it, one who thinks they did it, and unless it was Thorgar as stabbed Father Edmund, a dead man who was wrongly believed to 'ave done it.' Walkelin spoke assertively, and Catchpoll hid a smile. Coming along nicely, was Underserjeant Walkelin.

'Which means two people knew Thorgar was innocent, if he did not do it.' Bradecote folded his arms and sighed. 'This becomes more tangled. Would the knuckle-skin of the man who attacked first be broken, Catchpoll?'

'Not for sure, my lord, not if the man had wrapped a cloth about his fist a couple of times as well. If he planned the beatin' he might 'ave done that, 'acos afterwards a bruised hand would show 'is guilt even to villagers who never thinks about hows and whys with crimes.'

'I would say it was planned to a degree, because what could suddenly anger a man so much if he had an arranged meeting with his priest in the church, yet also the degree of violence looks uncontrolled. This is like – some boil that bursts. Whatever their reason, it had to be very, very strong.' Bradecote tried to think of a reason and failed.

'We is forgettin' that whoever washed and shrouded this body must 'ave seen the wound.' Walkelin was thinking his own way through events. 'So they knew it was not the beatin' as did for their priest. I wonder if they has already told everyone they made a mistake?'

'Not everyone has eyes like ours, and mayhap with quite a lot of blood smeared about they did not make the connection, though I doubts it,' Catchpoll cautioned. 'We must speak with whoever came and made all tidy. We also needs to find out what was used to stab 'im. That is no knife wound. It is smaller and round—'

'Like a *treowwyrhta's* awl?' suggested Walkelin.

'Just like that. I wonder if Pryderi found an awl missing or out of place this morning?' Catchpoll's eyes narrowed. 'If he did not know the priest died other than from being beaten, he would not connect the two, and probably just berate 'is son for not keeping all tidy.'

'Do we say that there is no chance that it was he or the lad who killed Father Edmund?' asked Bradecote, and raised a hand as Walkelin opened his mouth to respond. 'Yes, I know the man was "ill" yesterday, but I doubt he was seen to be so every minute of the afternoon. It even means that the boy Gwydion might possibly have been involved. What if the father had beaten the priest and the son finished him off? Unlikely, yes. Impossible, no.'

'Doesn't ring true to me, though, my lord, 'specially the second part. I knows Pryderi in Worcester, and he is not a man of violence or swift to wrath, and what could have raised a killin' passion against a priest he did not know in just a week?'

'I agree, Catchpoll, but the thought has to be entertained, even if to be dismissed.'

'If Pryderi's awl was used and replaced, then surely it cannot have been Thorgar as did the deed, for why would 'e come back to the body afterwards?' Walkelin was arranging his thoughts out loud.

'You are right, Walkelin. It makes Thorgar look suddenly even less guilty to us, though most of the villagers would have still assumed death was from the beating.' Bradecote wanted to be fair.

'The thing is, if Thorgar did not kill the priest, then someone else did, and the chances of it being someone just happenin' to be passin' by and with a sudden urge to commit murder are as likely as me bein' made Archbishop of Canterbury. It also means two knew they were hangin' an innocent man and was prepared to watch it done to save their own necks. Now that is nigh as good as another murder, to my mind.' Catchpoll looked grim.

'It will be interesting to see the faces of the villagers when they realise what they have done, if Thorgar is shown to be innocent, not that it will do his family much good. I would also say that if he was found with the body, but not seen in any act of violence, then a summary hanging was not according to law, but a village reeve might not know the difference.'

'Then best we speak with the reeve, the woman who raised the alarm, and also the washers of the corpse. Whatever their answers, I doubts we will be ridin' back to Worcester tomorrow. A pity that is, for I will miss my fish for dinner.' Catchpoll sighed.

Since it was the sowing time and the weather was again clement, most of the population were in the year's productive field, bent over with aching backs to dibble the peas into the earth or broadcasting the grains that would bring them wheat come late summer. This great field lay on the fertile land to the south and west of the village, though the border of osiers on the riverside spoke of the winters when flooding might conceal ridge and furrow beneath the rain-broadened Severn and duck and goose float serenely upon it. Catchpoll asked to 'make the introductions' because, he averred, he could make the lord Undersheriff sound even more important. Hugh Bradecote wryly commented that he had never felt ignored as an undersheriff, and always thought he looked suitably 'lordly'.

'Oh, there's no doubt you do, my lord, and especially on that horse o' yours. No amount of talkin' could increase your importance if you rode that hair shirt of a beast that Walkelin bestrides.' Catchpoll grinned.

As if insulted by this, Snægl shook his head, and the tremor ran along his shaggy mane to the withers.

'Ah, but that means I gathers up all as is afeard of a noble lord's power, and afeard of Serjeant Catchpoll's . . . er, bein' 'imself, and so they tells things to me, Underserjeant Walkelin, who looks to be on their side and rides the "hair shirt".' Walkelin spoke not in jest but all seriousness, though he allowed himself a small smile.

'That you do, Young Walkelin, that you do.' Catchpoll nodded, approvingly. 'Now, my guess is the reeve is the fair-haired man who is pointin' a lot and bendin' little. Shall we see if I am right, my lord?'

'Yes, though I agree with you, Catchpoll.' Bradecote smiled, then schooled his features into a suitably haughty 'lord Undersheriff' seriousness.

The sight of three horsemen riding towards them along one of the ridges of earth caused heads to rise in a ripple effect as one alerted the next. They stared, and Catchpoll made a cursory assessment of them.

'You, there, are you Selewine, the reeve of Ripple?' Catchpoll sounded the voice of authority, and seeing he was in company with a lordly-looking man on a fine beast, Selewine did not respond with a question about who wanted to know, but nodded, looking cautious.

'Then we needs to speak with you, aye, and all here, about the death of your priest, Father Edmund, and the hangin' of Thorgar the Ploughman. I am the lord Sheriff's Serjeant, come with the lord Sheriff's Underserjeant, and the lord Bradecote, lord Undersheriff of the shire.'

Bradecote thought Catchpoll had rather overstressed the 'lord' element, but the reaction was everything that Catchpoll could have wanted. Everyone stared at them with a mixture of awe and stupefaction. Not only had these important men come among them, but they knew everything that had happened only the previous afternoon.

'Everything was done right and proper,' declared Selewine, sounding defensive and wary. 'Pity it was to 'ave to do it, but there, that is the Law.' He paused. 'Why should the lord Sheriff wish to learn more of a village matter that is dealt with?'

'Suffice to say, he does.' Something about Selewine annoyed Hugh Bradecote, so he played the autocratic lord who could not care less what menials might think. He looked down his long nose, and from the height of his big horse, at the reeve and made him feel small, just as he intended. If this was the dunghill cock hereabouts, then he needed to know his dunghill was barely worth stepping around.

'I meant no discourtesy, my lord.' Selewine took a step back and belatedly grabbed the woollen cap from his head to clasp between his hands, revealing thinning hair with a pink scalp just showing through. The action was submissive, but his look was still questioning.

'The lord Bishop will also want to know all the details of the killing of a priest he himself sent to this parish,' Bradecote continued.

Walkelin felt something, as did Catchpoll, or rather an absence of something. What was it? Both made a mental note of it, whatever it was.

'Well, that is easy to do, and could 'ave been told to a clerk.' Selewine was still worried by the extent of shrieval power before him. 'He was beaten to death in the church by Thorgar the Ploughman, who was hanged for the deed.'

'So he was seen in the act of murder?' Bradecote raised

an eyebrow. 'Did he attack the priest in front of the whole congregation at Mass?'

'No, no, my lord, but as good as in the act. Widow Reed' – the reeve pointed towards a woman who paled but bobbed a curtsey – 'saw Thorgar kneeling over the body of poor Father Edmund and raised the alarm.'

'And where was it that you finally caught up with him?'

'Why, he did not run, my lord. We found him by the body.' Selewine looked surprised.

'So this violent killer just waited, nice and peaceable, to be taken, did 'e? Not common, that.' Catchpoll sounded quite casual. 'I wish as most of them we takes was as easy.'

'Indeed, Catchpoll. And he admitted his guilt straight away?' Bradecote once more addressed the reeve.

'No, that he did not, my lord.' Selewine responded, cautiously.

'He cried that he was *unscyldig* right up to the moment the noose tightened,' offered a male voice from among the villagers, who were now crowding together to hear what was said and in an unconsciously defensive act.

'The Law does not allow for summary justice, just because you decide someone is guilty of a crime, and especially if they do not admit guilt. The correct action was to hold this man, and send to Worcester for me to bring 'im in, and for investigation to be made.' Catchpoll looked grim.

'How do you know he killed the priest?' Bradecote kept up the questions.

'Because 'is hands were bloody, and Father Edmund's face were a mess, all bloody and broken.' Selewine felt a bit more confident about this, and a murmur of agreement went round the crowd.

'Where on 'is hands?' Catchpoll's voice was very even.

'What do you mean?' Selewine frowned.

'It is a simple question, Master Reeve, so answer the serjeant. Where was the blood on Thorgar's hands?' Bradecote was as calm.

'All over his palms and fingers.' Selewine held up a hand and pointed, as though Catchpoll might not know what a hand looked like.

'So you are saying the priest was slapped to death?' Catchpoll pounced.

'No, of course not but—'

'And was Thorgar searched for any weapon other than these, er, vicious palms?' Bradecote leant forward, one arm over his saddle bow.

'What need was there, my lord? There was nothin' on 'im when we stripped the body when it was taken down, other than his eatin' knife in his belt.'

'We have seen the body,' declared Bradecote, 'and Father Edmund died from a stab wound to the chest.'

'Well, I does not know why Thorgar did that too, but he must have used that knife, then.' Selewine held his ground.

'Except that the weapon used was not a knife, but a thin, sharp instrument.'

'Mayhap he hid it?' Selewine's confidence crumbled.

'And then went back to look long and lovingly at 'is handiwork? I thinks not,' scoffed Catchpoll.

'You mean we 'anged the wrong man?' The voice was female.

'Looks very like it.' Catchpoll turned his gaze from the reeve to the crowd and could almost see the cloud of collective guilt descend upon them as the rain-heavy mist might smother the tops of the distant Malvern Hills.

'Poor Thorgar.'

'He was always a good and quiet soul.'

'Helpful.'

The mutterings grew into an encomium.

'Yet you forgot all that and strung 'im up swift enough.' Catchpoll did not disguise his disapproval. 'And what we wants to know now is, since it looks very much as if Thorgar did not kill Father Edmund, who did?'

It was then that the villagers of Ripple became fearful.

It could not be said that Selewine looked fearful, but rather disbelieving.

'But how could we . . . ? We was sure enough . . . And who would want to kill Father Edmund?' He turned to his neighbours, and what all three of the lord Sheriff's men saw this time were quite a few faces that could imagine just such a thing. It was also interesting that Selewine did not seem to see it, or be of that faction. Finding out more about Father Edmund would be very useful, if folk would speak their thoughts.

'We would speak with any who knew of a grievance against Father Edmund, and the Widow Reed and whoever it was who washed and shrouded the body must come forward. We needs to know how the corpse looked afore it was tidied.' Catchpoll made it seem a small but useful detail.

'If you think you know anything that will aid us you may

speak with me, with Serjeant Catchpoll, or with Underserjeant Walkelin, and need not speak before all.' Bradecote realised this opened them up to receiving not just gossip but malice between neighbours, but he could not see any of these people stepping forward to denounce the cleric before all and sundry. He noticed several glances towards Walkelin, and correctly guessed that the timorous would be approaching him rather than his superiors.

'If it was a sharp thing, then the Welshmen did it.' It was a young, male voice. 'They has all manner of tools hard by the Church, and you know what they says about the Welsh.'

There were several nods, but as many looks of puzzlement. 'What they says about the Welsh' was clearly not widely known. However, it clearly sounded a good idea to many that whoever did this was not from the village, and there were mutterings.

'Well, I has 'eard many things said about the Welsh, and said some myself, but never have I 'eard that they kills priests for no reason, and the *treowwyrhta* is well thought of as a craftsman by the lord Bishop, so he would not risk losing 'is custom even by a suspicion of such a crime.' Catchpoll did not discount Pryderi, not until he had more knowledge, but he did not want him hounded by the Ripple community, even if he was Welsh.

'It looks very much as if one man has died unnecessarily because of leaping to conclusions. Leave this up to the Law.' Bradecote sounded stern. Feet were shuffled in the damp earth. 'And we would speak also with you, Master Reeve, alone. The priests' house is, I take it, empty until the return of your other priest?'

'Yes, my lord.'

'Then we will go there so as not to be a burden upon any

one household, but would have food and drink provided to us. You will show us the house, and when we have spoken privily with you, we will speak with the Widow Reed and the person who shrouded the body, who is . . . ?'

'Agnes, who is our healing woman.' Selewine pointed to a thin-framed dame of middle years, who pursed her lips. Bradecote hoped they would not stay so firmly closed upon questioning.

'We also need stabling for our horses.'

'Yes, my lord.' Selewine's normal cocksure manner had deserted him, although only briefly. 'If you will follow me.' He then turned to the crowd of villagers and raised his voice. 'And there is still another good hour or so of daylight, so them as is not called forward remember that talk is for the fireside and there is work to be done.'

Chapter Three

The priests' house was, unlike most of the village homes, of stone up to the height of a man's thigh, though it was thatched as all the other dwellings were and was of a generous size for just two men. It looked as if constructed in part with leftover stone from the original building of the church. Selewine opened the door and stood back for Bradecote and his subordinates to enter.

The chamber was sparsely furnished, as befitted men for whom worldly goods had no real meaning. There were two wooden cots at one end, each close to a side wall as if keeping as far from the other as possible, and between the head of each hung a wooden cross upon the end wall. A long, narrow chest, which might also serve as a seat, was set lengthwise down the middle as a very visible division of the space. There was a cold hearth, with the ashes from the last fire still upon the stone, a simple table, two stools, and a shelf with beakers, a jug, bowls and basic cooking utensils above pottery crocks that would contain flour and dried pease. There was a vague smell of old fish and, as Walkelin entered, a small, black cat rushed past him and went to snatch a fish head from behind a crock. It glared at them, back arched, since hissing was difficult with a mouth full of fish, daring them to take its prize, then made its escape.

'Father Ambrosius is a good fisherman, and generous with what he catches too, not only to our poor, but Oldmother Agatha's cat. I think she, the cat that is, likes to come and curl up on his lap and remind him she likes fish. Mind you, Father Edmund could not abide her presence. I wonder if that was half the appeal to Father Ambrosius.' Selewine gave a short laugh.

This might account for the smell, but there was something not right in the priests' house. The clergy were tidy, ascetic souls who liked things orderly, and yet the blanket on one bed was a little askew, the pissing-pot showing from beneath the other, and the chest showed the corner of a piece of charcoal-coloured cloth peeping from beneath the lid. Bradecote said nothing, but glanced at Catchpoll, and saw the flicker of mutual agreement cross his face. Someone other than a priest had been in, and had probably been seeking something. Well, they could think about that later. First, they needed to get all they could from Selewine the Reeve.

'How long have you been the reeve of Ripple?' Bradecote's first question made the man blink.

'Why, nigh on ten years, my lord, since my father died. He was reeve afore me.'

'And is it a peaceable manor? Do the folk get on with one another?'

'Aye, my lord, barrin' the odd squabble between women over the bushes they lays their washin' over, and lads who find they has eyes for the same girl. Ordinary stuff, my lord, and nothin' as would lead to a death.'

'And you have not had cause to think Thorgar violent.' This was not a question.

'No, my lord. A shock it was that he could turn like that. A big, peaceful lad, not unlike his oxen, other than he had more brains.' Selewine shook his head. 'There seemed no other explanation than he had killed Father Edmund, though, and everyone agreed it.'

'You mean nobody raised an objection once you put it before them,' growled Catchpoll. 'I knows sheep when I sees them, and the folk in that field are sheep on two legs. You shepherds 'em and they will be biddable. When did one last say nay to you, Master Reeve?'

'No, no. If you is tryin' to say it is all my fault Thorgar is dead you are wrong. Why, it were my brother Tofi who said first as 'e must hang, and it were my duty as reeve to see it done. And his daughter Mildred, who were as sweet as a maid might be on Thorgar and be a maid still, she cried clear and loud that Thorgar had been at odds with Father Edmund that very morning, raisin' his voice and wavin' his arms about, which were not like him at all. It all fitted.' There was a touch of desperation to Selewine's voice now.

'Then we must speak with this Mildred and hear from her own lips what she saw. Make sure she knows to come to us after the healer.' Bradecote paused. 'Is it not to your advantage that Thorgar, the only man grown in his household, is no longer present to object to your taking his sister to wife?' The question was put very evenly.

'How did . . . ? No, of course not,' spluttered Selewine, colouring.

'Well, you can see as why the lord Bradecote asks, Master Reeve, 'acos if there is no man to say you nay, the path looks a lot less stony. At least it does to me and Underserjeant Walkelin 'ere.' Catchpoll nodded towards Walkelin, who concurred.

'Not used to anyone sayin' you nay, I dare say.' Walkelin sounded very reasonable. 'Must 'ave been a surprise, and not a good one, eh?'

'It has nothin' to do with my decision.' Selewine was flustered.

'So it was your decision. Glad we sorted that out.' Catchpoll smiled, slowly, and with eyes that remained quartz hard. Logic said it had to have been, but it was good to keep Selewine worried and more eager to assist them. The man babbled about having no choice, being sorry and it not being his fault, and Catchpoll dismissed him to bring Mildred.

The Widow Reed was in her thirties, as best as could be judged by Bradecote, and the sort that missed having a husband, not just for the security of food upon the table and digging in the garden patch. She was like a flower just past full bloom, with petals a little bedraggled and browned, but still showing the form of its prime. She held a scrap of cloth, which she dabbed to her eyes even as she made her obeisance, and immediately launched into self-exculpation. It was not her fault Thorgar had been hanged.

'This is not about blame for his death, but about what you saw, and even did not see.' Bradecote wanted to make sure the Welsh apprentice, Gwydion, was absent as he had said. 'Why were you in the church?'

'It were time for None, and since we was not in the fields I thought it would be good for my soul to go and listen to poor Father Edmund say the Office.'

'Had the bell been rung?'

'It had not, but the rain were stopped and the sun come out a little, so I knew the hour was about right. I could always sit awhile in prayer if early. But it were odd that the bell was not rung. I did not think of it at the time, but oh, poor Father Edmund. Such an awful thing to happen.' The cloth was deployed to the corner of her eye.

'So you went to the church. Was anyone else about outside?' Bradecote did not specifically ask about the apprentice.

'Nobody. Mind you, the rain had only just stopped, which were why I decided to leave my spinnin' and go to church.'

'Are the Offices of the Day usually well attended?' Walkelin enquired.

'Not unless there is a saint's day or festival, though Compline sees more when it is after the day's work is over but afore we is all in our beds. Often it were only me and poor Father Edmund.'

'Did Father Ambrosius not attend also?'

'Oh, yes of course, but I did not count 'im, and also he is often over the river. I think poor Father Edmund were happier when he was. I ought not to say things of a priest, but I do not think Father Ambrosius liked poor Father Edmund.'

It was clear that to Widow Reed, the dead priest would always be 'poor Father Edmund'.

'And when you entered the church, what did you see, exactly?' Catchpoll wanted details.

'Thorgar, bent over poor Father Edmund's body.'

'And what did he do?'

'He turned around and looked at me. I screamed and he half got up and I ran outside crying "murder" and knocked upon Selewine the Reeve's door, and Tofi 'is brother's, and cried they must come quick. They went together to the church, bein' brave, and they said to knock upon folks' doors, so I did and everyone came out, and they dragged Thorgar from the church to the green and . . . he looked guilty. He was over the body.'

'Astride it? Holding up the shoulders?' Catchpoll pressed for more.

'No, not that. Sort of knelt close to the head and facing away from me, so I could see 'is back. Sort of under an armpit, for one of poor Father Edmund's arms was flung out.' The woman threw out her own arm to the side to illustrate this. 'I did not recognise it was Thorgar in the first moment, just a murderer, but of course I did when he faced me. So unlike him it was – to do it, not the look, you understand.' She looked from Catchpoll to Bradecote and back.

'So you knew Father Edmund was dead?' Bradecote guessed she had leapt from one conclusion to another but wanted to check.

'Well, 'e was not movin' and I could see blood upon the floor.'

'Did you see anything else? A weapon?'

'Nothing more, my lord. No stick or staff.'

'Or anything smaller?'

'No, but if you had seen the body, my lord, the bruises upon his poor body and head . . .'

'You saw those?' Bradecote frowned. The reeve had said it

was the village healer who had tended to the shrouding.

'I did. Mother Agnes went to do what was needed, but I-I wanted to do this last thing for poor Father Edmund also, so I joined 'er. Cruel it were, what were done to the poor man, so cruel.' She sniffed. 'There was blood everywhere, and one of 'is teeth was lost. I suppose it were swallowed, for I looked and could not find it in the habit or on the nave floor.'

'And who lifted the body onto the trestles, and indeed set them up?'

'Oh, the Welsh boy brought the trestles from where they is stored, for the workmen 'ad been told not to use them in their work. He offered the help. Poor Father Edmund was a slight man, not fat or bulky, and it was easy enough for the lad and Mother Agnes to roll him onto a blanket and carry him to the trestle table. He were very polite and asked if there were anything more we needed, then left. We removed the clothes,' she sighed, 'and washed the poor body, though it made the bruises show the more. Poor Father Edmund.' There was a pause. 'And poor Thorgar as well, of course, if he did not do it after all.'

'Thank you. If there is anything else you remember, come to us.' Bradecote dismissed her with a small smile of thanks, and Walkelin held open the door.

There was a woman outside, but she was not the healer, whom they expected. Mildred was a good-looking girl, the sort local young men would scramble to claim for a wife. She had a thick, glossy plait of raven black that lay upon her shoulder and peeped, not quite demurely, from under her coif, heavy lids with long lashes over violet eyes, and a figure that no man could fail to appreciate. She was also clearly aware that she drew that appreciation, but in the current situation was rather less bold than normal. She looked nervous, even a little frightened, and those violet eyes had shed tears recently.

She entered, made a deep obeisance to Bradecote, and offered up her name.

'I am Mildred, Tofi's daughter. Mother Agnes, she says she is sorry but she is seein' to Cuthwulf, whose back has gone again. Everyone offered to plant the pease for 'im, knowin' that back of his, but . . . Yellin' loud 'e was, when I left the field.'

'Then we will speak with you, Mildred. Now, you saw Thorgar arguing with Father Edmund the morning of the killing, yes?'

'I did, my lord.' She nodded, but sniffed, not once but twice, and then took a gulp of air and began sobbing loudly.

Bradecote's eyebrows flew up in surprise, and he glanced at his companions, who shrugged.

'Sit upon the stool and tell us what you saw. You need not be afraid of us.' Bradecote thought perhaps it was fear upsetting her.

She obeyed the first part of the command, but wailed, 'I should not 'ave spoken. It was spite, and God will judge me. Poor Thorgar!'

'So did you really see them argue, girl?' Catchpoll exuded 'firm oldfather'.

'Yes, yes, but I did not 'ave to tell it.'

'You do to us, because all truth is of use to us.' Bradecote thought this a pompous thing to say as the words left his lips, and he caught Catchpoll's choked back gurgle of laughter, but the girl was not attending to his every word but rather fighting her own guilt.

'I was takin' the pail to the midden. Guthlac, my little brother, had been sick and it stank. We told 'im not to eat the mushrooms mother dried and keeps for addin' to the pottage, but then Guthlac is greedy and disobedient. I felt no sympathy.'

'So you left the house for that reason.' Bradecote did not want to hear more of Guthlac's indisposition. 'How far from this house is that?'

'Oh, we lives but the first house along from the churchyard.' She pointed, but since there was a solid wall in the way that was not very helpful.

'You mean near where it comes to a point outside, not up where it is wider by the oak tree?'

At the mention of the oak tree Mildred began to cry again, and Bradecote cursed his own thoughtlessness.

'Come now. Give the lord Undersheriff an answer.' Catchpoll was encouraging rather than threatening.

'Yes.' She nodded. 'Next to the reeve's house, where my Uncle Selewine lives.' She clearly thought that the reeve's house was a landmark in the village that the world at large would know. 'I saw Thorgar walk down to knock upon this door and then Father Edmund opened it, and they spoke, not loudly. Then Thorgar began to wave his arms about and 'is voice grew louder. I never saw Thorgar angry ever before.'

'Did you hear what was shouted?' Bradecote could not keep a touch of hope from his voice.

'No, my lord. It was a wet and windy morning, and the wind took the words. I just 'eard them as loud and angry. Father Edmund opened 'is arms like this.' She spread her arms but with the palms facing forward, fending away rather than raised upward in any calling down of a benediction. 'He shook his head also and Thorgar did the same and pulled the piece of oilcloth up more on 'is shoulders and went along the path that goes beside the Ripple Brook. I did not linger, for it was wet.' She swallowed hard. 'If'n I had said nothin', Thorgar would not be dead.'

'Well, Mildred, that may well be blaming yourself without need. If you spoke up true, then you did right.' Bradecote, a man prone to self-blame, knew how much it tied one into knots inside.

'But I did it for the wrong reason, my lord. I was angry. Night afore, we met as often we did, just for a little while, and . . . and Thorgar said as I was a test. A test!' Mildred lost her sorrow in the residue of outrage. 'All these months when we was talkin' and cuddlin' and . . . I even offered—' She blushed, but not so much that Catchpoll thought it was the first offer she had ever made.

'What sort of test?' Walkelin was confused, and Mildred, who had ignored him thus far, looked at him.

'A test to see if he could resist the sin of fornication – "the Daughters of Eve", he said. Admitted he loved me, but loved God more, and that I should seek an 'usband elsewhere.' She clearly found this incomprehensible. 'Rejected, I was, and that made me want to speak up. It was wrong and God will judge me.'

'If it lies badly with your conscience, tell the priest, the other priest, Father Ambrosius. It does not sound a sin that is beyond penance and absolution.' Bradecote thought this the only suggestion he could make, and it served also as a dismissal. Mildred left, sniffing forlornly.

They had some time to ponder upon what might have angered Thorgar, and then there was a knock upon the planked oak, and upon Walkelin's opening it, a woman stepped within and, after glancing towards Catchpoll, looked straight at Bradecote.

Agnes, the village healer, was a woman best described as 'narrow'. She was on the tall side for a woman, with a long, narrow face, narrow shoulders and narrow hips. Her face showed no signs of a beauty faded, but every sign of resolution. Her lips were thin, her nose aquiline and pinched, and everything about her declared that this was a woman who realised early in life that men would always look first at others when looking for a wife. Her gaze, with eyes that were a surprisingly vivid blue, was firm and unflinching. She made an obeisance to him, and then stood as straight as a bullrush.

'I am Agnes, the healer in Ripple. Me, and the Widow Reed, washed and shrouded the body of Father Edmund.' She sounded matter of fact, though 'and the Widow Reed' was given in a tone that implied her presence had not been needed.

'Then we would ask you, mistress, about the state of the body afore it was cleaned, not least because yours will be eyes that see where others just looks.' Catchpoll was not flattering the woman but acknowledging her experience.

'There were a lot of blood about the face, and the nose were broke, which would account for much of it. The skin were puffed and bruised about the jaw and cheekbones, and a tooth gone. I reckon as the cheekbone might well 'ave been cracked.'

'Which one?' Catchpoll wanted every detail.

'The right, and I think that were from the kickin'. Many a bruise and broken face has I put mosses on over the years where men,' and Agnes gave a half snort, clearly unimpressed by the whole gender, 'has taken to usin' their fists on each other. The lost tooth and broken nose most like came from a fist, and Father Edmund were never a heavy man. I reckon as 'e fell back on the floor and were lucky then not to crack his skull open, not that it helped later. Then 'e got kicked good and proper. A man as kicks in another's head is blind drunk or mad angry.'

'You want to be a serjeant, mistress?' Walkelin, impressed by her observational skill and deductions, smiled at her.

'There's more to what you does, as there is to what I does, and we would neither of us be good at those parts, young man.' It was part the reproof of an elder, and part acknowledgement of a compliment. Agnes gave a half smile that twisted.

'So you know how he died.' Catchpoll looked her straight in the eye.

There was a pause.

'Aye, I knows. At first it were not somethin' as you would see, for there were a lot of broken skin and bloody bruises, but it were there, that little killin' hole. Never seen one afore but it were clear enough to them as sees.' She nodded towards Catchpoll.

'Did the Widow Reed not see it too?' Bradecote wanted to know whether the widow had held anything back.

'Her? Oh no. Too busy snivellin' and dabbin' at bits like you would a child's sore knee.' Clearly, Agnes had not found her a help.

54

'Then why did you accept her aid?'

'Could not stop the woman, not without much noise and foolishness. Since Will Reed died and then Father Edmund arrived, bit under a year past, she has been always at church, or rather always gazin' at the man. Some said she was thinkin' holy thoughts, but I doubts it. He would speak gently to 'er, mostly about the poor fare he and Father Ambrosius endured, and she would be forever leavin' bread or butter inside their door. If she thought that would give Father Edmund a soft spot for 'er she were a fool. Those eyes preferred much younger fruit on the tree.' This was said with strong disapproval and a very straight look at Catchpoll. 'Selewine the Reeve is not as clever as he likes to pretend, and is the father of sons, not daughters, Serjeant.'

'You mean Father Edmund broke his vow of chastity.' Bradecote frowned.

'Doubt any man is pure of thought, even the tonsured, not all the time, but there is thought and there is deed, and there are knowin' maids who makes eyes at men and little maids who knows nothin', as is right.'

The implication of her words made all three men frown.

'And any father who found out – that would be a good reason to be killin' mad,' Catchpoll murmured, 'so if the priest died after blows from fist and boot, it would fit easily.'

'Mistress, do you think Father Edmund would have died from the beating alone? You know more than we do.' Bradecote thought it a useful piece of additional information.

'It were bad, mighty bad. If there were breath in 'im when I saw 'im I might have made a guess, but dead is dead. Such blows could easily break somethin' deep inside and a man die days later. I would say an even chance, my lord, but it is just my thought on it.'

'And why did you not tell Selewine the Reeve that you had found a stab wound?'

'What good would it do, then? Poor Thorgar be dead and there is some things a healer cannot do. Bringin' back from the dead be one. The thing were done.'

'But Father Edmund's killer is still free.'

'And God will judge them upon the deed, whether foulest sin or one they can atone for. Do you think I would give cause for Selewine, or any of 'em, to seek another to dangle?' She folded her arms, and the bony elbows stuck out sharply.

'Did you think Thorgar guilty afore you saw the body, mistress?' It was Walkelin's question. 'You said "poor Thorgar" and I wondered . . .'

'Thorgar were a good lad, a good man. Took up the responsibility as man of the family when Alvar died, and with only fifteen summers to 'is name. Never gave any pain nor problem to anyone, not since the day he were born, and I were there. A big baby, he were, and a trial to 'is mother to get out into the world, but thereafter a son to be proud of.'

'Did you not raise this when the crowd was for a-hangin' Thorgar?' Walkelin frowned.

'I were not there, but at Naunton, up yonder, with a birth far from simple. Even if I 'ad been there, do you thinks they would have listened, the men that is?' She snorted. 'Men listens to me when their bellies ache, their bones ache or break, or their women are in the time of trial. Then they looks up to me, but at all other times I is just another woman to be told "What can you know?" Hah! They confuse brains with *bealluccas*, and that be plain fact.' Agnes' cheeks flew two spots of colour and she was clearly annoyed. Only after the words had come out did she consider her audience of three men. 'You may not like that,' she admitted, her gaze passed from Walkelin to Catchpoll and then to Bradecote, and then she added, 'my lord. I will say, upon my hope of Heaven, I do not think Thorgar killed Father Edmund.'

'But he has at least one sister, Osgyth.' Bradecote took no umbrage at her disparagement of men.

'The only sister, and a maid as none is likely to fool. She was also nigh on woman grown when Father Edmund came to Ripple.'

'But the maid, er, Mildred, said she saw him arguing with the priest the morning of the killing day.' Bradecote pressed her.

'I do not know why that would be, unless some word reached Thorgar of what few others know, but then why would he not raise a hand to 'im then? If you said to me Thorgar took a swing at him then and there, mayhap there could be a reason, but not later, and not a sneaky stabbin'.'

'Which leaves us with the one important question. Which men in Ripple would have cause, *just* cause,' Bradecote stressed 'just', to make it clear that such an act was at the least understandable, 'to beat Father Edmund senseless?' He did not say 'kill him'.

Agnes the Healer looked him straight in the eye and compressed her lips tight shut.

'We will find out. The Law needs to know, and justice be done.'

'Is those two the same, my lord? From where I stands, it looks as if justice be done already, whether whoever did the killin' knew that or not. The little maids in Ripple is safe now.'

'The trouble with that argument is that it means you could say that if a man of bad character is robbed and killed upon the road, then the killer ought not to be taken and hanged because the man he killed deserved no better. And who is to judge whether a man is good or bad of soul, other than God in Heaven?' Bradecote was all reason, and his words did make the woman frown, but then she shook her head.

'What you says is true, my lord, but we are in Ripple, this day and after that death, and I knows what is right. If the Law demands a penalty of me for that I must bear it.' She was resolute. They would have to make difficult discoveries for themselves.

'No penalty, mistress, but think upon what I have said, and you may come to change your mind.'

'Thank you for that, my lord.' Agnes dipped in a gawky curtsey and left. As the door shut behind her the three men looked at each other.

'Well, that gives us a reason for the murder, and why Selewine got so little response when he put out the question "Who would want to kill Father Edmund?" I thought something felt odd then.'

'It does, my lord, but part of me still worries at the stabbin' part.' Catchpoll frowned. 'It does not fit with a man with the red mist of ire goin' to beat whoever misused 'is little daughter. Fist and foot, yes. They gives a connection, a feel of the man takin' punishment if you likes. The stab wound is – sort of different. The other thing is that all of Ripple will be as ignorant as Selewine or as tight-lipped as Agnes.'

'But could we at least discount men like Selewine, with sons only, no children, or grown daughters?' Walkelin was trying to be positive.

'And have we considered it might have been more than one man? What if a group of—' Bradecote began but was cut short by Catchpoll.

'You might get a father and brothers, just might, but what man shares a shame upon a daughter like that, one that might well mean she finds it difficult to find a man when she is of an age to wed? In a village like this, memories is long but they also twist. It might be all pity now but later . . . and what father wants to admit they did not protect their child, even if in ignorance of the crime?' Catchpoll, a father and a grandfather several times over, was practical. Deep down, he did not think the priest deserved justice to be meted out for his killing, and agreed that it was better for the little maids of Ripple that he was gone, but justice was not about only those who deserved it. If the man had died after the beating, he might have wanted secretly to let it go, and duty would have been hard to do, but the stab wound niggled. It was not the act of a moment of total rage, stabbing a man who was already half dead and senseless. That was cold murder, and it gave less heaviness of heart to pursue the murderer.

'Besides a reason for killing, we also have some other useful information.' Bradecote ticked things off on his long fingers. 'Thorgar was not seen to strike the body, and if he was close up to the armpit and facing away, towards the head, it would be an odd position from which to have tried to make that stab wound. And if he had stabbed him, why still be there to be accused of murder? Second, the apprentice Gwydion might have been able to pick up the sharp instrument if it was something of his or his father's, if he saw it in the folds of the habit and the Widow Reed missed it, or it had rolled away. I do not say it is likely, but it is possible, and why was he so helpful?'

'My lord, I thinks that might just be Gwydion bein' a lad and curious. A good tale to tell other young men in years soon to come. "I saw this murdered priest and there was blood everywhere . . ."' Walkelin smiled the smile of one now both too grown up and also too used to dead bodies to think like that. 'Is that all we does for today, my lord?'

'I think we ought to visit Thorgar's family and tell them we do think him innocent. I know taking whoever did kill the priest will be the final proof, but we can give some ease since they will know their neighbours will soon look upon them as tainted by his deed.' Bradecote was still for a moment, thinking. 'And it was interesting what Mildred said about him seeing her as temptation. You cannot think that sort of man would kill a priest.'

'Unless that priest had defiled not only his vows to God but more than vows. Oh, I still think Thorgar did not do it, my lord, but being kind and even religious does not mean it is impossible.' Catchpoll was being even-handed.

'True. I wonder if his mother knew of his religious fervour? Let us go and find out, before – and I hope this happens – food is brought to us.'

Chapter Four

They knocked briefly at the reeve's door to ascertain which was the house of the late Thorgar. When Catchpoll knocked upon the one pointed out to them it was opened by Osgyth, who managed a wan smile and stood back to let them enter. It was she who introduced them to her mother and three siblings, a whey-faced boy with red-rimmed eyes, who was of about nine or ten, and two aged about seven or eight, who looked to be twins and stood, fearful, very close to their mother's skirts.

'We are come to tell you that whoever killed Father Edmund it is very unlikely it was your son,' Bradecote was quite formal, 'and all of Ripple will know it also.'

'But we knew he did not do it,' blurted out Osgyth, and her mother half raised one hand.

'We knew in our hearts, my lord, but your words will aid us in the time to come.' The mother sounded crushed. 'We will need the aid of friends and neighbours, for I am alas, but part a woman in strength and cannot work our land beyond pulling up garlic and onions from the garden and guiding the children in their weedin'.' She sighed. 'It pains me also that my son lies not in hallowed earth or with the benefit of the Last Rites. My boy would 'ave so wanted those, and even if Father Ambrosius had thought him guilty, which I doubts, since the good priest has known 'im since childhood, he would have given that sacrament if he had been 'ere.'

'Several people have marked upon Thorgar being devout.' This, thought Bradecote, was a fair distillation of what had been said of him.

'Ah, my poor son. Told me 'e had felt the touch of the Almighty and a callin'. Thorgar wanted, above all things, to be a monk in the Abbey at Tewkesbury.'

'He did?' Osgyth almost squeaked the question. 'He never said anythin'.'

'He did to me, 'is mother. Such a kind boy. He were keepin' back because 'e knew how much we needed him, and our village also for the ploughin', but these last few weeks something changed. He said that he had been sent a sign from Heaven that he ought to leave us this spring, but that we would not be lackin' as a result of it. He were filled with' – the woman paused for a moment and smiled at the memory – 'a glow of purpose. He were so happy, like a man on the verge of marriage. Oh, Thorgar!' Quite suddenly she broke, and one hand was lifted to cover her mouth as she cried. The twins joined in. Only Osgyth and the older boy stood quietly, taking it all in. Then Osgyth turned to Catchpoll.

'That is why 'e went to Tewkesbury Abbey yesterday morning, Serjeant Catchpoll.' She sounded almost triumphant. 'So my brother went to arrange his entry to joining the monks.'

'That makes sense, and they will be able to say what 'is plans were.' Catchpoll nodded.

'We are set upon trying to find out who really killed Father Edmund, and leaving Thorgar's name without stain, which is all we can now do for him. We will work as swiftly as we can but be thorough. God sees all, mistress, and will be merciful upon the good, wrongly condemned. I am sure Father Ambrosius will tell you that.' Bradecote was solemn.

The crying woman just nodded, and the three sheriff's men left, very aware how little they could realistically do for the family.

'So we need to find out just what Thorgar planned to do, and when, and perhaps why he sought out Father Edmund on his return.' Bradecote was planning. 'I think we do that first thing so that we can then concentrate upon this village itself with all the facts we have been able to gather. Walkelin, if the river flow has lessened enough, go early and bring back Father Ambrosius to his flock. He sounds a steadying hand and I think they need it, as well as him comforting the bereaved here. Now, let us eat and sleep.'

The morning dawned with a soft, white fleece of mist blanketing the vale of the Severn, though it did not delay the sheriff's men, who split up, Walkelin to cross the river to find Father Ambrosius, and Bradecote and Catchpoll heading south to Tewkesbury. Walkelin both relished his independent action, which showed the trust that his superiors had in him, and regretted not going with them to Tewkesbury, because he was as curious as they were to discover Thorgar's reason for going to the abbey. However, if he was the first to tell Father Ambrosius of his fellow priest's death he would also be the one to hear what manner of man Father Edmund was, and from the man who would know him better than any other. After all, they lived in the same house. Walkelin had been shocked by the previous day's revelations. Catchpoll had reminded him, quietly, that being in holy orders did not make a man a saint, and clerics were just like other men beneath the habit, and sometimes much worse. When he was still just a man-at-arms, Walkelin would have assumed all men of God to be godly and good, but he had learnt better now. Neither rank nor calling prevented men and women from not just sinning but law-breaking.

It was a thoughtful Walkelin who followed a muscular youth down to where a small boat was kept, upturned upon the bank. They passed the mill, where the lad cheerfully hailed a girl of about nine or ten with a wave of the hand and a smile, and confided to Walkelin that she was a sweet little thing and had been his sister's best friend.

'She 'as always been so swift to smile, and always singing to 'erself. Used to play with my poor sister, afore she died last autumn. Berthe, the girl's name is, but of late she is grown quiet and does not smile back as she used to.' The youth sighed. 'I suppose it is the growin' up girls does. I understood my little sister, and Berthe too, but I cannot do that when they grows into women, like Mildred, Tofi's daughter. She and me would play chase together when we was small, but now she looks at me as though I were a tick in the skirt-hem of 'er gown and if'n she speaks to me it is to say I understands nothin'. Worries me, that do. What if I has so little understandin' I never finds a maid to wed me?'

'You will find the right maid in time.' Walkelin, the successfully married man, could afford to sound almost paternal. 'Plenty of time afore you needs to think of bein' wed.' They came to the small boat, keel to the skies. 'Now, what happens if someone from the other side of the Severn wants to cross? The boat is here, but it is not a ferry, not as such.'

'Ah, there is one the other side also.' The lad righted the boat with surprising ease, and pushed it to the water's edge, indicating Walkelin should get in. 'Them in Holdfast and Queenhill knows where it lies, just as we do with this'n. Sort of belongs to the parish, and what with many havin' kin both sides, and priests goin' to and fro, they gets plenty of use. Most any of the men grown will row across easy enough, but we always has two, one to bring the boat back. Father Edmund never took up an oar, thinkin' as priests should not row, but Father Ambrosius takes his turn, though not the strongest man to look at. You would not think it, but 'e can row as well as me, and is over twice my age.' The youth, who had passed but sixteen or seventeen summers, made him sound ancient. ''E were born in the village, of course, and knows the river better than nearly anyone, but still . . . I miss Father Ambrosius, for 'e spends more time on the other side these days. I think 'e does – did – not like living with Father Edmund as much as with old Father Giraldus. I hopes whoever the lord Bishop sends will be more like Father Giraldus, soft spoken and thoughtful.'

'And Father Edmund was not?' Walkelin sounded suitably surprised, and was delighted to have a view of the dead man before even meeting Father Ambrosius.

'No. Father Edmund were always telling us we must do better, pray more, and that we must please the Lord much more in all we do. Father Edmund were . . . very eager. Father Ambrosius is another who is more calm and gentle. Never frightens anyone.'

'I cannot imagine a priest "frightenin'" his flock.' Walkelin thought the lad was exaggerating.

'Well, Father Edmund frightened my oldmother when she suggested 'e collect the dewfall right after a full moon and mix it with sheep's whey to treat his sunburn last summer. Told 'er that 'er soul would be forfeit if she spread heathen practices, and told 'er all the nasty things that would happen to 'er in Hell. Fair upset 'er that did.'

Walkelin decided that the late Father Edmund had not been an understanding cleric, as well as been a danger to girls, and wondered how forthcoming Father Ambrosius might be without gentle 'prodding'.

Walkelin's superiors did not take the track that was little more than a wide footpath and kept to the low ground nearer the river, but headed a little uphill to the Old Road, which was straight and faster for horsemen. It led them south, down into Tewkesbury and the crossing of the Avon at Mythe, where the ferryman wondered at a lord accompanied by a man who was clearly not his retainer. The answer to his unspoken question came when Catchpoll asked if he had heard the bad news from Ripple, in the manner of a man eager to gossip. Only when the ferryman sucked his teeth and said that he had, and a nasty business it was, and to think that he had taken the Ripple ploughman across the river and back the very day of the killing, did Catchpoll's tone change and his questions become specific. It was then he revealed that they were the lord Sheriff of Worcestershire's men, finding out about Thorgar the Ploughman's visit to Tewkesbury.

'You sure it was him?' Catchpoll had heard often enough from folk who liked the idea of being close, but not too close, to a crime, and turned a 'might have' into a 'I definitely saw'.

'Aye, for he came across sometimes on Holy Days, and not many men were built like Thorgar. Strong as an oak he were, and none so far shorter either.' The ferryman gave a short laugh, curtailed by the thought that laughing about a dead man, murderer though he was, was unseemly. 'Always pleasant, and paid me in eggs, good 'uns. He said his mother's hens were the finest in the whole parish, and Ripple parish covers almost to Upton and even east of the Old Road towards—'

'And how was he when you took 'im across last?' Catchpoll did not want to hear details of local geography, which he could sense were coming.

'Well, for Thorgar, he were a bit quiet, and not from bein' soaked wet by the rain that morn. Not his usual self, I would say, but then if you was plannin' to kill a priest you would be wonderin' about what horrors of Hell would be your lot at your end of days, whether or not anyone found you out. Not a man as I ever saw angered, but there was a frown to his brow and a set to the mouth that was not happy.'

'Did he say why he was coming to Tewkesbury on this occasion?' Bradecote joined the questioning.

The ferryman just shook his head, and added 'No, my lord' as an afterthought.

'And did he look happier on 'is return?' This, thought Catchpoll, was of greater importance.

'He did, leastways he looked sort of relieved, as if a burden was lifted off those broad shoulders o' his. I will say this, he did not look like a man about to murder anyone. I has to say fair. If'n he killed the priest mayhap some madness afflicted the man of a sudden. It makes no sense otherwise, truly it don't.' The ferryman sighed, pocketed the coin that was proffered, and tied his craft so that the two horses could be led off.

Tewkesbury's abbey, with the spring sunlight giving its fresh Caen stonework a warm and creamy-golden glow, dominated the town in a benign manner. The tower was almost complete, and masons, ant-like at this distance, could be seen as dark blemishes upon the construction. Earl Robert of Gloucester's own father-in-law had endowed the rebuilding, and lay within its walls, and it was assured of Earl Robert's patronage. It was a community that was thriving, and exuded power.

As the shrieval pair made their way along the main street towards it, a stocky and slightly bow-legged man watched them, his expression stony. He began to follow them, his walking pace sufficiently swift not to fall behind the two horses, walking easily on a loose rein, and drew close as they entered the precincts of the abbey. Catchpoll, sensing a gimlet gaze upon his back, turned as the man approached.

'And what brings you over the shire border?' The man's deep tone was guarded, if not slightly antagonistic.

'Questions, just questions. We is not treadin' upon the authority of Earl Robert. The lord Bradecote,' Catchpoll indicated his superior with a gesture of his hand, 'and me just wants to ask questions as might be important to a killin' in

Ripple. None here is under suspicion.'

The man gave a slight nod, which might have been acceptance of this statement, but focused upon the man who had dismounted from the steel grey horse. His eyes evaluated, and Bradecote felt they did so just as Catchpoll's did. He made a guess.

'Are you Earl Robert's serjeant?'

'I am, my lord. Wulfram the Taker.'

'What Catchpoll says is true, Serjeant. We seek only information from the Master of Novices and perhaps Abbot Roger, which may make our path the clearer concerning—'

'The death of the priest? I heard of it in Twyning yestereve. But the man as done it is hanged.' There was just a hint of doubt in the voice.

'You knows as well as I does,' murmured Catchpoll, 'that not every man that sees a hempen noose afore the Justices in Eyre decides upon it is guilty. We wants to be sure, that is all.'

'Fair enough. I will say that the hanged man was known a little in Twyning, for he had kin there on his oldmother's side, and heads were shaken over it more in disbelief than at the wickedness of the deed. You may be right to ferret deep.'

'And you were not in Twyning for any reason that might cross over into Ripple, I take it?' Bradecote thought it best to ask.

'No, my lord.' Wulfram shook his head. 'Just a simple case of a man as disliked his neighbour tuppin' his wife and beat the man so as his nose will never be straight again. Came and made loud complaint, did Master Tupper, so I went to look into it at the lord Undersheriff's command, and there is no cause to bring in the cuckolded 'usband. He has not so much as taken his hand to the wife's arse, which is good, and his tithing all swear he is by nature a gentle man not given to violence, whilst the complainin' man is distrusted even by the village priest, and I reckons as three hearty cheers was given by every 'usband of a comely wife and father of pretty daughters in Twyning that he has paid a price. I reckoned as one broken nose and some bruises was fair justice, and the Law would not be served by lettin' a man, one who does not see that other men's wives and daughters are not for his takin', set hisself up as a righteous victim. I told him if I had been the 'usband, I would have broken more 'n his nose and I never wants to see him again.'

Bradecote smiled, slowly. He might look very different to Catchpoll, but here was another man who was a serjeant to the core.

'Since I know another who would have done the same,' he glanced at Catchpoll, 'I can say the lord Undersheriff of Gloucestershire is a lucky man.'

'Not all men realise how lucky they are, my lord.' Wulfram permitted himself the hint of a chuckle. 'I hope as you gets answers as aid you.' With which he nodded, combining a farewell to Catchpoll and an obeisance to Bradecote, and went back out into Tewkesbury's thoroughfares.

'Have you come across Wulfram the Taker often, Catchpoll?'

'Off and on these last dozen years and more. Been a bit more difficult since Earl Robert came north and burnt Worcester, and Earl Waleran returned the favour and came to Tewkesbury, though he did not burn more 'n Earl Robert's hall, so we does not take ale together, but he knows the craft well enough. And if he thought it right to mention what Twyning folk think of

Thorgar, it is worth us bearin' in mind.'

'Very true. Now, I wonder who Thorgar spoke to here. Would he have had access to Abbot Roger?' Bradecote thought it unlikely.

'Brother Porter will know. I never entered a "monks' nest" without finding Brother Porter knew everything that set a serjeant on his merry way.' Catchpoll grinned, and, taking the reins of Bradecote's grey as well as his own mount, went to the porter's little gateside cell. Bradecote realised it was not a subservient act on Catchpoll's part but more that it made Catchpoll of greater interest to the nosy brother within. A few minutes later Catchpoll was handing the horses to a lay brother to take to the stables, and reported to the undersheriff that Thorgar came to speak with the Master of Novices, and that worthy had been sent for.

The monk who approached them soon afterwards was a kindly-looking man with a waddling gait, who knew the younger novices mimicked him behind his back and called him 'Brother Duck'. His tonsure was freckled as if he had been sprinkled with the dust of desiccated autumn leaves, and was ringed by red hair now faded to the colour of pinkish sandstone. He looked very benign, and a little indolent.

'You wish to speak to me? I am Brother Cuthbert, the Master of Novices in this House.' He took in Bradecote's garb and mien, and spread his hands in a gesture both welcoming and placating. 'Ask what you will, my lord, and I will do my best to answer, though I doubt any information from within these walls could be of use to the lord Sheriff of Worcestershire.'

'You were visited, the day before yesterday, by Thorgar the Ploughman, from Ripple.' Bradecote chose not to begin with a question.

'I was. He is wishful to join us here, and I took him to see Father Abbot, because he was in some distress about his gift upon entry.'

The sheriff's men noted the present tense. Brother Cuthbert had not heard the gossip that had passed over the ferry into Tewkesbury.

'He will not be comin' to you now, Brother, for he was hanged that afternoon for killin' the priest of Ripple, or one of 'em, to be exact.' Catchpoll did not soften the blow, and his face was grim.

'Hanged? For murder? No, no, surely not? Oh dear, dear. I cannot believe it of him. It must be a mistake.' Brother Cuthbert's voice shook, and his hands clasped together tightly.

'If it was, it was a mistake that he paid for with his life, Brother. I think it best we speak with Father Abbot as well, and hear all that Thorgar had to say.' Bradecote did not make it a command, for he saw no need to do so.

'Indeed, my lord, and such a shock as it will be to him also. Oh dear, oh dear. Do follow me.'

They followed Brother Cuthbert, curtailing their own pace to his. He led them to a building near to the west end of the church, which provided the Abbot of Tewkesbury with a chamber where he might entertain noble guests, and a solar where he might work in some privacy. The monk knocked upon this door and awaited a call to enter. He entered, but closed the door behind him, which made Catchpoll scowl.

'This is not a matter of "Would you like to see . . . ?" It is not a visit to be polite,' he growled.

'Oh, he will see us. The good Brother Cuthbert will simply

want him to know the news from Ripple beforehand.' Bradecote was quite at ease, perhaps because his rank meant far fewer doors had ever remained closed to him. He was proved right without them loitering. The door was opened and a Benedictine with ink-stained fingers, clearly the abbot's clerk, came out. Brother Cuthbert, blithely unaware of any discourtesy, bade them enter.

Abbot Roger was seated at a table with a vellum document set aside upon it. He was a man in his mid-forties, sinewy rather than thin, with an air of authority which declared that not only was he in a position of power but knew how to wield it. Some clerics looked as if they were hiding from the world, but Abbot Roger was not one of them. At the same time, he did appear genuinely shocked at what he had just heard. He gestured to Father Cuthbert to push forward the second chair in the chamber for the lord Undersheriff, and gave a formal greeting, but then continued immediately.

'This is most upsetting. You are sure that Thorgar committed this foul sin? I cannot believe it of him.'

'No, Father, not sure, but it did, at first viewing, seem likely, and it was believed enough by the villagers to see him hanged for it. He swore his innocence to the last, but then, would not any man seek to avoid a noose about his neck?' Bradecote's was the voice of reason.

The abbot shook his head, and the undersheriff could not decide whether it was from wishing to cast the thought from him or rejection of the possibility of Thorgar's guilt. He wondered at it, but Abbot Roger's next words cast mere wondering aside.

'As Brother Cuthbert will have told you, it is true that Thorgar came here the day before yesterday, in the morning. He came to

Brother Cuthbert as the Master of Novices, who then brought him before me to discuss his dilemma.'

'And what was his dilemma, Father?' Bradecote managed to avoid sounding over eager, but it took an effort.

'Thorgar was an earnest young man who felt the calling from God. He spoke of it most feelingly. He was a ploughman and I assumed he would come to us as a lay brother, and serve God through his labours in our fields and granges, and obedience alone, but he wished above all things to be a choir monk, reciting all the Offices in full each day with his brethren in the church. His own priest had begun to teach him Latin and Thorgar said he was amazed at how well he had been able to assimilate it. Thorgar recalled another priest, the one who had served his village when he was but a boy, speaking of a simple shepherd called Cædmon, in the early days of the Church in these isles, and he was God-given the gift of poetry and song. Thorgar did not think some miracle would enable him to be a second Cædmon, though he sought to take that name within these walls, but he had a true passion for what God called upon him to do. He said it was both a hard decision and easy, since how could he not obey Heaven itself, but he knew it would be hard for his family, since his father is dead, his younger brothers too young to take his place, and his mother crippled. He said it was that which had held him back until now, but that two things made him change his mind. The first was that he was being tempted by the flesh, and feared to sin with a particular maid of Ripple who was very much a Daughter of Eve – and persuasive.' Abbot Roger frowned. It might have been at the sin of women, but then again perhaps it was trying to recall what sinful thoughts about women might be, and Brother

Cuthbert tutted. 'What finally made his decision for him was a Sign.'

'And what was that, Father?' Catchpoll's brows furrowed far more than the cleric's.

'A silver chalice. That a matter of rejoicing should lead to this . . .' The abbot sighed and steepled his fingers and closed his eyes, and Bradecote and Catchpoll exchanged glances, unsure whether he was praying or merely setting his thoughts in order. There was silence in the chamber, so complete that a house sparrow felt confident enough to land in the narrow opening of the window, where the shutter had been opened to let in the spring sunshine, and chirruped for some moments before fluttering away.

'Tell us anything that you think of meaning, even if not what passed between you in that meeting, Father, but in some order, since we must understand and remember it all.' Bradecote smiled, ruefully. 'Our task, our duty, is to see that the killer of Father Edmund is brought to justice. Perhaps he has been already, but if Thorgar was innocent, then we have to discover whether he was made to seem guilty by the true guilty man, or whether it was mischance.'

'And it makes a mighty difference to Thorgar's family, for he lies in unconsecrated ground, being condemned as a murderer.' Catchpoll added his mite.

'Yes, that must be so.' Abbot Roger shook his head at the thought. 'From what I saw of him, Thorgar seemed a truly honest and devout young man in whom the Calling was almost overwhelming. He actually wept tears at my feet, and I said . . . but you need it in order. I am sorry.' He half smiled.

'You will be unaware of certain events and history which may have great bearing upon all that has happened. While Thorgar was ploughing, the day after Lady Day, and by chance his own strips, allotted but last year, his ploughshare turned up not just the good earth but a silver chalice and several secular silver items.' The latter were said in a tone that indicated their lesser importance. 'He said the ground had been ploughed many times, by him and his father before him as village ploughman, but it was only now that the chalice appeared. He had been tormented by the thought that if he brought a gift of a piglet, or sold one for coin at market, his family would suffer from the loss, but if he brought the chalice to us, they would not be disadvantaged, for it had not been expected.

'He told nobody of the find except his priest, Father Edmund, to whom he gave it for safekeeping. It seems there was an old tale in the village about a priest hiding a newly given chalice when the heathen Danes came down the Severn at the time when the Lady Aethelflæd had the capital of Mercia in Gloucester. The good priest was drowned in an accident shortly after and none knew where he had buried the silver. The lord Bishop of Worcester had a new chalice made, one with a design of wavy lines as a remembrance of that priest and his loss in the river. It is the one used now. I think the story has become almost a fireside tale in Ripple, only half believed. Thorgar was convinced the chalice came to him not by chance but the Will of God, that he might bring it as his gift here upon entering the Order. He decided that when next there was no working in the fields he would bring it, even if he did not himself join us until at least he had sown the family's strips and given them the oddments of coin. However, when he went to Father Edmund the morning it rained too hard to plough, Father Edmund, who had now learnt of the tale, told him that the chalice belonged to the lord Bishop of Worcester, and must be returned to him. He said that perhaps the lord Bishop would put Thorgar forward to St Mary's Priory in Worcester, for finding it, but Thorgar was adamant that he had been called to serve in Tewkesbury.

'Thorgar doubted the ownership of the chalice, though I myself told him that the priest was correct. That was when he wept at my feet. I told him not to be distressed, for it did not mean he had to go to the priory at Worcester, or mean his vocation was not real. I then suggested that if he brought one of the secular pieces of silver as his gift, we would be as delighted to take him. Had I said nothing was needed he would have felt accepted out of pity, but we would have taken him thus, for he showed such a need to be one of us.' Abbot Roger paused. 'I can say that, when he left me, he was no longer agitated, and indeed looking forward to entering this House. He said that he would apologise to Father Edmund for arguing over where the chalice should go and would bring some piece of silver here before Whitsuntide, by which time he felt he could leave his family. He was not a man planning murder, I assure you.' The Benedictine frowned for a moment and then said, very deliberately. 'If, in your judgement. Thorgar was innocent and wrongly hanged, we would still accept his earthly remains, and bury him within our precincts. We will pray for him, guilty or innocent, for if the former he needs our prayers so much the more.'

'Thank you, Father. I think that might be a comfort, to his mother especially.' Bradecote was taken slightly aback at the offer. If Abbot Roger clearly felt that the man he had interviewed but two days previously was not a killer, that carried weight. 'What you have said, and your reading of Thorgar's character, means much, sufficient for us to look even deeper into the killing of Father Edmund. What we are seeking now is why the priest was murdered and, if Thorgar merely discovered the crime, why the rest of Ripple was able to believe that a man, of whom nothing bad has yet been said, should be strung up for that murder.'

'Perhaps Ripple is a village of sheep, not goats, and easily persuaded by an assertive minority. After all, Our Lord was greeted with hosannas upon Palm Sunday, and yet crucified within a week. Those who might have saved the Son of God chose Barabbas the criminal.'

'Very true, Father. We must therefore look for goats with motives.' Bradecote gave a small, twisted smile.

'I pray that your investigations bring truth to light, and we will pray for that as for Thorgar, and of course for Father Edmund.' There was the slightest hesitation before the priest's name was added.

'Is there anything you know of Father Edmund, Father Abbot?' Bradecote was swift to pick up upon the pause.

'Oh no, and he was an appointee of Bishop Simon, who is a discriminating man and would make a careful choice. However, he has not been in the parish very long, less than a year. Father Giraldus, who served with Father Ambrosius for many years, was much loved and missed. I think a man not fully settled in a village might more easily make a mistake that roused the sin of anger in a parishioner, that is all.'

'Thank you. Every small thing aids us, Father. We will let you know what we finally discover, and if Thorgar's wish may be granted, even after his death, he may yet come to you.'

With which Bradecote's smile lengthened, and Brother Cuthbert, taking this as his cue, ushered them out into the hazy sunshine.

'There is one thing that Father Abbot did not tell you, my lord, for he does not know it. When Thorgar spoke of being tempted by a young woman, he said that he had not been totally innocent, and had responded to her advances – a little.'

'You mean he kissed the girl. Since the lad had not taken vows there was nothing to be ashamed about.' Catchpoll was pragmatic, and this was not news to them, though he gave no indication of it.

'Ah yes.' Brother Cuthbert blushed a little. 'But what is important is that he turned from her, rejected her. I doubt that pleased her, or mayhap her kin? They might speak against the young man out of spite?'

'True, Brother. That is worth the knowing.' Catchpoll smiled his thanks, though a Catchpoll smile was not a thing of beauty. 'We shall see what we shall see.'

It was a thoughtful pair who returned to the ferryman and then retraced their steps to Ripple to find out whether Walkelin had returned with Father Ambrosius.

Chapter Five

Walkelin was not the worrying sort, but right now he was at least concerned. Having followed his youthful ferryman's directions into Queenhill, he had knocked upon several doors to ask after Father Ambrosius, or at least a woman whose babe was coming. Most folk were out at their labours, but a woman, nearly bent double with age, had directed him to the home of Oswy the Shepherd.

Oswy himself was not at home, but the eldest child, a girl of about ten, opened the door to Walkelin. She looked worn, worried and weary, and Walkelin wondered if she was in fact older than he had thought, and just small. He gave his name and office. A weak voice called from the bed, and the girl let him in. Oswy's wife lived, but looked exhausted not just by a long and exhausting travail, but also by the cumulative effect of all those that went before, for Walkelin counted six under the age of tithing, if you included the swaddled infant in the crib. Oswy the Shepherd seemed to be breeding a flock of children to rival the number of lambs out at grass. Walkelin did not think the woman herself would be able to give him the answers he needed, and looked to the girl.

'I come seeking Father Ambrosius and he is needed for a burial in Ripple.' Walkelin thought he was being very clever, not spreading the news of the murder before he had to in the wider community. 'I heard as he was come here to pray for your mother in her time of trial, but where is he now? Did someone else call for him and he moved on elsewhere?'

'He were here until yesterday about noontide, Master Underserjeant. The babe arrived at last late the night afore, thanks to the good Father's prayers, but Mother scarce even noticed the babe put to the breast, she were so weak. He prayed at the bedside till dawn, and then slept for an hour hisself. Father went to attend the sheep then, and Mother awoke a mite afore midday and took a little thin pottage, and Father Ambrosius and me took the babe and she were baprised in the church. He said then that all was secure in the hands of God and he would depart. I left him there and thought he went back to Ripple.' The girl looked thoughtful. 'He were tired, as was we all, but he looked to me as though there were somethin' more than weariness to 'im, a sort of weight upon the shoulders. Such a kindly man is Father Ambrosius, always understandin' and even makes the little 'uns laugh, but he looked – grim and sort of sad.' The girl shook her head. 'I hopes he feels better soon.'

Walkelin thanked the girl, gave his good wishes for mother and infant, and returned to the river, where wisps of mist still lingered, drifting like ghosts seeking the lost within the river's flow. He stared at the small boat resting near to where he had been landed. He ought to have asked the shepherd if he would row him across, but he could go and find a villager in the fields. Father Ambrosius must have done that too, if he crossed at all. Could Father Ambrosius have been called to another house, unexpectedly, as he was returning? Instead of going directly to the fields, Walkelin knocked first on every single door. There was no answer except from the old woman, who complained that she had told him once already, and that was an end to it. She slammed the door in his face. Walkelin sighed. He could see in the distance where the Queenhill villagers were labouring, so he went to ask both for a ferryman and if any had seen the priest since noontide the day before. He was met with shaking heads and denials as he went among them, until a child piped up that he had seen the priest.

'Father Amb'sus were walkin' by the river, with a little sack or bag over 'is shoulder. I thought 'e were goin' back to Ripple.'

'You are sure of the bag?' Walkelin was puzzled.

The child nodded.

'And the sun was right up in the sky afore a big rain cloud came and covered it.'

'And I will row you over, Underserjeant, if it be the lord Sheriff's business.' A broad-chested man eased his back as he made the offer.

Walkelin thanked child and man both, and in company with the man began to retrace his steps back once more to the river, thinking, ordering his thoughts. If Father Ambrosius had gone from the church, it was more likely that whatever he was carrying had been there rather than hidden under a bush or up a tree. He asked the man to wait briefly at the boat for him, and made a swift detour to the church, which was a simple, austere stone building. There was an altar with a wooden cross upon it, and a small aumbry set into one wall, where the vessels for the Sacrament were kept, carefully covered with a cloth. It was otherwise bare. If the priest had left anything within and a parishioner had entered, would they not have seen it? Walkelin could not make any good sense of it all, and it was a pensive underserjeant who climbed into the rowing boat.

The big man began to row with long, apparently easy strokes, but commented on the river being 'right full and strong'. As they neared the eastern bank a vessel came into view coming downstream under sail. The man raised a hand in familiar greeting as it drew closer.

'You gets to know the craft that plies up and down, by the look and the sail, though I only knows the name of steersmen whose boats have landed folk or goods. This is the lord King's manor, held of the lord Bishop, and some years back, in the last year of King Henry, he had new slates brought upriver for the chapel roof. I doubts King Stephen has time to think about little manors like ours these days.'

Walkelin agreed and considered whether Father Ambrosius had hailed a boat on the river trade and gone up- or downriver. The main thing was that he was gone, and there were too many options as to where.

Bradecote and Catchpoll found Walkelin at the priests' house, which they expected, but had not thought he would be alone.

'I am sorry, my lord. I can neither work out why Father Ambrosius did not return here, which way he went, or what it was he took with him.' Walkelin looked a little dejected.

'Well, it is possible that with the knowledge we bring from Tewkesbury we might at least make a guess about that last part.' Bradecote was making connections even as he let Catchpoll recount to Walkelin what they had learnt. 'If, and it is merely a possibility, Father Edmund thought that Thorgar would want to take the chalice, and was strong enough to do so by force, he might have given it to Father Ambrosius to keep out of temptation's way across the Severn.'

'Or else, my lord, since it does not seem that the two priests was on close terms, Father Ambrosius might have taken the chalice without Father Edmund knowing of it.' Catchpoll saw an alternative scenario.

'From what was said to me, my lord, Father Edmund was very eager to show folk how much they failed, and I suppose how righteous he was . . .' Walkelin offered.

'Which was also a cover for the evil he was doin',' growled Catchpoll.

'Yes, Serjeant. What I means is, if he possessed the chalice and said it belonged to the lord Bishop, would he not want to hand it back hisself, and be praised for the deed? Bringin' hisself to his bishop's notice for a good thing would make it less likely that bad things would be quickly believed.'

'That follows, Walkelin.' Bradecote was approving. 'And if Father Ambrosius were to take the chalice instead—'

'Ha, that would rankle.' Catchpoll smiled at the thought.

'What if Father Ambrosius discovered what we have,

about Father Edmund?' Walkelin let his thoughts flow. 'I was thinkin' that whatever was in the bag was taken from the Queenhill church, and if you wants to hide anything in a church, well a chalice put beneath the cloth with the other vessels would not be noticed, but is there any chance that Father Ambrosius, spoken of as a strong rower, rowed back alone, killed Father Edmund and took the chalice in haste from the house? He was seen by the child "by" the river, so he may have brought it back over and—'

'Why would the priest take the chalice to the other side afore hailin' a passin' boat?' Catchpoll did not like the idea.

''Acos everyone knew he were that side of the river, and it meant there could be no connection to the death. Boats docs not come like the Offices, the same time every day. Waitin' this side would be a risk.'

'I grant that what you say has a grain of sense to it, Walkelin, but surely the more likely thing is that Father Ambrosius has gone north, to be the one to return the chalice to Bishop Simon? We also have to wonder whether the other items, the secular ones, were also taken. Someone surely searched this house in a hurry for something, but it was not a seeking that had everything strewn about.' Bradecote rubbed his forefinger along the side of his nose and then sighed. 'Yesterday we arrived with a mystery of why anyone would kill a priest. Today we have two very different but very likely possibilities and now this, which just adds to the tangle. Not only is Father Ambrosius under at least some suspicion, but he may have useful information about Father Edmund. It is most likely that he will return in the next few days, but we would look very foolish if he simply disappears, and we are ferreting here pointlessly.'

'Do you want me to go back to Worcester, my lord, and find Father Ambrosius?' Walkelin did not sound eager, though part of him was wondering if that might give him a night at home with Eluned.

'In so many ways no, Walkelin, because I think you will be the one to whom most will be revealed, but as long as you take Serjeant Catchpoll's horse, not your own, you will be the swifter. I doubt Serjeant Catchpoll likes riding far at speed.'

'That I does not, my lord. Jiggles me about and makes my knees ache the more.'

'Then we make the best we can of this. Walkelin, ride straight away to Worcester and if the lord Bishop is not to be found there, go to the lord Sheriff, and have one of his clerks write a message to Bishop Simon requesting that if Father Ambrosius comes to him, he is to send him straight back to Ripple, and not on foot. If he does not come to him at all within three days, he is asked to inform the lord Sheriff of it. That way we show we are aware of the priest's importance in this, and you can, at the worst, set off back here at dawn tomorrow and be with us again mid-forenoon.'

Parts of this were to Walkelin's taste, namely the idea that he might indeed remain overnight in Worcester, but less palatable was the thought of having to go before William de Beauchamp and request the services of one of his scribes and a messenger.

'Very good, my lord. I will be off.' He left, his face intent.

'And I think we need to speak with Pryderi and his son.

If we can be sure of the sharp weapon that killed Father Edmund rather than assuming, it will sit better with me.'

'Aye, my lord. And we needs to speak with the lad about his aidin' of the women with the body. Young eyes sometimes sees things others miss, and we wants to be very sure that the awl, or thing like an awl, was not picked up then, in innocence or in guilt. When that is cleared up, we has two things to discover that nobody will want to tell us; who feared for their daughters and who else knew about this find of treasure.'

Bradecote sat down on one of the simple stools and leant forward, gazing at the cold hearth and dimly registering that someone had come in and removed the ash from the previous evening's fire and laid a fresh one. He ran his long fingers through his hair and was silent, thinking. Catchpoll let him think, and took the opportunity to sit as well.

'There are what, two dozen homes to Ripple? If we visit each one when they come back from their labours, asking each household if they saw anything unusual the day of the priest's death, then we can see how many are those with young girls in the family,' decided Bradecote, eventually. 'That way we do not let them know that we know about the priest's misdeeds, and we reduce the number of possible outraged fathers and brothers.' He held up a hand as Catchpoll opened his mouth to speak. 'Yes, Catchpoll, I know other kin might be the hand of retribution, but it is far less likely. How we ask about a find of silver without starting the whole village on a hunt for it and ignoring the deaths as past and done, I do not know.'

'Not sure that is possible, my lord. I remembers goin' up

north of the shire, way back in my serjeanting-apprentice days. Three men died, and all from greed after one of 'em dug up some fine-worked piece of gold and gems that had once been part of a wealthy lord's sword pommel. The man as found it was killed by his neighbour, who said it had been in the ground on his side of the garden border, and that man in turn was killed by his sister's husband after he bragged about it over a beaker. The folk were shocked by the deaths but more interested in digging up their gardens. I doubts anything came of that 'cept a better crop of cabbages next season, but there. We took the brother-in-law and he was hanged, but though we knew why each killed the other, we never laid eyes on the treasure that began it all. The wife of the hanged man swore oath she had not got it and would not want it, for it was cursed. She said she cast the thing into the river, as far out as she could, and we believed 'er. She was right to do it, for if not cursed, then such things always bring out the worst in folk.'

'Father Ambrosius might have come to the same view, Catchpoll, and decided that he would remove what would be a cause of sinning in his parish.'

'True, my lord. Let us hope Walkelin is successful.'

'Amen to that. Now, we will go and speak again with Pryderi, and come sunset will take half the village each and knock upon doors.'

'My lord, in the time between, might we speak again with Thorgar's mother? She will not be in the field, and we can both tell 'er of Father Abbot's offer, and it might be there are things she would tell us about her son more easily without his sister and brothers about and kept back when we spoke yesterday.'

'Fair enough.'

Pryderi was busy with chisel and mallet and singing what might almost have been a lullaby to the wood. His words meant nothing to the sheriff's pair, since he sang in Welsh, but it was the singing of a man untroubled. He looked up as undersheriff and serjeant filled the open entrance to his temporary workshop, and his singing ceased.

'Where's your son, Pryderi?' Catchpoll did not make the question sound ominous.

'In the church. I set him to measuring for the next joint. Got good eyes, 'as Gwydion, especially in the dimmer light.'

'We are hoping those good eyes may be of use to us.' Bradecote sounded equally unthreatening. 'And we would like to know if any of your tools are missing, or were out of place when you returned to your work yesterday.'

'Why would anyone 'ere steal my tools, my lord? None in Ripple could use them so—'

'We doesn't think it was theft, Pryderi, more a sort of borrowin',' interrupted Catchpoll. 'Was anythin' not quite as you would expect it?'

Pryderi frowned, and looked at his bench as if recalling how it had appeared to him the previous morning. Bradecote and Catchpoll could almost see his mind working. Eventually he spoke.

'No, Serjeant Catchpoll. Gwydion was 'ere first, for I was delayed by an old dame who asked in charity for me to help her with her water pail from the well. Slopping it so much her skirts was wet, she was. In Christian charity I could not refuse 'er. My boy did not mention anything not right. Has this to do with Father Edmund?' Pryderi's brows gathered in a worried frown.

'Turns out that for all the blood and beating, he was stabbed to death, and not with a knife blade. It was a thin, sharp instrument, such as an awl, that killed him.' Bradecote looked at the treewright a little more intently.

'*Diw*!' Pryderi crossed himself. 'Upon my good oath, my lord, I knew nothing of the death until everyone gathered with the man they hanged for it. I came out of Tofi's house at the shouting, I did, and it was said Father Edmund was beaten to death then.' He paused. 'Do you mean they hanged the wrong man? There's bad.' He shook his head. 'If you wants to look at my tools, 'ere they be, but if any hand used one in murder it was not mine.' It was less an offer than a challenge.

'Well, we will, in case somethin' was put back neater than expected. We wants to know exactly what it was that was used.' Catchpoll stepped forward, and took up a likely looking awl, peering close at the haft and at where the steel met wood. If thrust in hard, such a weapon might well sink in that far and leave a trace of blood, even if wiped clean.

'Everyone knew we was working and in the church, Serjeant Catchpoll. Anyone might have taken one of my tools, seeing nobody by 'ere, with Gwydion up that hill there, proving his courage to that daughter of Tofi's. Time is come where I must speak with the lad about maids.' This was said in a reluctant tone and accompanied by a sigh.

'You said before that you had been here for only a week. Had you ever worked on Ripple church before?' Bradecote thought it worth asking.

'Never, my lord. I came downriver with all that I needed other than the wood, and with permission to fell two oaks if needed for the work. Thankful I am that the lord Bishop has the right to take timber from the Chase for repairs. As it stands, I think the tree we took is a fine one and I will not need more. I think that was the problem when the treewright who first made the trusses in the porticus did the work. If 'e worked with what there was and no more, well, by the end the timber was not so suitable. We works with fresh timber, still with sap in it, see. It makes it easier to work, but over time it dries out and in places there are shakes, splits, formed. My guess is the man knew that they would need replacing, but it would be long after he was in the earth. Not 'is problem, and not really judgement on 'is skill.'

'Ah.' Catchpoll, now inspecting a second awl, exhaled not with relief but satisfaction, and held it up like a prize. Bradecote and its owner both gazed at it, not quite sure what they were missing.

'This would be the thing, my lord. Whoever used it did wipe it, but in haste. There is a mite of dried blood right up close to the haft, and the haft itself is slightly darker where a bloodstained finger left a mark. You can just about make out the little lines. That would most like be blood from the beatin' wounds as spread about so much. Hard it would be to avoid gettin' any on you. I wonder if Thorgar had it on the knees of his braies?'

'Had what, Serjeant?' Gwydion, screwing up his eyes a little as he adjusted to the better outdoor light, had turned the corner from the west door, and approached. He looked curious rather than cautious.

'*Bydd yn ofalus*,' murmured Pryderi, but with an urgency that gave away he was uttering a warning, even though the sheriff's pair could not understand the words.

Gwydion stared at his father for a moment, blinked, and then looked questioningly back at Catchpoll.

'You did not tell us yesterday that you helped the women take up Father Edmund's body, lad.'

'No, Serjeant, but . . . but everything was over then. The man as did it was hanged, and one of them, the women, came out and asked if I would help. It was the scraggy one as is the healer in the village. I was just tidying away as the light went. When it gets to sunset it is foolish to keep working with sharp tools. I could not say no to 'er.'

'You sure about that, lad?' Catchpoll's eyes narrowed to slits. 'The healer came and asked for aid? Strange that, for she is a very independent soul, and the other woman said as you offered to assist. Tell things true now. Was it that you went in to them?'

Gwydion looked guilty and nodded.

'I sort of wanted to see . . .' His voice trailed off. It made sense, a youth's curiosity.

'Were there plenty of candles lit in the church, so the women could strip and wash the body?' This was Bradecote's question.

'Aye, my lord.'

'And did they ask for trestles from you?' He wanted to see if the truth was now being given.

'No, for there are two, and a broad board also, kept in the south porticus for funeral use. I was showed them by Father Edmund himself, for I was told, and twice, not to use them instead of a ladder. Not that they would have raised me high enough.'

'So the light was good, and your father here says you have keen eyes. When you went into the nave and saw the body, what exactly did you see? Describe it to us.' It was a command, but gently given.

'There was the other woman by the body, and she was crying sort of soft and quiet, which made the thin one tell her not to be foolish. The body, well it was strange to think it 'ad been Father Edmund, always nosing about and telling us our craft as though 'e was in charge. Even said that as Bishop Simon appointed him, we must answer to him in the lord Bishop's place. You told him, *tad*, what you thought of that.' The lad smiled, briefly. 'No more words would come from that mouth. The face was all colours 'cept normal – purple and blue and bloodied and sort of grey, and sort of out of shape a bit. I saw a fight in Worcester once where two men hit each other till one lay senseless, but neither of 'em looked as bad as Father Edmund.' Gwydion seemed caught between horror and a ghoulish fascination. It seemed a natural mix of emotions in a youth of his age. 'Not a big man, Father Edmund, and I thought it would be easy for three of us to lift 'im, though the crying woman did not aid us in the end. Thing is, somehow the priest seemed heavier, dead.'

'When you lifted the body, was anything else visible on the floor other than the blood?'

'No, my lord, the floor showed the blood, that is all.'

Catchpoll noticed Gwydion's momentary glance downwards, and a hint of relief in his voice, as though that question was easier to answer than others that might have been posed.

'So where was it?' Catchpoll's weary voice sounded as though he was bored with waiting for the information he needed, though in truth he was making a guess, but Gwydion gasped.

'I found it. That is all. It 'ad rolled against the base of the tall stand for a big candle. I thought it a silly place for it, and then wondered why Father Edmund 'ad taken it into the church. I suppose it was just another little thing to complain about. If it was put away and then he "found" it next day, he could say we disobeyed the order not to keep any of our tools in the church. Very strict he was about that. And it would get me in trouble for not putting everything away tidy. I picked it up as I left, when the thin woman thanked me and told me I was not needed more.'

It was a logical answer if Gwydion had no knowledge of the stabbing, and had not caught Catchpoll's comments on the awl, but it was also interesting to hear that the apprentice thought the priest might do something mean-spirited. It added to the less than pleasant picture of his character that was appearing. Of course, there was the small chance that Gwydion's hearing was as acute as his sight, and he had heard what Catchpoll had said and concocted a story that did not lie about the awl being picked up and returned, but made it innocently done. One of the two women might have caught his action out of the corner of their eye and reported it, which would be how Catchpoll was able to ambush with his question. All this was being worked through in Catchpoll's mind, until he was distracted by Bradecote's blunt question.

'Father Edmund does not appear to have been a – charitable priest. Are you sorry he is dead, both of you?' Bradecote looked from son to father and back. 'It is an honest answer I want, not to say it means guilt.'

Gwydion shuffled his feet and looked at the ground. Pryderi folded his arms and looked boldly at the undersheriff.

'Did I want the man dead, and would I 'ave done the deed? No, my lord, for such a thing is a mortal sin as I cannot think Heaven would ever forgive, but am I glad Father Edmund is not 'ere any more – I am. Met a lot of priests I have over the years, in my craft, and none was as plain full of sly malice as that man.'

'Fair enough. And you, Gwydion?' Bradecote pressed for the son's answer.

'Like my *tad* says, my lord. We can work without being prodded with a sharp stick, so to say. I-I think I am more glad he is dead, for think what the lives of all the folk of Ripple must 'ave been like with it all the time. Mean and nasty, I call it.' Gwydion managed to look Bradecote in the eye and held the gaze firmly.

'Thank you. One question more. How much longer will you be working on the church?'

'I reckon as another three or four days, my lord. I told the lord Bishop's clerk as directed me that it depended upon the number of trusses that were like to give way. From what was reported to me, I thought there might be more. The average man, or priest for that matter, does not see what a treewright sees, and only those timbers worst affected might be noticed. If there were joints set to fail in the next year or so, well, they ought to be replaced also. That is just what I found, too, and it makes sense, if they came from the same tree.'

'Well, I would rather you remain until we have taken who killed Father Edmund, in case we have any other questions to ask, but I hope that will not mean keeping you beyond the conclusion of your work.' Bradecote saw Catchpoll's flicker of a questioning look and explained as they walked away and left the treewright and his lad to their labours.

'I know, Catchpoll, but, if we are fortunate, what I said is true, and if we are not, well, it was a less harsh way of telling Pryderi to stay put until given leave to go and it means he has an interest in this being over soon. If he hears anything, he would bring it to us the faster.'

'True enough, my lord.' Catchpoll sucked his teeth. 'What we heard does not mean either of 'em could not 'ave done it, but on balance I think what was said was honest, and it was their awl but not the hand of father or son that thrust it into the priest's chest. Which leaves us with our two reasons why 'e was killed, and I am not happy with the death, my lord, not happy at all. What I means is that the killin' wound and the beatin' does not work as one thing and whether you wanted to beat a man to a bloody mess for a daughter's lost innocence, or to get a man to reveal the hidin' place of silver, pushin' an awl between his ribs as well seems – disconnected. Once the priest is dead you cannot try again to make the man give up the secret, and if you has nigh on killed a man with fist and foot, why stab 'im after?'

'Because you want him dead and that makes it beyond doubt, and also makes it harder to untangle if we arrive.' It was the best answer Bradecote could think up.

'But most folk who kill in the moment does not think of afterwards. Father Edmund's death was not long planned; no, I would swear a good oath this was not planned days afore the deed, mayhap not even many hours.' Catchpoll was not convinced.

'And we have to consider how they thought the death would have been discovered and what done, since they could not have guessed that Thorgar would happen to go to the church and be found, apparently, to those who do not really consider possibilities, guilty.'

'Indeed, my lord. So our killer was lucky. Yet they were also unlucky, for so far none 'as said a bad word about Thorgar, which means sayin' nothin' and watchin' a rope go about 'is neck would not sit easy with a man as only killed in mad rage and feelin' justified by the priest's foul actions. Might make it easier to get a confession if a conscience is sore pricked by that.'

'We can hope so, Catchpoll. Now let us go and speak as we planned with Thorgar's mother and learn what we can not only about her son but about her neighbours.'

Chapter Six

When they knocked upon the door of the ploughman's home they were not called to enter, but had to wait until the door was opened, and were met with apologies from the crippled woman within. She was not alone, for the sickly-looking boy was curled up on the bed, his arms wrapped about his body in a self-embrace.

'My lord, I be sorry, but I did not want to let anyone else in, unless it be Mother Agnes for our poor Baldred, and I am slow of tread. Almost a stream it were, last eve and this morn also, first thing afore everyone went to the field, all folk sayin' as they never thought Thorgar could be guilty and how it were such a shame. Not one of 'em opened their lips when it mattered, though, and oh, I so wanted to throw that back at 'em, but without their aid this family may starve if we cannot grow enough to keep us and pay our due portion to the lord Bishop as overlord.' Thorgar's mother put her good hand to her cheek. 'What did I do so wrong that God 'as punished me with takin' a good 'usband and a good son and afflictin' me so as I is but of little use?'

'No cause is there to think that any of it is a punishment.' Catchpoll never thought that deaths were brought about by the 'guilt' of the victim's nearest and dearest, though sometimes it was true that it was through their foolishness.

'But Father Edmund said as my weakness of limb were a punishment and a sign from God to be more obedient to Him.' Her voice trembled a little, and Catchpoll gently pressed her to sit upon the bench that was placed against the wall. There was no fire, though it was laid, and the dark chamber was cold.

'From what we are hearing, mistress, Father Edmund said a lot of things that were just to make him feel more important and others unhappy.' Bradecote paused for a moment and then continued. 'Had Thorgar spoken to him about his calling to become a monk?'

'Yes. He said at first Father Edmund said that wanting to become a choir monk was pride, and sinful, and he ought to think only of doin' what he was bred to do, and be a lay brother. He did stress that to labour within the community of the brethren was itself prayer and of value.' The proud mother smiled, a twisted, sad smile. 'He wavered when Thorgar spoke of the shepherd who wrote a famous poem and became a saint at Whitby, centuries ago. Never thought Thorgar would know of that. Thorgar's belief in his callin' was so strong, it sort of lit 'im up inside, if you understands. Father Ambrosius told me few men are granted the joy that such a God-given command creates.'

'But he was going to leave you and yet said you would be

provided for. How could that have been, since now you are in such straits?' Bradecote wanted to find out if Thorgar had been as open with his mother about the treasure he had found as he had his calling to the Benedictine life.

'I-I knows not. He was sure of it, and I cannot think what he meant. He would not 'ave abandoned us to beggin' the aid of our neighbours.' The woman got up as the boy on the bed groaned, and went haltingly to sit upon the edge, caress his brow and murmur soft words, though she attended to Catchpoll when he spoke again.

'And afore all this, would you say your neighbours was good folk?' enquired Catchpoll, casually. 'Who lives next to you?'

'Oldmother Agatha, and 'er blessed cat as uses my garden for its needs. She is a good, kind woman, but is now near-sightless and 'erself aided by family. Ulf, the eldest son, fathered eight, and the oldest two lads live with 'er. They say 'tis to make more room, though all but the poor old soul knows it is to look after 'er.'

'A man of many sons, eh?' The question was a leading one, and drew forth just what Catchpoll hoped for.

'Indeed, though there's the three girls, or was. One died last autumn and one 'as gone to Ruyhale as wife to a fine young man with five good sows worth the keepin' over winter, but there is still little Emma to be a boon to 'er mother and old enough to be useful. There's room for the boys now, at 'ome, but I thinks Ulf Shortfinger fears 'is mother will knock over a lamp and set all aflame, or fall over that cat and not be found for a forenoon.'

'And on the other side?'

'Wilf the Worrier. Always fears the worst even when things is goin' well. If'n the harvest is good, Wilf will be tellin' all as the next year will see the crops ruined and no bread from June. Not surprised 'is wife went off last Michaelmas, only that she stayed with 'im so long.'

'Went off? Ran off with another man?' Catchpoll sounded suitably shocked and intrigued in one. It was, as he revealed to his superior afterwards, a very good way to get women to gossip.

'Well, not with any man of Ripple, that is for sure. Wilf said as she was always sayin' she wished she 'ad gone with her sister as went to Worcester to find work in a burgess's house about the year afore the old king died, and said life would 'ave been easier than livin' with 'is worryin' all day, every day. There's truth in that, though Eadild and her sister, Leofcwen, was ever dreamin' fanciful things, and I doubts livin' in Worcester is any better 'n Ripple. Tewkesbury be too big and noisy for me. Wilf is convinced she went to Worcester.'

'And she told no other woman she was off?' Catchpoll, aware that Wilf was clearly not going to be the outraged father of daughters, still felt his suspicious mind stirring, not least because the only Leofcwen he knew of in Worcester who was not born and bred there had been a whore that worked the Foregate and had been found huddled in an alley and frozen to death three years past. If Eadild had come to Worcester and been asking after Leofcwen he felt he was likely to have heard of it in the whispers of the streets.

'No. Here one day, pullin' up onions from the garden for

the pottage and gone the next, though I thinks Wilf did not admit it for a good week. Told me three times she was laid up in bed with a chill afore 'e admitted she was gone. Fends for hisself now, does Wilf, though a bad pottage he would make, I doubts not. I offered to get Osgyth to take up the vegetables from the garden and set a pottage at least every other day, but the offer was refused, and quite grumpily too. No aid will I get from Wilf.'

'Perhaps it is not your near neighbours who will be of assistance.' Bradecote, without Catchpoll's knowledge of the inhabitants of Worcester, or his degree of natural suspicion, fleetingly considered the small possibility that Wilf the Worrier might have killed his wife, but dismissed it as a distraction from the matter in hand. 'It is not so large a community that families are not connected, by blood or indeed just friendship. Have you kindred, or is there kindred of your husband?'

'My kinfolk lives in Naunton and Twyning, my lord, and a niece comes often on Holy Days with news and a goose egg or two, for my sister has fine geese, but they cannot be of practical help. Alvar was an only son. His mother could not keep a child in 'er, poor woman, and Alvar was treated almost as a miracle when he were born. There are wider kin, o' course, but their own families comes first, and what time could they spare to work our strips when they are out from dawn to dusk?' One shoulder was permanently drooping, but the good one now matched it. She looked utterly defeated, and neither undersheriff nor serjeant could find anything to say that did not sound merely a general hope. The only consolation they could offer was the offer from Abbot Roger of a place for her dead son in consecrated ground among the Benedictines in Tewkesbury.

'But Thorgar is already buried.' His mother looked confused.

'For so short a time it would be easy to fetch 'im up again and send the body to the monks.' Catchpoll phrased it as generally as possible, since imagining the disinterment would not be pleasant for a mother.

'But we need there to be no doubt in any mind, and that means we need to take whoever killed Father Edmund.' Bradecote made a decision. 'We came wondering why a priest might be killed, but things have come to light which mean that in this case we do have at least one probable reason. Does all Ripple know of his . . . preferences?'

Thorgar's mother looked blankly at them, then pursed her lips.

'He was less strict with those who fawned and treated 'im as if he was "Bishop Edmund". The Widow Reed, now she was always makin' food and takin' it to their door when she knew Father Edmund was within. Father Ambrosius said as she was too generous, and they were humble clergy who ought not eat so well. Said it gentle, but meant it, not that it made a mite of difference. Mind you, I cannot think any would kill Father Edmund for not bein' fair.'

It was obvious that Father Edmund's proclivities had not reached her ears, and Bradecote assumed that was because she did not mix as those who were still out in the field this afternoon would do. If Osgyth knew, she may have decided not to tell her mother about it.

They left with a sense that the murdered Father Edmund, whose killer they sought, was less worthy of their endeavours than Thorgar, whose death seemed increasingly to be a mixture of misfortune and the inability of his neighbours to think.

'It is clear that Thorgar did not tell of the treasure find, other than to Father Edmund, since he did not even tell 'is mother of it, which makes it less likely someone killed Father Edmund to find it, even more so when you thinks the killer would also 'ave needed to know that Thorgar had given it to the priest for safekeepin'.' Catchpoll made a low, growling noise in his throat. 'My lord, if we takes the real killer, I wants to get them as buried Thorgar up by the Old Road to dig 'im back up again and shrouded proper. They can take it in turns with the handcart to get 'im to Tewkesbury Abbey, unless they uses a boat. They was so swift to condemn a man they knew to be good, and for a-killin' a man many knew to be bad.' Catchpoll shook his head at the ways of the majority.

'Yes, I agree, Catchpoll. We have another situation where Justice and the Law are not the same thing. At least we have but one good reason for the killing. Agnes the Healer was absolutely convinced of the priest's wrongdoings, and would be the one most likely to know, if families kept quiet through shame, but if this was happening in Ripple, why did Father Edmund live so long? I mean, it would only take someone to push him out of the ferrying boat into the Severn and say it was a terrible accident, or even just hit him on the head and cast the body into the river with a bag of stones tied to him, and then "bemoan" he had disappeared.'

Catchpoll laughed, and Bradecote frowned at him.

'I do not jest, Catchpoll.'

'No, my lord, I knows that, but since you took up undersheriffin' you has learnt to think like those we take. You would not have thought of ways to conceal a killin' afore. Most folk do not, for which I give thanks to Heaven, or else I would never get a peaceful night in my own bed.' The laugh died and Catchpoll became more serious. 'My guess is that it would be mothers as would find out what the priest did, and make a sensible guess that if they told their 'usbands then the result would be a rope-danglin' and their children left fatherless. They would keep quiet, except to the healin' woman if she was needed.'

Bradecote stopped in his tracks.

'Catchpoll, does that not mean we need to consider Agnes as the one who used the awl? She was in Naunton, so she says. But even if that was true, and it would be easy to confirm, for the woman she aided, or her family, could tell us when she left, it is not much over a mile to Naunton, and we would only get a vague "mid afternoon" or "before noontide".'

'True, my lord,' conceded Catchpoll, grudgingly, 'but we comes back to the question Young Walkelin would put – "Why now?" I grants you she could, and she would know as the priest would be in the church to say None, but why was she there at all?'

'We can but guess, Catchpoll, but think on this. The death of Thorgar came about by him being in the wrong place at the wrong time, not some plot and plan. It could not be otherwise. If we apply the same thinking to the death of Father Edmund, what if Agnes comes to the church, thinking to give thanks for the safe delivery of a child that has been difficult, and she finds him senseless upon the floor. She knows just what sort of man he is, and the horrors he wreaks. She sees her chance to protect the innocents of Ripple. None has seen her arrive and the temporary workshop is empty. She goes back out, takes an awl, does the deed and then takes a way back that avoids anyone being likely to see her, and "arrives" back in Ripple some hours later. Who would think to go and ask how long the travail was in Naunton?'

''Ceptin' us, my lord.' Catchpoll's face worked ruminatively. 'Would she be capable of it? I would say yes, for she is a tough and practical woman. Has to be in her craft. Not afraid of blood, neither. Nor is she one of the "sheep" who does not think for themselves. Plenty of wits in that 'ead.' His expression became a grimace. 'Remember what she said too, about justice bein' done and if the Law demanded a penalty of 'er she must bear it. Thing is, my lord, and I 'ate to say it, I really would not want it to be true, what you says, for if it is, then I tends to agree with the woman's thinkin'. Mind you, I doubts many would think things through as you has just done, even Agnes the Healer. You thinks like a serjeant now, and that is different to other folk.' He brightened.

'But we still need to speak with her more, and get exactly what she did and when that day, and check it as much as we can.' There was a pause as they both considered the situation. 'Catchpoll, there is another option, and I like it perhaps even less.'

'And that is, my lord?'

'If a father came intent upon retribution for a daughter

foully mistreated, could he have brought her to see that done? Not seeing it as murder but justice. The priest lies senseless but not dead. It takes no great strength to thrust an awl into a man, and in the right frame of mind a girl could do it. You get a woman beyond scared, beyond angry and they grow ice cold, fiercer than any man.' Bradecote was thinking of his Christina, and how she had confronted Baldwin de Malfleur. 'It might be true for a girl.' He did not sound quite as certain on this point.

'And again I hopes you is wrong, my lord.' Catchpoll looked at the sky, not seeking some sign from God, but judging the time of day. 'I reckon there is but an hour afore folk returns from the field. The women might come back earlier to get the pottage cookin' and you does not want to be chasin' hens about in the dark to get them all safely in the hen house.'

'I think any woman in Ripple would be wary of revealing to us how much they knew of Father Edmund's vices with us seeking his killer, so it would be best to have all a household together, then we can see for ourselves which were at risk from Father Edmund without asking the obvious question. It will be very interesting to hear what Father Ambrosius knew, or suspected. Would loyalty to his parishioners outweigh loyalty to his Order, and avoiding a public scandal?'

'We must hope as Walkelin returns with 'im on the morrow, my lord. Very useful it will be, to be sure, but I am not sure how much further it will get us. Now, I am goin' to knock again at Widow Ploughman's door and ask directions for Agnes the Healer, reason bein', let me see, ah yes, you, my lord, is goin' down with a nasty ache of the head, very nasty.'

'A very good reason to ask for her direction, Catchpoll. And I am so very happy that my well-being is so important to you.' Bradecote grinned.

Catchpoll said nothing, but had to suppress a laugh.

Agnes the Healer was not to be found at her humble dwelling, and Serjeant Catchpoll did not want to loiter outside with a very obvious rain cloud scudding up the Severn valley towards them, so he and his superior went back to the priests' house, which felt, now they knew so much about Father Edmund, as if it contained the vestige of a malign presence.

'I imagine Bishop Simon will be both shocked and grieved when he hears of the actions of the man he appointed, though if Father Edmund came from the cloister there would have been no temptation for him and no sign of what his true nature might be.'

'Aye, and most like he will give a prayer of thanks that the bastard did not end with all knowin' what was done. Tidier this way, and done without makin' too much of the priest as a victim, which will be what Bishop Simon and all the clerics will want remembered. 'Tis never about the victims of a man under a vow of chastity and in a position of power in a small community.'

'Have you ever come across crimes like this before, Catchpoll? Involving a priest, I mean.'

'Once or twice, but under Benefit of Clergy they was put before a Church Court, not the Justices in Eyre, and though in cases of murder they always used to be cast out and handed over to us for punishment like any ordinary man, they never did so for this. No doubt their Court set them a great penance, and would say that puttin' them back in a monastery kept them from further sin, but that was not justice, not in my eyes,' growled Catchpoll, and spat onto the hearthstone in disgust. Bradecote, now the father of a daughter, agreed with him. It was a very grim-faced pair who a while later went out into the lessening daylight to begin knocking on the doors of the inhabitants of Ripple. They divided and took what looked to be half the houses each, agreeing to meet back at the priests' house before trying the door of Agnes the Healer once more.

It could not be said that they were greeted with welcoming faces. Some, especially the women now taking up the other half of their daily toil in feeding the family, glanced up resentfully from chopping onions and wondering if they had used too little barley and would receive complaint that bellies were not yet filled at the end of the meal, and there was, among the men, a hangdog look that implied they felt a certain communal guilt about Thorgar that they would rather forget. Being reminded of it by the Law was not welcome at all. Almost nobody had anything to divulge about the day of the killing, since it had been a day when the rain had kept each to their own holding, venturing no further than the gardens of their small plots to hoe the first signs of weeds from among their remaining cabbages and sow their turnips, or remaining indoors to mend, spin or weave. There was one exception, and that was a child. The boy, who stared at Bradecote with the indifference to rank that only a small child could possess, made his announcement in a piping treble.

'I see'd Father Edmund hit upon the door of Guthlac's

house and when the door was opened the Father shouted inside.'

'Don't you be oath-trustin' of the lad, my lord. What 'e says might well be true in part, but it could be it was three days or six days past. You cannot trust a lad of six summers, not with time.' The boy's father looked reprovingly at the child, whose lip trembled.

'No,' Bradecote held up a hand, in case the father forbade further speech, and looked at the child in a fatherly way, as he would at his own son, even if Gilbert was far younger. 'Tell me, are you sure it was the day when Father Edmund died?'

The child glanced at his father and then nodded. 'I went to the door and opened it 'cos I wanted to go and play with Guthlac, but Mother said we would get muddy and I must stay 'ere and play with my sister instead.' He did not look very impressed by this, but then the sister in question was a toddler.

'I see. And did you hear what Father Edmund was shouting about?' Clearly Guthlac was not the householder.

'No, 'cos I could not understand 'is words.'

'Thank you.' Bradecote turned to the father again. 'So Guthlac is the son of . . . ?'

'Tofi, my lord. His youngest. Gundred came of tithing age at Candlemas, and there's Godric in between.'

'Did they name them to be confusing?' Bradecote was sure he would apply the wrong one.

'You would think so, my lord. Their daughters are Mildred, woman grown now, and little Mald, who is but two years older 'n little Guthlac.'

'We will ask Tofi what was shouted.' Bradecote wondered why Tofi had not mentioned the priest shouting at his door on the day of the killing.

It happened that Tofi's door was one being knocked upon by Catchpoll. It was opened by Tofi himself, who looked to be in a poor temper, and his words proved it.

'What do you want, Serjeant?' He scowled, which did not improve the look of his heavily pock-scarred face, but Catchpoll looked positively cheery, mostly to show he did not care how Tofi felt.

'We is tryin' to find out every little thing as was noticed the day Father Edmund was killed. Your girl Mildred told us she saw Thorgar and the priest have words, but did anyone else see him about the village, visitin' someone sick or even just carryin' a pail? Little things helps.'

'Nothin' I can tell you.'

'Then let me step in and ask everyone. Mayhap your wife saw—'

'My wife was busy here. What cause would she 'ave to look out the door?' Tofi did not move.

'I saw Father Edmund go to say Matins and Sext and return from both.' The voice from within was young and with a Welsh lilt. Catchpoll made to step into the gloom of the little house, and Tofi did not stop him. Gwydion was whittling a stick in the firelight as the pottage bubbled, and had an audience of three boys and a little girl of about eight, though she watched from a distance, being seated next to her mother on a bench. She looked mouse-quiet and not a happy

111

child, thought Catchpoll. 'I did not tell you earlier,' continued Gwydion, 'since a priest would do that every day, see, at those times.' He clearly did not think further explanation was needed and turned his focus back to the stick, though the children now stared at their visitor, dimly aware his presence was not welcomed. Pryderi, almost invisible in the darkest corner, groaned, but Catchpoll did not think the lad had tried to conceal anything.

'So nobody saw anythin', not even your healer about 'er visits.' Catchpoll sighed, in the manner of one dejected, but his eyes were watchful.

'I doesn't need to 'ave looked out to know that she would 'ave gone first thing to Oldmother Agatha. There's an ulcer on her leg, what came after she fell over that cat of hers afore Lady Day, poor soul.' Tofi's wife, darning a tear in a cotte by the light of a rush lamp, looked up from her work. Catchpoll could see that Mildred got her looks from her mother, but the woman looked worn and jaded. Mildred herself entered the house at that moment, venting her frustration before she became aware of Catchpoll.

'If'n Uncle Selewine does not take a new wife soon, I may do for 'im with the ladle, that is for sure. Grumble, grumble, that is all I gets. Oh!' Seeing Catchpoll, she reddened. 'I did not mean . . .' She looked worried.

'No, girl, that I knows.' He smiled, but she did not find it relieved her at all. 'Now, Tofi, what were you a-doin' while your wife was "busy"?'

'I dug a few more turnips out of the clamp, and I worked our garden patch once the rain lessened a bit. Too wet the earth were to plough or to sow grain, but I took a hoe to the weeds and it kept me from a naggin' tongue.' His voice was bitter and he gave his wife a resentful look, but she just hunched her shoulders and sniffed. The little girl shuddered, and snuggled in closer to her mother, to the detriment of the darning.

'He did that, Serjeant, but it had little to do with the rain and more to do with a sore head from too much ale.' There was clearly antagonism between husband and wife over that.

It corroborated, thought Catchpoll, Gwydion's claim that Pryderi had not been the only one who had drunk too heavily the evening before the killing day, but it did not provide any gem of information.

He had not planned to visit Selewine the Reeve, since he knew the man had only sons, but it was only next door, and it was always possible that the boys might have seen some small thing. If Tofi had been unwilling to let the serjeant into his home, Selewine was positively antagonistic.

'Why pester me when we is about to eat?'

'I sees no ladle in your hand, and if there was you would be eatin' scarce-cooked pottage. I saw young Mildred next door just come in from doin' a wife's task and gettin' no thanks for it. I reckon as that there pottage needs longer over the fire than I will be here askin' questions.'

Selewine made a sound between a grunt and growl and reluctantly let Catchpoll within. There was a decided difference between the home of Selewine and his brother, and the absence of a woman to care about it was clear. Catchpoll knew his wife would have pursed her lips and shaken her head at the state of it, though it was not, to the average man's eye, such a mess as to make one feel any need to apologise for it.

'So, ask your questions and leave us be, Serjeant Catchpoll.' Selewine folded his arms and the boys, two of them, the younger about the same size as his cousin Guthlac, looked watchful. Their father in a poor mood had to be treated with care to avoid a clip about the ear.

'I wants to know if any of you,' and Catchpoll looked at the boys in turn before returning his gaze to Selewine, 'saw Father Edmund on the day he died, or anything that seemed odd.' He wondered if children had been lost in between, for the older lad looked about tithing age.

Selewine was tight-lipped and the boys looked blankly at him, but then the younger child put up his hand as if asking permission to speak, and said, in a soft whisper, 'I saw when 'e took Oldmother Agatha's cat back to 'er.'

'Fool boy. Father Edmund would rather carry an adder than that cat. Loathed it and shooed it away whenever it came close. It made him sneeze, and that were undignified. You is lyin' or dreamin'. Don't you take anythin' the lad says as true, Serjeant. Of an age to tell all manner of lies, even if without wickedness behind it.' Selewine glared at his son.

'But I saw, I did.' The boy began to cry, softly, and his brother folded his arms and looked upon him with disgust for being so babyish.

'When was it, and what exactly did you see?' Catchpoll asked, gently, and held up his hand to prevent Selewine interrupting.

'It were middle forenoon. I wanted to see if the rain would

stop soon. I saw Father Edmund with the cat under one arm and a little sack under the other, with bread I s'pose.'

'Hah! Oldmother Agatha wants for nothin', not to eat. The family sees to that. Serjeant, this is just the child makin' things up.' Selewine glared at his son, whose lip was now trembling. 'And do not you start tryin' to get that cat to come and plead for food here, Frewin.'

'If 'e does I will throw water over it, Father.' The older boy sounded as though this would be fun rather than a duty.

'Aye, you do that.' Selewine clearly approved of this idea. He then turned to face Catchpoll. 'Anythin' else, Serjeant?'

'No. Not for tonight.' Catchpoll saw how the qualification annoyed the reeve, and was glad of it.

Meanwhile, Bradecote was being offered a beaker of mulled cider in the house of Ulf Shortfinger, a man missing his right middle finger beyond the first joint. Bradecote did not refuse, though he realised that it was a ploy by Ulf's wife to make him feel more welcomed than he really was. She looked harassed, and not just because of the six progeny in the small house. A seventh, whom Walkelin would have identified as his young ferryman, had been exiting as Bradecote was about to knock upon the door, and shook his head as he was asked, in passing, if he had seen anything relevant. It was a very male household, and it was possible that this was the reason the little girl Emma hung about her mother's skirts, but the single glance she gave Bradecote was genuinely fearful, and not because she understood his rank. There was tension in both mother and daughter, but it was not the same as that in Ulf

Shortfinger, whose wariness seemed to owe more to having the lord Undersheriff of Worcestershire in his home than fear of revealing anything criminal.

He was a sturdy individual, with an open expression and more goodwill than any great intelligence, from what Bradecote could discern. He could give no information on the day of the killing, but sounded genuinely sorry that he could not help. His wife, who just shook her head, seemed the more likely to be holding back, and the sons, the younger of whom had abandoned what was a boisterous rough and tumble as soon as Bradecote entered their home, averred that they had fed the pig, brought water from the well and chopped firewood, but had not seen Father Edmund. It was when they said that name that the little girl froze, and visibly held her breath. Bradecote had no doubt she was a victim, but doubted her father knew of it. Now that the priest was dead, he hoped that time might aid her but, other than putting her in his prayers, he felt he was powerless to help in any way. He thanked Ulf Shortfinger for the hospitality, and left, knowing that a pair of small, haunted eyes followed him to the door and no doubt remained staring at it after it was closed behind him.

Chapter Seven

It was the better part of dark when the sheriff's men met back at the priests' house. Bradecote was about to enter, and turned, rubbing his gloved hands together to warm his fingers. The rain cloud had, as if it now wished to stalk its prey and then deluge them, slowed its advance up the valley of the Severn from the south and west, and shrouded the pale face of the waxing gibbous moon.

'Anything useful, Catchpoll?' His voice was quiet, though he realised there was no need for it to be so. The gloom simply made everything feel covert.

'Possibly, my lord, and there be five families with young daughters. The only information that affects Agnes is that she is visitin' Oldmother Agatha most days to tend an ulcerous leg. It will be interestin' to hear if she tells us that in the tale of 'er day of the murder. Sort of lets us know if she is just givin' us the whole or parts.'

'Agreed. I discovered three households with daughters who would be at risk.' Bradecote sighed. 'Let us try the healer again.

I hope she is home, for I do not want to linger in the cold.'

Catchpoll knocked with a confident thud upon her door. After a short delay it was opened, revealing Agnes the Healer wiping her hands upon her skirts.

'Ah. Well you 'ad best come in rather than stand there waitin' to get wet, the both of you.' Agnes did not look worried by their arrival, more slightly annoyed. Apparently considering that she had not sounded at all deferential to the lord Undersheriff, she made a beckoning gesture within and then went to draw a stool closer to the hearth, where a pot simmered gently and an aroma of herbs made Bradecote's mouth water, and invited him to sit. She did not extend this courtesy to Catchpoll.

The chamber was not simply tidy, it was neat to the point of being precisely ordered. Bradecote felt the stool would be moved back to its exact original position as soon as they left. There was a plank bench along the south wall, set beneath the small, shuttered window opening, no doubt to enable the healer to work in the light when the days were longer and less damp, and pots of assorted sizes were set along it, each the same distance from its neighbour.

'What need is there to speak with me again today, my lord? I said what I had to say in the church.' The appellation was respectful, though the tone was not.

'I have no doubt that you did, but we want to know whether you had warned all the mothers of daughters in Ripple about Father Edmund.'

'Men thinks women cannot keep from gossip, but we is better at keepin' silent, when needed.'

'Are you sayin' you did not warn 'em, or that those you

warned did not speak of it?' Catchpoll's eyes narrowed as he looked at the woman.

'I'll give you credit to see and think better 'n most, Serjeant, so no doubt you has the right answer anyways.' She stared back at him.

'We are not here to play with words, mistress. I want your answer.' Bradecote did not try to charm this woman, who clearly had a poor view of men.

'I never told anyone the private things of another, my lord. 'Tis like the priest and the Confession. Mind you, that does not mean I did not drop a warnin' word in the ear of them with most to guard.'

'Was that general, about men, or did you mention Father Edmund by name?'

'I gave the name, for warnin' about them as took vows might cast doubt upon Father Ambrosius, who is a good man.'

This was like pulling up water from a well using a bucket with a hole.

'And how many innocents in Ripple have you knowledge of, who came in too close contact with Father Edmund?'

'Four, but you will get no names from me. The first was late last summer, leastways that were when I was called to treat the poor mite, but I thinks it were some months earlier as happened. She would not eat, and were strikin' herself with withies till the skin were raw. Said she were wicked and destined for Damnation, and it were that serpent-priest told 'er so. A girl of eight summers, wicked? Hah! And you know why she were "wicked"? All 'acos she lifted her skirts above her little knees to paddle in the brook when it was real burnin' sun afore the field was cut for hay, and he saw her and were "tempted" by it. Could 'ave been worse, just, but a child that age obeys a priest, whatever they says to do. Not right, not right at all it were, and afterwards the poor little soul feared to tell anyone, for she were told God would strike down someone she loved if she spoke of it. Clever, that were, since folk dies often enough and even young 'uns knows death visits old and young, rich and poor alike.'

'But she told you, or her mother.' Catchpoll looked grim.

'Me, in the end, and I told 'er poor mother, who wanted it kept secret for the shame of it. Someone put the idea into that little mind about wickedness, and Father Edmund was all for frightenin' simple folk with the Vengeance of God. Hmm. Well, he will find out about that for 'imself now, and I for one will not pray for his black soul.'

'And the others? Did he – do worse?' Bradecote felt besmirched just asking the question.

'I could not swear oath to it, for one girl still will not speak of it, just stares through you like you was a ghost, but from what I saw of bruises, it is possible. Others he hurt, and more 'n once, but most of all, he made them loathe themselves, put all the "guilt" upon the innocent, ruined their trust, even in the Lord God above. One girl lost her best friend to sickness a few weeks later, and is still convinced, months later, it is her fault she died! Not fit to be a priest, not fit to be a man!' Agnes's voice held real anger and was driven low by it.

'He is neither now, and the Law needs to know by whose hand. It need not follow that whoever beat him dealt the fatal wound. A woman could do that. From what you have said, you would have reason, almost the strongest reason, since you know so much, to take the chance to protect the innocents of this parish. Nor are you one who can be afraid of blood.' Bradecote was open with her. 'You even said that if the Law demanded a penalty of you, you must bear it. Did you kill Father Edmund, Agnes?' Bradecote asked the all-important question.

'I did not.'

'Then tell us all you did that day so we can prove it.' Catchpoll sounded on her side, which at heart, he was. Serjeanting sometimes meant going against the heart in support of the truth.

Agnes looked at him, then back at the lord Undersheriff, and there was silence as she made up her mind what to do. Then she spoke.

'Like priests, I gets a knock at the door all hours. I was called to Naunton just after dawn by Cerdic the Smith, who wanted sympathy for trippin' over three times on the way in the partlight. Would not 'ave been so if the man came the night afore, as he ought, and so I told 'im. The poor wife had been in travail all the day and night and was near done to death with it all. When it came to the pushin' part she were too weak to get it done timely. I did what I could but the babe came out very limp and took a lot of rubbin' to get a yell from it, and the mother is as weak as the babe. I were with them until past the middle of the afternoon, makin' things to give strength and ease and I left not knowin' if both will be alive in a week. Cerdic the Smith is a fool. There's six children to 'is loins afore this, and the wife is a slip of a thing who struggles pushin' babes out into the world. I told 'im last time that if he loved his wife he should stick it in cold water, like he does quenchin' the iron, when the need took 'im, and leave the poor woman be. Only the Grace of God has let her last this long.' Agnes shook her head.

'I wonder you did not go to the church to give thanks for the safe delivery and pray for mother and child.' Bradecote looked thoughtful.

'God don't listen to prayers only within the walls of a church, my lord. I prays more than most, seein' and doin' as I does, and I misses more Holy Days than anyone else in the parish. Father Ambrosius told me long ago that the Benedictines say that to work is to pray and all my work is a prayer and God listens.' She crossed herself. 'Assuredly He listens.'

'Did anyone see you when you came back to Ripple?'

'See? No, my lord, not see, since I went to Oldmother Agatha, whose eyes are all milky, to salve a leg ulcer, and she were wonderin' why I had not visited first thing as usual, and I was not swiftly back, for I did not take the track but went due west across the fields to pick some new growth of a plant that is most effective picked young, and came back through Uckinghall. Then the grandsons came in, all words at once, and told of the killin' and the hangin'. That was the first I knew.'

'So you did not see the burying of Thorgar up by the Old Road?' Bradecote frowned.

'No. As I says, I did not come that way.'

'And why did you offer to deal with the body of the priest?'

'Because I am the one most used to bodies, my lord. Laid out fewer than I has seen come into the world, but not by many, and besides, it were good to see that he died hard.

Could 'ave done without the Widow Reed actin' like a saint had passed, mind you.' She sniffed, disdainfully.

'We will speak with the smith and Oldmother Agatha.'

'You do that, my lord, and they will say I speaks true enough.'

'Then we will leave you to that good pottage.' Bradecote gave the faintest of smiles, and she dipped an obeisance as they left.

Bradecote and Catchpoll returned to the priests' house in subdued mood. Catchpoll lit the fire in the hearth, and they watched the flame scramble through the kindling, tasting and then consuming it hungrily. He held his hands to the first warmth and sucked his teeth.

'We gets back to four families where a father might 'ave found out a nasty truth and taken action, my lord, and our door knockin' gave us over twice that number. Does we confront them all and spread the knowledge of what happened in Ripple?'

'I think over time it will come out anyway, Catchpoll, but I would not want to make it any harder for the girls involved. I would say that with two of the three families with young daughters that I saw, the girls looked like any other child, playing with their siblings and merely curious about me, a strange man in their home. Only with the third was the girl shy and watchful, and . . . different. That was Emma, the daughter of Ulf Shortfinger. She froze when Father Edmund's name was mentioned. However, I do not think it likely Ulf himself knows anything. He is not the sort to conceal well, and it would fit if, as Agnes the Healer told us, the women wanted everything kept close and private.'

'Trouble is, my lord, by those ways of whittlin' down the suspects, I falls short by one. The daughter of Leofwin looked at me, eye to eye, for a moment and I 'as seen that look afore in a maid. It is fear mixed with distrust and a dull loathin'. She never spoke a word, and she went and slipped 'er arm through her mother's, to be close. Leofwin is a broad-shouldered man, and the wife looked scared. Now, that might be in case Leofwin finds out now, or he found out and acted upon it.'

'That gives us one. The other?'

'Tofi, who was only slightly less unhappy to see me than Selewine.'

'But Selewine has only sons, Catchpoll. Why visit him?'

'We was askin' about anyone seein' the priest the mornin' of his death, so Selewine's sons might be of use too. Turns out I were right to ask, for the younger son swears he saw Father Edmund take the cat back to Oldmother Agatha early on the mornin' of the murder. Selewine did not believe a word of it, since the priest disliked the cat, but if it were shut up in the old woman's house it would not be pesterin' at his own, or bein' let in by the Widow Reed deliverin' honey cakes or such to please 'im.'

'I see. But Tofi's young daughter – Mald was the name I was given.'

'Not a cheerful home, Tofi's. The wife looks tired, most of all with Tofi, and the little girl, this Mald, kept right up close with 'er. Little soul looked – hollow, like some does in grief. She did not draw close like the boys to watch Gwydion whittlin' somethin', and you knows that children love to watch when Young Walkelin does that, so it says much she stayed back.'

'We can look closer for the fourth victim if we need to after speaking with Tofi, Ulf Shortfinger and Leofwin. With luck it will not be needed.'

'And does we check what Agnes the Healer said first, my lord?'

'It would be tidier if we did, and it need not take long at all if we ride, even if you have only Snægl.'

'Fair enough, my lord. And I hopes we sees Young Walkelin and Father Ambrosius early too.'

There was a knock upon the door, and Mildred came in with bowls covered with cloths to keep out the mizzle now falling in the darkness outside. One of her brothers followed with a pair of beakers and a jug, his focus all on not spilling a drop of the ale within. The pottage was good, but it did not aid sleep.

Walkelin, meanwhile, with the benefit of Catchpoll's rather more eager mount, had reached Worcester a little after None, instructed a castle groom to take care of his horse, and gone to the bishop's residence to the north of the cathedral. It was an old building, looking a little dilapidated except for its chapel, where its roof was pristine. There had been rumours of the lord Bishop having a new and grander palace built, but with Worcester having already been set aflame once since the Empress Maud began to challenge King Stephen for the throne, no doubt Bishop Simon feared any expense might be wasted should the strife return to Worcester.

Walkelin was relieved to hear that Bishop Simon had returned late that morning, which would save him making representations to William de Beauchamp for the use of one of his clerks and a mounted messenger. He was less pleased to be received politely, but without any sign that he would be allowed to speak directly with the august prelate. The clerk to whom he had been brought, probably the lord Bishop's chief scribe, patently thought that he did not look the sort of person to be ushered swiftly before a bishop.

'I am here on behalf of the lord Sheriff.' Walkelin considered this was not the time to be talking only of an undersheriff. 'The lord Bishop will have been told of the killin' of Father Edmund of Ripple, and it is of the greatest importance that I speak with the lord Bishop in person, swiftly. The lord Sheriff also needs to know if Father Ambrosius of Ripple has come to the lord Bishop today.'

The clerk was silent, but Walkelin caught a flicker of interest, or was it concern, cross the man's ascetic countenance. There was no vibrancy to the man, as though he was as lacking in life as the quills he might scratch across a piece of vellum.

'This is not just to tell the lord Bishop of progress. It may be very important in catchin' who murdered Father Edmund in his own church.' Walkelin looked as commanding and authoritative as he could. The cleric wavered. 'If I cannot see the lord Bishop I will return to the castle and tell the lord Sheriff that you would not let me see 'im. I represent the lord Sheriff and he represents the lord King. Would you keep King Stephen out?' Walkelin dimly remembered the lord Bradecote using this chain of authority, and deployed it.

'I-I will see if the lord Bishop can spare you a short time.' The clerk scurried away, and Walkelin was both astounded at his success and very pleased with himself. The man returned in a few minutes and led Walkelin to a hall that was not so very unlike that in the castle. Walkelin told himself he was now at ease speaking with abbots and nearly as much at ease as anyone might be with William de Beauchamp, depending upon the lord Sheriff's mood, so this was not a task to leave him tongue-tied.

Bishop Simon was a thoughtful-looking man, and Walkelin decided he was never one to rush a decision. He sat, impassive enough, with his hands lightly folded on his lap, though one finger end tapped very lightly on the back of the other hand. Walkelin made a deep obeisance and came forward.

'I am told that it is important that you speak with me.' The bishop's voice was very calm and even, though a little dry.

'Yes, my lord. I am Underserjeant Walkelin, and I have come most urgently to ask if Father Ambrosius of Ripple has also sought to speak with you this afternoon.'

'He has.' Even as the wave of relief flooded over Walkelin, he caught the slightly watchful look dawn in Bishop Simon's grey eyes. 'I have sent him to the priory to rest tonight before he returns to his parish.' The bishop turned slightly to dismiss the clerk, who had remained as if needed to protect his superior. 'You may leave us.'

The clerk seemed a little surprised, but obeyed. Walkelin waited until the door shut behind him before he continued.

'And did he bring something with 'im, my lord, a chalice of silver?'

'Yes, and he explained why. I think that in many ways he was correct to do so, for it appears that its bringing up from the earth has brought up greed and sin after it, though to have removed it without Father Edmund's knowledge was wrong, however good the motive. It pains me to think the gift of one who sat where I sit now should become tainted.'

'But Father Ambrosius did not know of the death of Father Edmund.' It was half a statement and half a question.

'No, he did not, until I told him of it, and he was very shocked at the news.'

'So did 'e see the chalice as a temptation?' Walkelin wondered what exactly the priest had believed.

'I cannot say what he thought, only that he told me that the story of the priest who buried it and other valuables, to keep from the heathens, had been passed down the generations and, like most stories that become a legend, grown in the process. He said if it was known that the treasure was found it would corrupt, and set neighbour against neighbour in the sin of greed.'

'And when he heard of the death of Father Edmund, did he say anything other than it was a shock?'

Bishop Simon's lips pursed.

'My lord, I will say what is known. It seems that Father Edmund betrayed 'is position as priest and not only broke the vows of a Benedictine and committed foul sins, but broke the King's laws also.' Walkelin, a young man whose expression was usually cheerful and approachable, looked grim, and his eyes did not waver from the bishop.

Bishop Simon sighed and closed his eyes. The tapping fingertip ceased its motion. There was silence, and Walkelin, not sure whether this meant the prelate was praying, did not like to interrupt. Eventually the bishop spoke, his voice heavy with disapproval and, thought Walkelin, embarrassment.

'Father Edmund cannot defend himself, and I bear that in mind, but Father Ambrosius set before me his fears and belief that his fellow priest was guilty of more than sinful thoughts about women. Such thoughts, transient ones, afflict many who take their vows, for some find celibacy easy and natural and for others the struggle is a sign of their commitment to God. If only all could be as the Blessed Wulfstan who, in Worcester itself, resisted a foolish and sinful woman, and who wrote so eloquently how a priest should conduct himself.' The sigh was repeated, even more heavily. 'To break the vow in any deed is another matter, and to even look with lust upon an innocent is beyond comprehension.' He now shook his head.

Walkelin, who did not understand every single word of what Bishop Simon said and – whilst like everyone in Worcester, knew of 'their' St Wulfstan – had no idea of any writings, hoped he understood the sentiment.

'So if Father Edmund had not been killed, would you have replaced him, my lord?'

'That is not a matter for the Law, Underserjeant. Father Edmund faces the judgement of God, and He sees all things, knows all things. What would have happened is no longer important.'

'He does, my lord, as will we all,' Walkelin crossed himself, 'but—'

'I would not have left Father Edmund as a parish priest, Underserjeant. I can see it was that which troubles you. The trust which must exist between parishioners and their priest was broken, so he could not remain in Ripple, and I myself would feel in error to send him to another parish where other innocents, and his own soul, might be put in jeopardy.'

Walkelin sighed with relief, but a final question occurred to him.

'One thing more, my lord. Did Father Ambrosius bring any other things, besides the chalice?'

'No. He said there was other "treasure", but it was all clearly without connection to the Church.'

'Thank you, my lord. I will leave you n—'

'I have a question for you, Underserjeant.'

'You do, my lord?' Walkelin's surprise was obvious.

'Yes. A young woman came seeking me, not only to tell of the death of Father Edmund, but saying that her brother had been falsely hanged for the crime. Since you have not told me the matter is closed, am I to assume she was correct and he was innocent?'

'Almost could I swear my oath upon it, my lord, though only when the true killer is taken will it be proven. Thorgar was a young man of faith who felt a great callin' to take the cowl at Tewkesbury, and Abbot Roger had spoken with 'im about it. Abbot Roger says he would be pleased to give Thorgar's body a home in death, if innocence be proven and the body is taken from a murderer's grave. The monks of Tewkesbury pray for 'im.'

'Abbot Roger is a good judge of men. I will assuredly also pray for the soul of Thorgar.'

'And we will bring you news as soon as we may of all that is discovered, my lord.'

Bishop Simon nodded in gracious acceptance of this, and,

making a further obeisance, Walkelin withdrew to go in search of Father Ambrosius at the Priory of St Mary.

Walkelin thought there was time before Compline to speak with Father Ambrosius, so knocked confidently at the priory gate and called forth Brother Porter, who in turn waylaid a novice and sent him in search of their priestly guest.

The young man returned shortly afterwards, followed by a tall man, perhaps a little over two score years in age, whose tonsure did not need shaving, having but a narrow ring of wispy, black hair about his baldness, with black brows which were both sparse and of long hairs, and who stuck his neck forward, all of which made Walkelin think of a heron. At first glance it was difficult to match this man to the description given by Walkelin's youthful ferryman that morning of a strong rower, but then the lad had also said that Father Ambrosius looked less capable than he was. Studying him more carefully, Walkelin noted that his hands, which were large, showed callouses upon the palms as the priest outstretched his arms in questioning welcome. This was a man of deeds as well as prayer.

'You have need of me, my son?' The voice was deep, with the accent of Worcestershire overlaid by the more precise speech of the trained priest, and was slightly surprised in tone.

'I do, Father. I am Underserjeant Walkelin, and have been sent to ask you about . . .' Walkelin, aware of the novice lingering in case he was required further, decided it prudent to remain vague, 'events in Ripple.'

'Ah.' Clearly not slow of wits, Father Ambrosius thanked the novice and dismissed him gently before looking again at

Walkelin. 'Thank you. What has happened ought not to be a source of gossip, which happens even within cloisters, alas.' The man sighed, and folded his big, capable hands before him.

'Father, you brought the silver chalice that Thorgar found to Bishop Simon, and your concerns about Father Edmund also. I must ask you about both things. Did Father Edmund give you the chalice, to bring here or keep secure elsewhere?'

'No, he did not.' Father Ambrosius frowned, his dark brows gathering. 'Was it a form of stealing? I hope not, though I accept that it might seem that way. You see, that "treasure" is cursed.' He saw Walkelin's own eyebrows rise in some amazement. 'Ah, not by some words of intended evil, but because over the many, many years it has been spoken of in Ripple it has become something to be coveted.' He smiled, though it was a twisted smile. 'Providence ordained that it should be discovered by the young man in Ripple least likely to succumb to greed, and who saw it only as Divine Guidance, approval of his deep feelings of need to enter the cloister. However, he was in error in one respect, for he could not give to Tewkesbury what belonged still to the Lord Bishop of Worcester. I am sure Thorgar will see that.'

'Then you do not know, Father?' Walkelin's surprise was even greater this time. 'You were told that Father Edmund was dead by violence, yes?'

'I was, and I will pray for a soul for whom much prayer is needed.' This was said heavily.

'But you were not told by whom?'

'No.'

'Then you must know that Thorgar was hanged for the killin'' of Father Edmund.' Walkelin did not immediately say that he was actually innocent, wanting to see the cleric's first reaction.

Father Ambrosius's face paled, and he crossed himself with a shaking hand.

'Thorgar? No, no, he would not, could not – I have known Thorgar since he was a small boy, and even then he was not a violent or aggressive child. As he grew taller and broader, why, he grew more gentle of action and deed. I was not surprised that he was called to a life of prayer. Thorgar, Underserjeant, simply could not kill another.'

'Your readin' of Thorgar seems to tally with what we has found, Father. It seems very unlikely that Thorgar committed the murder, but when 'e was found by the body, none said as you do, though now nobody says other than Thorgar was a good son and a gentle soul. So you see, I needs to know all that you can tell me about what took place in Ripple these last few days, and I needs to take you back to Ripple first thing tomorrow.'

'Indeed. My duty is to return straight away and give both comfort to Thorgar's family and keep the village together. Oh dear, oh dear.'

'So tell me, Father, everything you can about the chalice and its findin', and also what you knows about Father Edmund. Not that it will be news to me or the lord Undersheriff, but how much was known and how much just – suspicionin'?'

'He had told me he had been given something "most precious" for safekeeping, but I did not know what it was until he spoke of it the evening before I was called to Queenhill. He told me, and I fear it was in a very gloating way, that Thorgar had come to him, while I was away at a deathbed in Ruyhale, and said that he had been granted a Sign from Heaven because his plough had turned up silver, on one of his own strips for the year. Father Edmund did not know it was "The Priest's Treasure" that had lain there for generations. Thorgar had told him he feared that if it was known about, there would be arguments and ill-feeling about it, and so he brought the chalice, as a sacramental item, for safekeeping to his village priest. It was his intent to take it as his offering to Tewkesbury Abbey for his admission to be a choir monk. There was mention of a small amount of other silver without religious meaning, a few coins and cloak clasps I suppose, which would provide for his family. He said they could buy at least two good sows and a goat with it, and then exchange piglets and cheese for labour when he was not there to work the land. Father Edmund was not' – he paused to seek the right word – 'kind about Thorgar's wish to become a choir monk. In fact, he mocked it in a way I felt was quite wrong. He did not know about the history of the items, other than they were buried a long time ago, but I did. I was the one who told him the story and that the chalice belonged to Bishop Simon as Lord Bishop of Worcester. This made him smile, and it was not a nice smile.' Father Ambrosius sighed. 'Father Edmund came to Ripple a little under a year ago, upon the death of good Father Giraldus.' He crossed himself again. 'I was born in Ripple and came here to this priory as a youth, not very unlike poor Thorgar, but for me it was always the ministry that called me. My father was the reeve's brother, and I am kindred to Selewine, though I would not boast of it, nor have I ever given him lesser penance because of it. So I knew the people and the old stories. I was appointed as a fresh young priest by

Bishop Simon's predecessor, Bishop Theulf, to serve with Father Giraldus, who was very experienced. I think Bishop Simon had a similar thought when he sent Father Edmund, who had been ordained barely a year when he arrived. It was my duty as a good Christian and a brother priest to make him welcome and be in charity with him but, I confess, I could not. I have prayed much and done private penance for my thoughts, but no, I could not like him, and recently I had cause to think him a danger to his flock, at least to the lambs.' Father Ambrosius reddened. 'I did not know what to do. It was all things that came to me under the sanctity of the Confession, and none would willingly come forward and say to the world what had happened in their family, and also who would believe me? I had not his sly and silver tongue, for Father Edmund could beguile like the Serpent of Eden. I think he was aware that his misdeeds might come to light, and I sensed that when he heard about the chalice belonging to the lord Bishop of Worcester, he saw a way to put himself forward in a good way so that anything said against him might be treated as mere unpleasant gossip.'

'So you took the chalice and brought it here to Worcester instead.' Walkelin saw this as perfectly sensible.

'Yes. I thought it best, but now . . . My act may have caused two deaths. May I be forgiven.' Father Ambrosius closed his eyes as if in pain, and his knuckles showed white as he clasped his hands tightly together.

'But Father, unless another knew of the chalice, then Father Edmund was not killed by one seekin' it.' Walkelin said this to be consoling, but it had his brain turning over yet again how a vengeful beating was ended with the cold and calculated stabbing of a man rendered defenceless. It was then that it hit him, and made his heart sink. Had a small hand driven that awl under the ribs, encouraged to show that the erstwhile victim was no longer powerless and would be victimised no more?

'. . . and I still think the accursed treasure is involved, Underserjeant.'

Walkelin nodded, though he had not been listening.

'I can take you up behind me on my horse, Father. Could you be ready to leave after Prime in the morning?'

'Yes.'

'Then be outside the gate and I will meet you there.' Walkelin gave a friendly nod and turned to go.

'God grant that no more harm is done in Ripple.'

'Amen to that, Father.' Walkelin sought his own abode in a more thoughtful than happy mood, where he was greeted warmly by his new wife, though his mother worried that dividing the meal between three rather than two might mean he had less than a grown man might, in her view, need. Eluned, it had to be said, was very good at distracting him and so, when he eventually slept, he slept well, and more soundly than his superiors.

Chapter Eight

Whilst he left his bed, and a sleepy Eluned, with the natural reluctance of a man newly married, the next morning Walkelin was eager to restore Father Ambrosius to Ripple, and went to saddle his horse in the castle stables before the bell for Prime began to toll. As he crossed the bailey he was taken aback to see William de Beauchamp, with a fur-trimmed cloak about his shoulders, emerge from the other side, bellowing to know why his horse was not already being walked up and down in readiness for him. He reminded Walkelin of a bull broken loose in the shambles and daring any man to approach him. Espying Walkelin, he halted, mid bellow, and pointed an accusatory finger at him. At least he did not paw the ground.

'And what are you doing here, Underserjeant?'

Walkelin ran forward, half stumbling on the cobbles, and grabbed the woollen cap from his head as he made a deep obeisance.

'My lord, I was sent back yesterday afternoon to speak with the lord Bishop and to find the priest of Ripple.' Remembering he was now an underserjeant, Walkelin controlled the urge to rush his words.

'But he is dead.' De Beauchamp's scowl deepened.

'Ah no, my lord, the other priest, for there are two in the parish.'

'And he, the second one, is in Worcester?' William de Beauchamp's annoyance and eagerness to depart were curtailed by curiosity.

'My lord, he returned a silver chalice to the lord Bishop, one that the man as was strung up, wrongly, dug out of the ground with the plough.'

'The lord Bishop's chalice was buried in a field? Were you ale-sodden last night?' It all sounded ridiculous to de Beauchamp.

'Oh no, my lord, oath-truth I was not. The chalice was the gift of a Bishop of Worcester 'undreds of years ago and was buried to keep it from an army of pagan Danes, and never found after, not till Thorgar's ploughshare turned it up from the earth again. The lord Bishop, way back, had replaced the lost one, so the priests saw it belonged to Bishop Simon as is lord Bishop of Worcester now.'

William de Beauchamp grunted his comprehension, but his mind was assessing whether the find might in fact belong to the King. However, the idea of going to Bishop Simon and asking for it back sounded petty, and a succession of bishops probably counted the same as descent by blood. For the sake of one piece of silverware it would be best to leave things as they stood. He moved on to the next piece of information.

'So the sister was right, was she? The hanged man was not the killer?'

'My lord, we thinks so indeed.'

William de Beauchamp noted the inclusive 'we' and the scowl lifted a little. His horse was led out from the stables and he waved it away, as if the groom were a summer fly, telling him to walk the beast up and down.

'I will not be long.' The lord Sheriff looked again at Walkelin. 'I will not stand and get cold while you tell me what advances have been made. Come.' He crossed the bailey to the guardroom, and, upon entering, demanded that everyone else be about their duties and get out, then removed a leather gauntlet and held a hand to take the warmth that came from the still-glowing brazier that had been a source of warmth for the night watch, in between their shifts upon the chill battlements.

'So?'

'The ploughman, Thorgar, did not kill the priest, and there is two reasons why someone did kill Father Edmund. Either they thought 'e knew where the chalice and other treasure was, or—'

'There was more than the chalice?' This sounded much more clearly treasure trove, and de Beauchamp, who was by nature avaricious, instantly began to wonder how much of the treasure might not actually be sent to the King's treasury. 'What else is there?'

'I does not know all, my lord. The only two as did is dead now, but the lord Bradecote was told at Tewkesbury Abbey it was arm torcs and silver coin.'

'Tewkesbury Abbey?'

Walkelin explained Thorgar's desire for admission to the abbey.

'Well, Abbot Roger could not accept the gift, because it belongs to the lord King.'

'It does, my lord?' Walkelin voiced his surprise. He had never heard of the law of treasure trove, and doubted Serjeant Catchpoll or the lord Undersheriff knew of it either.

'Yes. If it was buried with the intent to retrieve it later, and was lost, then unless the owners are known and can prove their right, it is the property of the King. So when the items are found, Underserjeant, make sure they are brought to me.'

'Yes, my lord.' Privately, Walkelin thought that King Stephen did not need a few more pieces of silver, since kings must have whole rooms full of it, but accepted the ruling.

'You said there was a second reason. That was . . . ?' De Beauchamp moved on.

'Ah, that, my lord, was they found out what the priest 'ad done.' Walkelin looked severe, and far less 'Walkelin-like' than usual.

'Which was?' Walkelin's demeanour meant that de Beauchamp did not think it was getting merry on the wine for the Sacrament.

'Takin' advantage of little girls, my lord. My lord Bradecote and Serjeant Catchpoll are discoverin' more, but the village healer knew things and Father Ambrosius, the priest I came to find, would not give details as came to 'im from Confession, but was deeply troubled and reported it to the lord Bishop.'

'I would have liked to see the look on Bishop Simon's face when he heard.' De Beauchamp gave a small smile. 'He appoints the priests to Ripple so he sent a wolf among the lambs.'

'Well, he looked mightily unhappy when I spoke with 'im, my lord.'

De Beauchamp's smile lengthened for a moment, then he was deadly serious once more, and grim of visage. 'This is messy and unpleasant and . . . I will be back in Worcester in two or three days. I hope this is cleared up swiftly, though the Law will seem on the wrong side to many if the latter is the reason for the death. Off you go.'

'At once, my lord.' Walkelin went to fetch his horse, and was still able to be outside the priory gate before Father Ambrosius emerged, looking doubtfully at the animal upon which he was to be a second burden.

Bradecote and Catchpoll were saddling their own horses at first light, keen to establish the veracity, or otherwise, of Agnes the Healer's story before confronting the men who would have had cause to attack Father Edmund. Bradecote's steel grey greeted him with a whinny, which made Catchpoll laugh and say that the animal was clearly unimpressed sharing the stable with the ox team. It fidgeted as it was saddled and gave a half-hearted buck when Bradecote mounted, but a firm hand and gentle words calmed it, and Catchpoll did not get the chance to see his superior cast ignominiously into the damp, red-brown earth.

There was a chill in the air, but also the freshness of spring, and Bradecote rejoiced in it, in a way he knew Catchpoll, a townsman born and bred, could not. Hugh Bradecote was as connected to the seasons and the land as those who worked it with their labour, and as aware of the importance of weather suited to that season. There was so much that was finely balanced in the rural life, rather more than the urban one, and Bradecote gave up a heartfelt thanks that the spring, despite a few days of heavy rain, was unfurling the first leaves and warming the earth for planting.

The pair cantered up the gentle incline towards the Old Road, and received a raised hand of acknowledgement from the shepherd, who was now aware of who they were. Bradecote dropped his horse's pace and turned to call to Catchpoll, who, having to ride Snægl in the absence of his own horse, was lagging behind.

'Catchpoll, we could speak with the shepherd as we return, if we need further confirmation of the healer's timings.'

'Aye, my lord, that is true, though I am hopin' as we will get all we needs in Naunton.'

They reached the Old Road, and before the turning to Naunton there stood a lone dwelling with a large, open-fronted workshop next to it, and a wheel attached to the outer wall on the south side, advertising its purpose.

A voice raised in loud complaint from within made Bradecote's horse jib.

'If'n I told you once I told you endless times, not that way, boy. Are you sure you is a son of mine?' This was followed by a loud, hissing sigh. 'Never a wheelwright will you make, Wystan, and glad I am to possess other sons as loves the wood. Why your brother needs must go—'

'Mornin',' Catchpoll interrupted the wheelwright's complaints quite casually.

The wheelwright looked up from the part-repaired cartwheel, having mentally ignored any hooves not accompanied by the sound of rumbling wheels. His eyes narrowed a little as he saw the man who had spoken was at the side of a well-dressed and mounted man who was obviously lordly. He gave a nod and pulled the green, woollen cap from his head, nudging the lad at his side to do likewise.

'Mornin'.' The wheelwright was cagey, since these men would clearly not be requiring a wheel made or repaired.

'This is the lord Undersheriff of Worcestershire, and I am the lord Sheriff's Serjeant, come to look into the death of the priest in Ripple.'

'Be that so? None 'as come our way and spoken of it, though we is part of the parish. Which priest? Not Father Ambrosius, I hopes.' The wheelwright frowned.

'No. It was Father Edmund.' Bradecote noted the slight relaxation in the wheelwright's shoulders. Not popular even in the wider parish, then, Father Edmund. 'A man was hanged for the murder, but Thorgar the Ploughman was not the killer, and we seek who was.' Bradecote was a little surprised that news had not reached thus far from Ripple itself, since it had gone south to Tewkesbury swiftly enough, but if none had reason to leave the village in this direction the gossip was yet to spread. His surprise increased as the wheelwright's son paled, and actually gasped in shock.

'Thorgar? But none would think Thorgar could kill. Big he is – was – but gentle of spirit and kind also.' Wystan was clearly stunned.

'You knew him well, then?'

'Not so very well, my lord, but whenever the ox cart came for repairs or any handcart from Ripple, it were Thorgar who came with it. Laughed, 'e did, sayin' as when the cart were too small for the oxen, 'e acted their part. Not a steep way up from Ripple, but not easy for the weak or women. I like the beasts,' the lad cast a swift sideways glance at his father, and Bradecote surmised this was seen as wayward by the wheelwright, 'and we got on well. I would say we was friendly. I will pray for a good soul lost.' The lad crossed himself.

'We are on our way to see the smith in Naunton,' Bradecote did not make it clear whether this was to nail a loose horseshoe or ask questions, 'but you must see most who pass this way.'

'If I am at my work but not so lost in it as to be "passer-blind", my lord.' The wheelwright did not wish to be thought obstructive if he could not answer the question that was obviously coming.

'Have you seen the healer of Ripple come this way in the last few days?'

'Not comin', my lord, though come she must 'ave, for I saw 'er on the way back to Ripple three days past now, good hours after noontide. Looked tired, poor woman. If Father Ambrosius is good for our souls in this parish, it is Mother Agnes as cares for our bodies, right enough. There be no other healer this side of the river even to Croome. Not soft of word, oh no, but none better 'earted nor swift of mind is there from Worcester to Tewkesbury. Fixed my arm, she did, five years back, and if the mend 'ad been poor I would not be at my craft now. Never say she be missin'!' The wheelwright looked genuinely concerned.

'Oh no, but we is just seein' where all the folk of Ripple was if not in the Great Field the day Father Edmund died.'

Catchpoll made sure the enquiry sounded of mild interest not major importance.

'Hmm. I takes it bad, as any in the parish would, that a question be asked over Mother Agnes, even if'n it comes from you, my lord.' The wheelwright nodded respectfully as he said this.

'Which is to the healer's credit, but we are the Law and do not know her character as you all do, so the question was asked.' Bradecote took no offence, for none was intended. This man was just speaking up for someone held in high regard by the locality. 'We will not keep you from your work further.' Bradecote's own nod indicated the interchange was ended, and he set his heels gently to the grey horse's flank and trotted away, with Catchpoll half raising a hand as his own farewell. They did not hear Wystan beg leave to abandon his ham-fisted woodworking and go down to Ripple before the sun dipped behind the Malvern Hills to the west.

Cerdic the Smith's strength lay in his arm not his brain. He took things day by day, and was thus often taken by surprise the way matters turned out. At present he was a harassed man, for his wife was still weak and bedridden, and her sister had taken over the home and care of his brood of young children. What with the different bustle and the mewling of the babe in the crib, the only place he felt any peace was by the inferno in his forge and with the steady 'breathing' of his bellows as he tended the fire, his fire. His fire was his companion who never judged, berated or pleaded with him, but was always there for him. He fed it, and nurtured it, and it rewarded him. The scorched hairs on his forearms and the scattered, white scars were as the marks from an overeager hound whose play had become too boisterous, except his beast was a dragon. When his name was called by an authoritative male voice, he turned from it, felt its heat upon his back, and his stance looked to Catchpoll as though the man was protecting the glowing red behind him.

Catchpoll did not ask the man's name. He was clearly the smith, and there would not be two in a small village that was not much more than a cluster of homes, huddling together as if for warmth.

'This is the lord Undersheriff of Worcestershire, and I am the lord Sheriff's Serjeant. We—'

''Tis not my fault,' cried Cerdic, and dropped the heavy pincers that had been in his hand.

'What is not your fault?' Catchpoll could not resist asking the question, even though he knew it might lead them far from the path of questions about Agnes the Healer.

'Anythin'.' Cerdic's eyes rolled like those of a frightened horse.

As an answer it was at least comprehensive.

'Ah.' Catchpoll gave a small sigh. 'Well, you will be glad to know we is not come to drag you off in chains, but to ask a simple question of you.'

'Ask. Ask and I will answer true, my lords.' Cerdic elevated Catchpoll, which was not entirely to that worthy's taste, but he let it pass.

'You called upon the services of Mistress Agnes, the healer in Ripple, a few days past, when your wife was in travail.' Bradecote spoke up.

'I did, my lord.' Cerdic now sounded amazed, as though they

had discovered this fact through some augury.

'We want to know when she came and when she left. That is all.' Bradecote's voice was very calm and even.

'Oh.' The man before them sagged with relief, rather like emptying bellows. For a moment he gathered what wits he possessed, and then he spoke, and it was in a more normal voice.

'My wife never finds it easy, come her time, though you would think it would be easier when six 'as come that way afore. All day and night it went on, and I went to Ripple even afore it were light, good husband that I am. Not that I were praised for it. Three times I near broke bones, fallin' over in my rush in the bare light. My wife is lucky all I did were twist an ankle and not break my neck and leave 'er a widow with seven mouths to feed, but no credit did I get for it from Old Bony Elbows, nor did she offer anythin' for my ankle, despite 'er craft. Praised all over she is, but I wonder what it is they does when it comes to babes. I mean, babes just – comes. For all anyone knows, she just sits and watches and says soothin' words.' Cerdic was clearly not of the local majority. Whilst neither of his auditors had watched a midwife at work, they knew there was more to it than patting hands and bathing foreheads, and wives would not treat such women so reverentially if their services had not been greatly valued in the most trying circumstances. However, Agnes the Healer was not a woman who pandered to the male of the species, and especially foolish ones. From what she had told them, Cerdic had probably been berated at length on the way to Naunton, and he felt mistreated.

'So you came home and then how long was it afore the babe arrived and Mistress Agnes set off back to Ripple?' Catchpoll decided to give the healer a respectful title, just to show the Law also accorded the woman that respect.

'Child arrived about noontide, but it were some hours after that she left. Do you know, the woman brought the afterbirth out and cast it into my forge fire.' This was obviously tantamount to sacrilege to the smith. 'Didn't burn well for two days after, and I does not blame it.' He shook his head.

'So how many hours before sunset did she leave you?' Bradecote wanted the most accurate guess of time.

'Enough that there were no fear she might fall as I did. I would say less than two but more than one, my lord.'

'Thank you. And how does your wife and child?'

'Fair, my lord. The babe is much stronger, but my wife is weak still.' The smith looked taken aback that a lord had asked such a question, and decided he would tell his wife later. That must surely make her feel better.

Undersheriff and Serjeant left the man to his glowing fire and mounted to trot back to Ripple, aware that their next interviews would be far from easy.

It was only just after they had taken the Ripple track off The Old Road that Bradecote and Catchpoll were hailed from behind and turned to see Walkelin trotting towards them. As he drew close they saw that he had a cleric up behind him, one whose bony white shins showed where his habit had ridden up as he sat astride the horse's hindquarters. He had clearly been successful in locating Father Ambrosius.

'I has spoken with the lord Bishop, my lord,' announced Walkelin, with just a hint of pride at having managed this when alone, 'and told all that is now known, or leastways was when I left Ripple. Father Ambrosius 'ere did take the chalice to the palace and returned it to the lord Bishop, but only that. The other things must still be in Ripple, somewheres.'

'Good. That helps us a little,' Bradecote responded, then addressed the priest. 'We would speak with you, Father, before you go about your flock.'

'I hope that it does not take long, my lord, for I would visit Thorgar's family and give what comfort I can in their grieving.'

'All but his mother are likely in the fields until eventide.'

'Let me see.' The priest closed his eyes, though it did not seem he prayed. 'No, my lord, for this is not one of the days when all work under the eye of the reeve and upon the lord Bishop's holding. This early in the year, many will tend their gardens for at least part of the day. There is a good chance all are about their home.'

Bradecote inwardly chastised himself for not considering this. On his own manors, at least at Bradecote, his steward was not rigid in the days when the villagers toiled on the lord's land, but judged it by weather and Holy Days, so that it never fell that no work could be done on one or the other for more than five days in a row. Such an arrangement was not universal.

'Well, we have no desire to delay you, Father, just to add more things to our store of knowledge that will discover who killed your fellow priest.'

'Of course, of course. We could begin even now, yes?'

'Indeed. I am sure you have told much of this to the Underserjeant, but I wish to know when you found out about the treasure that Thorgar found, where you yourself found the chalice, and how much you knew, or suspected, of Father Edmund's wrongdoings.'

'The first is easier to speak of, my lord,' admitted the priest, heavily. 'I knew nothing until Father Edmund told me that Thorgar had brought a thing that was "most precious" to him for safekeeping. He always liked to feel superior, not just over those in his parish, but me as well. At the first I put it down to him being new and unsure, and I had the advantage of being born in Ripple and being part of it all my life, excepting the cloistered years leading to my ordination. We are all of us sinners, my lord, and listing the sins of another is uncharitable, even if they are no longer living, but Father Edmund – I could not like the man, though I tried hard to be in charity with him. He used people to his own ends in so many ways, and I came to fear, rather late, that the worst of them were terrible sins, not just encouraging the poor Widow Reed to bring him her baking. He wanted everyone to know he was better than they were, more elevated. A parish priest is, on one level, different, but as a man no better or more important than any soul within his pastoral care. We serve them, not they us.' Father Ambrosius sighed. 'Father Edmund did not see that.'

'So did you ask him what the "important thing" was or discover it by other means?' Bradecote was less interested in hearing all Father Ambrosius's views on his brother priest's pastoral abilities.

'Ah, well I just waited.' Father Ambrosius gave a small, tight smile. 'You see, if you did not rise to the bait and looked eager, eventually he just had to give more. After Vespers, the night before I was called to Queenhill, he told me it was a silver chalice of some antiquity. I knew what it must be, since the tale has been told around the hearths of Ripple for the better part of two hundred and fifty years, and in the telling it grew. I remember hearing it as a child, and there were descriptions of such things as only a king would possess, even a crown on one evening, though that was laughed at. The thing is, what was imagined was far more valuable than simple folk would ever have owned. As such it would give rise to covetousness, jealousy and other evils. I feared what it might do, and I told him so, also that it had been a gift to the parish from the lord Bishop of Worcester, and thus belonged to our bishop now. This pleased him mightily, and he smiled, his thoughts showing. He would take it and present it as though he had been vital in its restoration, and put his name in the lord Bishop's mind in a good way.'

'And this led to you taking it, to prevent both the sin in your parish and the craftiness of Father Edmund. I see. Now tell us how you did so.' Bradecote guided the man's thoughts.

'I knew not how, until I was sent for to go over to Queenhill, where it might be that I was needed to administer the Last Rites, and immediate baptism of an infant that would not take more than a breath or two, though God be thanked both mother and babe are with us still. Father Edmund was about to collect our bread from the morning baking and then visit Oldmother Agatha, and I told him I would likely be away over the night. When he went out, I took my chance, thinking it most likely he had hidden it in our home, for none would steal from us. I found the chalice beneath his bed, in the far corner, and wrapped in a dark cloth. I took it, not counting it as theft because it did not belong to Father Edmund, nor even to poor Thorgar, and I took it with me over the river and placed it in the church until my duty there was done. Then I took a boat upriver and – you know all, my lord.'

'Which leaves the other matter,' growled Catchpoll.

'Nearly all of that is not for any man to hear, for it came within the sanctity of Confession, and not from he who committed the great sins. At first it was just vague odd things that hinted at something I dare not imagine, but then they gathered as the storm clouds do before a downpour and I was deeply troubled.'

'But did not go to your bishop.' Catchpoll was still grim.

'No, for I had no proof, and I could not break the Confessional even to my superior. All I would be doing was accusing a man who could deny all.'

'Yet you did speak of it when you took the chalice to the lord Bishop.' Bradecote wondered at this.

'Yes. It had been a long night with the woman in travail in Queenhill, and I fell asleep in the boat so that the master of it had to shake me awake at Worcester. When I slept, I had a dream, and it was Father Giraldus, who was my mentor and priest with me before Father Edmund. He was weeping and holding the hand of a child, a little girl, whose face I could not see. When I went before Bishop Simon, I felt good Father Giraldus was with me in spirit and urging me to speak, so I did.'

They were now passing the first squat homes of the village, and Father Ambrosius let out a sigh that was not so much sadness as relief to be home, among those he knew as if one wide kindred.

'I will go to the church first, my lord, and pray for guidance in what I say to poor Thorgar's family. The Welshman and his son must have nearly finished the repairs, and the quicker for not having everything watched over and no doubt complained about.'

'Father Edmund found fault with their work?' Bradecote frowned.

'I think so, from the tone, my lord, but I could not say for sure, since he used his mother tongue with them and I could not understand a single word of it.' Father Ambrosius shook his head.

'Father Edmund was Welsh?' Walkelin, who had been silent throughout, spoke out so suddenly and loudly that Father Ambrosius let go of his hold about Walkelin's waist and slipped unceremoniously off the hindquarters of the horse, landing in a heap. 'I am sorry, Father.' Walkelin dismounted swiftly and helped the man to his feet.

'Why did we not know this?' demanded Bradecote.

'Most like 'acos nobody thought it mattered, my lord, and bein' Welsh is no reason to kill a man.' Catchpoll said this with a hint of reluctance, but then Catchpoll distrusted all things Welsh on principle. 'Mind you, I consider it a mite strange that neither Pryderi nor his lad mentioned it.'

'My lord,' interrupted Father Ambrosius, hurriedly. 'Father Edmund was not Welsh, except when he wanted to be, for his father was English and it was his mother as was Welsh. His English was as fair as mine, but he was able to slip into the tongue he learnt at his mother's knee if he wished. I am not sure anyone in Ripple even knows, other than myself, who heard him with the treewright. They could not have told you.'

'I see. Well, there is no reason why the pair would have

wanted him dead, and many others whose reason was strong, so it matters not. Father, we will not keep you from your prayers.'

The priest, dusting earth from his habit, nodded his head as acknowledgement of dismissal, and took his leave. Bradecote and Catchpoll also dismounted, and the three sheriff's men led their horses to the ox stable. In its peaceful gloom they discussed how to proceed.

'I would not have us ask our questions with the children involved present, and we are not trying to find out exactly what they endured. We ask nothing of them.' Bradecote felt to do so would be cruel and unfair.

'Aye, my lord. So we asks the fathers to speak with us in the priests' house, where nobody else hears.' Catchpoll saw this as a simple solution. 'Which means sending Walkelin to the church to ask Father Ambrosius to knock and not enter unless bidden.'

'But Serjeant, would the fathers like it even less, speaking in the very place that the man one of 'em killed used to live?' Walkelin realised as he spoke that his choice of words would not please Serjeant Catchpoll.

'Whether they "like it" matters not.' Catchpoll did indeed correct him, but sounded grumpy, which was unusual when about to speak with those suspected of crime. Bradecote correctly surmised that he had little liking for what they had to do, and he felt the same.

'Tofi's is the nearest house. We will begin with him, and at least we have the easier introduction of asking him why Father Edmund was banging upon his door and shouting on the morning of his death.'

Chapter Nine

Selewine the Reeve had been patient. He told himself so, and
believed it. To have visited Thorgar's family immediately after
the hanging would have seemed callous, since his was the
word that had confirmed the sentence and he had overseen the
carrying out of it. He would, he knew, have met with a swift
rejection of his offer. Now several days had passed, and the
reality of their situation would be taking hold in minds at first
overwhelmed by grief. Yes, he had been wise.

It was in confident mood that he told his older son to keep an
eye on his sibling and went to hammer upon the door of a house
in mourning. Osgyth opened the door, already frowning at the
vehemence of the claim to be admitted, and as soon as she saw
who it was, tried to shut the door in the reeve's face. He was too
swift for her and, with foot and outstretched arm, thwarted her
attempt.

'Now then, Osgyth, remember who I am.' He tried to make

it sound a mild reproof rather than a threat, but failed.

'Oh, I remember who you are Master Reeve, which is just why I wants to shut this door,' Osgyth spat back at him, eyes flashing. He laughed, which he knew would annoy her the more. He had no illusions that the girl would welcome him with open arms, but this would be a decision made upon the grounds of good sense, not emotion, and it would be her mother who would persuade her to accept.

'I can stand here all evenin', and all you is doin' is losin' what warmth you can afford on that there fire. Now, let me in, like a good girl, that I might speak with your mother.' He was intentionally patronising, reducing her from woman to child, diminishing her importance. Osgyth fumed, but stepped back.

'The reeve is come, Mother, to tell us what we knows already – that he condemned Thorgar, an innocent man, to a death unshriven and a grave unconsecrated.'

'You has more sense than to believe that, Win.' Selewine addressed Thorgar's mother.

A flicker passed over the woman's face. Since her widowhood she had somehow become 'Winflæd', and the diminutive, used in her youth and always by her husband, Alvar, had been buried also. She had sense enough to know that Selewine used it with intent, but the sound of it rippled through her as a tingling shudder.

'Do I?' The words were just to buy her a few moments to calm herself.

'You do. Sorry I am as it were done, but from what was known, was seen, was said, there was no other way. The laws is clear.'

'What were said by my brother, a man who nobody ever said a bad word about, were that 'e swore he were *unscyldig*, and he were ignored, not given time for other things to come to light. It was a death in haste, and at your biddin'.' Osgyth clenched her fists and her face contorted in anger.

'Not as pretty when you look like that. Careful it does not stay on you.' It was a taunt.

'I would rather be ugly than have a man like you lust after me,' she threw back at him.

The three younger children cowered, the twins instinctively drawing together until shoulder touched shoulder. Their older brother, who was laid upon the bed, still sickly and pale of face, gripped the worn sheepskin that covered him and pulled it right over his head. Their sister Osgyth was known to have a temper, and they were used to it, but the reeve, as well as being the most important person they knew, was now the most threatening, even though no threat had been spoken openly.

'You say that, Osgyth, but would you see your mother and brothers starve because you could not find a husband to see them safe and fed?' Her silence at that pleased him. He turned back to her mother. 'The girl possesses spirit, too much mayhap, but time softens such things. She speaks all thoughts and keeps none close. You keeps an older and wiser head on you, Win. Life is not as we wants it, but as it is. Otherwise I would not be seekin' a third wife but be very content with my first, God rest 'er soul.' Selewine crossed himself. 'You are crippled and cannot manage as other widows manage. There are the three little 'uns, and I knows what it is like with young boys to keep under control.' There was a pause, and he said,

157

more slowly, 'Unless you keeps treasure beneath that bed, to buy both food and a man's aid, you knows what lies before you all – the gripes that comes when no food lies in the belly, cold when there is not even the strength to scour the wood for kindlin'. You and I both know it be a path with one end, and mighty difficult to turn about on. If there was a choice, I am sure you would choose different, but there is not, and you do not need to part with your flesh and blood treasure,' he pointed at Osgyth but kept his eyes on her mother, 'for there is room in my house for all, and your boys can join mine and you can be spared work.' He was watching her closely, exclusively. 'I will not press you now, for I understands you must think on it, talk about it, but give me your answer in a few days. If you do not, or it be nay, then I will find a wife elsewhere, in Saxon's Lode or Uckinghall, and will not lift a finger when the worst befalls the family of Alvar.'

'It will be nay,' shouted Osgyth, 'though you wait till the Day of Judgement.'

'Hush, Osgyth.' Her mother's reproof was soft, but effective. The girl was shocked that it had passed her lips at all. Was her mother even considering the match? She paled.

Selewine did not smile outwardly, and left sombre-faced, but once outside he nodded, approving his own words and demeanour.

'I wonder if the girl makes a decent pottage?' he murmured to himself, rubbing his hands together, and then frowned as a thought struck him.

* * *

The door of Tofi's house was opened by Mildred, whose welcoming look froze on her pretty face. Catchpoll guessed quite a few of the local young men knocked upon Tofi's door with messages they were happy to bring from their parents in the hope that they might exchange smiles with the local beauty, or just stare at her in awed silence. Some women just had a certain something beyond mere good looks, but it was better if they did not acknowledge it, since it made them the teasing sort, as Mildred clearly was.

'Mother, 'tis the lord Undersheriff,' she called out, even as she bowed her head and dipped in a curtsey, and it sounded a warning. Perhaps it was just because of his elevated rank, but neither Bradecote nor Catchpoll believed that was the case. She stepped back, but not too quickly.

The chamber, when their eyes accustomed to the low light, was occupied only by the worn-looking woman who was Tofi's wife, and the mouse-like Mald, who now almost enveloped herself in her mother's skirts so that only the top of her head and her fingers gripping the cloth were visible. It made an obeisance almost impossible.

'My lord?' The woman sounded nervous.

'We seek your husband, mistress.' Bradecote did not say why and saw the colour fade from her face and her body stiffen, and that in turn made the little girl, aware of the tension in her mother, begin to whimper. 'Is he perhaps in your garden?'

She nodded, and laid a hand on top of the little girl's head. It was probably just an instinctive act, but it felt more significant.

'Thank you.' Bradecote was courteous. He did not have to be so, but felt this was a woman accorded little courtesy in life, and whom he had frightened. Catchpoll would, he knew, tell him not to be a fool and feel sorry for folk, and it struck him less often these days. He acknowledged to himself that he was hardening, which was both a good thing as an undersheriff, and perhaps a bad thing as a man.

The trio went around the building to the garden at its rear, agreeing that as long as the boys were not present, there would be no need to take Tofi to the priests' house. In fact, all three children were working. The eldest boy was raking a strip of earth to a tilth as the other two were pressing beans into the prepared surface, while their father dug the rougher ground. It was a scene of industry, though not peaceful, since the two bean planters were engaged in a heated argument on the verge of a fraternal fight. Catchpoll hailed Tofi, who was facing away from them. He turned quickly, a complaint ready on his lips, but at the sight of the lord Undersheriff this remained unvoiced, though his expression was not welcoming. His nod was respectful but wary.

'We have questions to ask you, Tofi, and they are best asked without other ears to hear. The boys would be better indoors.' Bradecote preferred to be slightly cryptic, so that it would be less likely the children would take notice.

'I has them workin', my lord, and I doesn't want—'

'They will go in to their mother,' Catchpoll commanded, in a low growl that had all three youngsters look up, as they would if a bad-tempered dog approached.

Tofi opened his mouth, and then, seeing the uncompromising expressions on the faces of the lord Sheriff's men, shut it again, pursing his lips to show that he was obeying, but with extreme reluctance.

'You lads go back indoors now, and be useful to your mother.' He spoke gruffly, and when the eldest looked at him as though to question why, he repeated the command, louder. Only when he had seen them go round the side of the house and heard a door shut did he look at the three men before him.

'What questions – my lord?' It was not the voice of one who would divulge anything willingly.

'Can you provide oath swearers that you did not go to the church around the time of None the day Father Edmund was killed?' It was the easiest question to pose, though Bradecote doubted it would give the answer that meant any more were superfluous.

'I cannot, but then nor could any man in Ripple that day. The ground was too wet for plough or plantin', and we did things about our homes, in the gardens where there was clearin' and such, or indoors.'

'Did no man exchange a word with you in the afternoon? Not even your brother next door?' Even one witness would be a start.

'Selewine and me gets on quiet, but we lives closer than we is as brothers. Since his second wife died last year, mine cooks extra or our Mildred makes pottage next door so as neither Selewine nor the boys starves, and the children sometimes play together, but – we is not close. You would think, after two wives, and comely ones at that, Selewine would be content to woo a widow eager to be the reeve's wife, a good cook and able to spin and sew, not aim foolishly for that Osgyth, who is barely as old as Mildred. Two wives buried and the chance of

161

a third when most of us is chained to the first long after their looks is gone and you has forgot what it was that made 'em catch your eye all those years back.' Tofi shook his head, but received no sympathetic response from his auditors. 'Mind you, I heard Selewine whistlin' to hisself that forenoon, and that's a rare thing. I suppose 'e went and looked over the lord Bishop's ground just to be sure we could not work it that day, but his mind was on a different ploughin' and sowin' seed, if you gets me.' He gave a lascivious laugh.

Bradecote did not ask if Tofi's wife would vouch for him, since a wife would not risk the loss of a husband when she had a brood of children to feed, even if the marriage was not easy.

'What can you tell us about the priests, Father Ambrosius and Father Edmund? Were they alike?'

This question made Catchpoll glance at his superior, for a moment puzzled, then he lowered his eyes so that the glint could not be seen.

'Alike? Oh no. Father Ambrosius is one of us, part of our family kindred even, and Father Edmund would never 'ave become one of us in a lifetime. You would think as the newer priest, Father Edmund, would 'ave been more watchful of the way things is done, but no. Frightenin', that's the word for 'im, when he wanted to be. Not to the men, o' course, but the womenfolk seemed to shrink when he gave penance, and he were forever goin' on about women bein' the reason men sins since Adam. Ha, funny thing for a man to set on when never a wife has 'e put up with. The wife said as she would only confess to Father Ambrosius most of this last year and would rather be unshriven than go to Father Edmund.' Tofi paused. 'I doesn't think Father Edmund will be 'mourned in Ripple, not like old Father Giraldus was.'

'Was your daughter Mildred afraid of him?' Bradecote made the question merely an additional one.

'Not so much as 'er mother, but then Mildred – ha, I thinks if'n Father Edmund chastised her as a Daughter of Eve she would flash those eyes of hers and make 'im regret the vow of chastity.' Tofi laughed, and it was that which finally decided the sheriff's men that Tofi had no idea what had happened, and most likely to his own little girl. Bradecote's first thought was that any father who could not see what they saw was not worthy of the name, but then they knew of the priest's proclivities and were thus aware of the unthinkable. It would not be the thing which leapt to mind.

'We have one other question for you. Why was Father Edmund banging on your door and loud-voiced the morning of the day he died?'

'That I cannot say, my lord.'

'You can hardly have not heard him, for others in the village did so.'

'I heard the noise right enough, oh yes, and it fair made my poor head nigh on burst, it did. The ale flowed a bit the night previous, and the Welshman and me was not at our best. In fact, 'e were unable even to stand without spewin', and the wife was mighty shrill with us both.' Tofi winced even at the memory. 'I suppose the priest were beratin' the treewright for not bein' at work upon the church, but that is just a guess, for it were all in the Welsh tongue and not one word would I know of it. Odd mind, that Father Edmund should know it, and odder still use it when the Welshman speaks good English. Aye, and even when drunk.' Tofi gave a small chuckle at this.

The sheriff's men left him still pondering on this question.

Bradecote decided it would be better if he went back to the priests' house, so that when men were called from their homes it looked simply a case of a high and mighty lord not wanting to present himself at the door, and less significant that what would be said was not for young ears.

The interview with Ulf Shortfinger was short and gave nothing, though not through any reticence on Ulf's part. Having checked that he was not in his garden, Catchpoll and Walkelin rapped upon the oak and were bidden enter without hesitation. It was a rather crowded but patently happy home, with the exception of the unnatural quietness of his daughter Emma. When asked to come to speak before the lord Undersheriff again, Ulf looked a little daunted, but not worried, though his wife bit her lip. He came with the sheriff's men perfectly willingly, though shaking his head as he walked with them.

'I cannot think of anythin' more I could say as might be of use to the lord Undersheriff, try as I might.' Ulf sounded as though this would be treated as a failing.

'Well, sometimes we discovers things sideways, so to speak,' confided Catchpoll. 'Askin' questions folk think unconnected can lead us where we would be.'

Ulf, much to Catchpoll's relief, did not enquire why only he, and not his wife or children, would face these new questions. When they entered the priests' house, Ulf snatched off his woollen cap, bowed deeply and immediately repeated that he was very happy to be helpful but had no idea how.

Bradecote, seated, since he felt that showed sufficient 'lordliness' to establish power and control, was to the point.

'My questions are not about the day of Father Edmund's death, but rather about how he fitted in, not being a local man like Father Ambrosius. Do you think he was as well liked, and was there anything said among the men of Ripple that makes you think anyone would do him harm?'

'Ah well, my lord, I cannot say as Father Edmund ever felt "one of us" as Father Ambrosius does, but that were not 'is fault, just the way things was. Many of us, even if we was young 'uns at the time, could remember Father Ambrosius afore he went off and took the cowl, and changed 'is name. A godly man he is, and better 'n us, but we knows as he understands us. Father Edmund' – Ulf shook his head sadly – 'always rubbed the fur the wrong way, if you gets me. Made folk feel small, and seemed to like it. You would think as 'e was the Archbishop of Canteryberry, so much better than us 'e acted. A few of the women felt different, for the man knew the best way to get better fare was to be sweet to the best cooks, but most – I can say as my wife likes us to stand right at the back when Father Edmund preaches – preached. She says as she feels he always looks at 'er when talkin' of Damnation, which is – was, often. Frightens our little Emma too, all that talk of punishment. Father Ambrosius encourages us to do better, not threatens us for our weaknesses.'

'Some priests is like that,' muttered Catchpoll, thereby showing he understood Ulf's position.

'Aye, and that be a pity, is what I says. Be that as it may, I does not know of any man in Ripple as spoke openly about 'im, just we would sometimes wish we had two like Father Ambrosius, as we sat over our ale.'

'Thank you. That gives us a better picture of Father Edmund.' Bradecote gave a small smile. 'I do not think we need to keep you longer.'

Ulf, a little surprised but very relieved, left, wondering how he had helped.

Leofwin, when he appeared before the lord Undersheriff, looked thoughtful, or perhaps watchful. When he spoke it was after a pause to consider his words. He was a big man, one who would have been quite capable of beating a man like Father Edmund into a senseless heap. Bradecote posed the same questions as he had to Ulf, and small muscles in the man's face worked as he formed his answer. It was telling.

'Father Edmund should not 'ave been sent to a parish. Far better a man like that be within walls and with his brothers about 'im.'

'And what is "like that", Leofwin?' The question was posed firmly but not unkindly.

'A man who breaks his vows.' Leofwin looked down at the floor, and when he looked up again there was a dull, angry fire in his eyes that he could not conceal.

'Tell us.' Bradecote did not ask which vows had been broken. Somehow that seemed wrong, though he would be exact if nothing was forthcoming.

'The vow of chastity, my lord. A man as takes the cowl should leave women alone, and 'specially so when their parish priest. My wife is a good woman, and loyal. One day when she was down by the river, washing clothes, he came and peered at 'er from among the reeds, when her skirts was kirtled up to keep dry and her ankles bare. She told me he sneezed and it showed where 'e was. Frightened 'er it did, and with our little Hild there too. Then he went on at 'er about women needin' to be cleansed of their sin, and came and laid hands on 'er body, which were wrong. My wife told me later, and only her pleadin' stopped me from confrontin' the snake. She wanted me to know why she and Hild wanted nothin' to do with 'im, but if I took a fist to 'im then all the village would find out why and she did not want the shame of it. Does not mean I is not glad the man is dead, but I did not kill 'im. To my mind, if 'e laid hands on my wife, well no doubt there was others, and mayhap worse happened. Whatever the Law says, I count whoever killed Father Edmund did right for all of us.' His voice and look challenged the three men before him to say otherwise.

'Is there any way you can prove that it was not you, though? Did any see you that afternoon about the time for None?'

'See? Well, not see, my lord. Oldmother Agatha, poor soul, can see no more 'n a bit of dark and light, and her leg be bad, but she likes a little air and comes to 'er door sometimes, and leans against the doorpost, and feels it on 'er old face. I were comin' back with kindlin' wood and saw the poor old soul there, and called out, and she said it smelt good after rain, and had I seen Agnes, since she 'ad not been to change the bandage on her leg that morn. Well, Mother Agnes is much called for not just in Ripple, so I said as most like there was an urgent need of 'er elsewhere, but she would be sure to visit as soon as she could. Oldmother Agatha agreed, and I carried the wood back to chop fine.'

It rang true enough, even if the exact time was impossible to judge, and the old woman might have spoken with him as he was going to the church with murder in mind. However, if his wife had given a reason some time ago why they should keep from Father Edmund, it made no sense that he would wait months and then do something that had all the marks of uncontrolled anger. Bradecote sent him home.

'Do you think it was the wife that the priest assaulted, Catchpoll? I do not.' Bradecote stared at the closed door.

'No, my lord, but if she needed a reason to keep the child well out of the way of the bastard, it was sound, and she would be able to make it not quite so bad as a man would go and commit murder feelin' in the right of it. Thing is, if that were months back . . .' Catchpoll shook his head.

'I agree. It would give no reason to act now. The trouble is, Catchpoll, that if neither Tofi, Ulf or Leofwin is the revenging father, our whole motive crumbles to dust.' Bradecote rang his long fingers through his hair.

'But what about the miller's daughter?' Walkelin asked, looking from one to the other.

'What miller?' Bradecote and Catchpoll responded in unison.

'Down by the river, not far from the ferryin' point. There's a mill and the lad who took me over t'other side told me about a girl called . . .' Walkelin paused for a moment, retrieving the information from its storage in his head, 'Berthe. He said she had been a friend of his sister as died last autumn, and was a lively, happy little soul, but nowadays never smiled and did not even wave at 'im.'

'And the dead friend would be the daughter of Ulf Shortfinger, the one who died last autumn.' Bradecote stood up. 'Why did we not consider anyone not actually in the village, but of the parish, Catchpoll?'

'Well, my lord, if the miller is not our man, we may 'ave to cast the net much wider, but to my mind, if it had been a man of Naunton or Uckinghall, it would be more likely they would follow the priest when out, and deal with 'im then, not come into Ripple and risk bein' seen where they was not usually.'

'A fair point, Catchpoll. Walkelin, lead us to the mill.'

They set off towards the river, and did not see that they were watched.

Wystan, who was not a naturally argumentative young man, had weathered a slightly heated conversation with his father, which had resulted in the latter eventually hunching his shoulders and giving grudging permission for his son to abandon his labours early. This concession had been the cause for further infelicitous comparisons with his two older brothers, the elder currently supporting his new wife at the deathbed of the oldmother who had raised her in Twyning, and the other one who had been industriously working the family field strips. It was where Wystan preferred to be, but he understood that as the youngest son he was essentially filling in for his older siblings. As the afternoon glided softly towards the early spring eventide he strode purposefully to Ripple and then found himself at a loss, since he did not know which was the house of Thorgar the Ploughman. He knocked upon a door which was not answered, for not everyone was yet home for the day, but at the second a man who recognised him vaguely as 'from up on the Old Road', directed him to the right dwelling. He stood for several moments rehearsing in his mind what he might say, and then rapped upon the weathered oak, hoping his knock sounded neither too timorous nor too aggressive. The door was opened, not by a woman of maternal years, but a girl nearly his own age. He blinked, and all the words he had prepared melted into nothing. He swallowed hard and just stared. She looked as though she was expecting someone else. There was an uncomfortable silence.

'Yes?' The word was a challenge rather than a question. The girl, who was quite tall for a girl, Wystan decided, and had eyes that reminded him of Thorgar's, was a lot more prickly than her easy-going brother. That would be the grief, thought Wystan.

'I am Wystan, son of Arnulf the Wheelwright, and I am – was – a friend of your brother, Thorgar. I am come to say I would never believe Thorgar could do somethin' bad, even if it were not proved so, and . . . and I offer myself to you – no, I mean,' he blushed furiously at the girl's shocked expression, 'to your family to aid with the work.' His words came out in a garbled rush. 'I know Thorgar's brothers are too young to guide the plough, but I could.' There was an edge of eagerness in the last statement that overcame his shyness.

'What is it, Osgyth?' An older woman's voice, hidden beyond the half-opened door, gave Wystan the name of this cautious doorkeeper.

''Tis a lad from the wheelwright up on the Old Road, Mother,' Osgyth called back.

'Then bring our visitor within.'

Osgyth stood back, reluctantly, and Wystan, snatching his cap from his head for the second time that day, stepped into the gloomy chamber. A woman much the age of his own mother, but with one side of her face no longer quite matching the other, as though it had lost all power to smile or frown, was seated near the hearth, a wooden spoon in her right hand.

'Mistress, I knew Thorgar for a good man and a kind one. When we met, it was as friends. In this dark time, I cannot do anything for Thorgar beyond pray for 'is good soul, but I can be of aid to 'is kinfolk as will miss not just the son and brother, but the man to work.' With this woman before him, not glaring at him like the fierce daughter, the words crafted on his walk returned to him.

'But you have family of your own.' The woman's voice was kind, but tired and sad.

'Aye, but I am the third son, and least of use in my father's eyes. From now till all is gathered in, I could work for you. And I has my father's agreement to it.'

'So you would work "for us". For what in return? We could not pay coin or food.' Osgyth folded her arms and looked very sceptical. In the back of her mind was also what Selewine had 'offered', which was aid in exchange for her. Wystan looked too young to be thinking of a wife, but young men thought of other things than marriage, given any encouragement.

'For neither, and 'acos I knows that if Thorgar could do a good deed for another he would, and if this were all the other way about, Thorgar would be in front of my mother as I am before yours.' This time he did not wilt before her.

'You say you would aid us, and in the field you could do

more 'n the boys,' there was a moment's pause, 'more 'n me, but you offered to guide the plough, yet am I right you has never done so afore?' Osgyth was now more doubtful than belligerent.

'I am strong of shoulder and arm as all the men become in my family, in our craft. I doubts I will plough as straight or as tight in the headland turns as a man experienced, but it is not like makin' wheels, with lots of things to remember in order, many skills to master.' Wystan did not say he had not been good at the remembering or the mastering thus far.

'And would you expect to live with us?' Osgyth had one final question.

'No. For one thing 'tis not so far back to my own folk and fireside, and if I lived and ate with you, then I would be another mouth to feed.'

'Your offer is generous, Wystan. Are you sure of this?' Osgyth's mother looked straight at the youth.

'I am, mistress.'

'Then we are in your debt.'

'But the ox team belongs to the village, Mother. It must be the reeve's decision who cares for the beasts and guides the ploughshare.' It had suddenly occurred to Osgyth that Selewine the Reeve would not agree to anything which would diminish his power over the family, or might stipulate that he would only agree if he got what he wanted, which was her.

'Yes. You are right, Osgyth. That must go before the whole village, but the aid with our land can be agreed now, and if everyone sees 'im and understands why Wystan is with us, that may sway them.' Osgyth was never one to do other than face a challenge head on, but her mother had learnt with age that sometimes a more circuitous way reached the goal. Selewine might indeed say no, but those whose strips had not been ploughed might be grateful for another doing the work and not adding to their own workload.

'Then I will be at the door by the time Ripple folk is ready to start the day's work.' Wystan stepped closer to the woman and held out his hand to shake the older woman's as head of the household, though part of him felt it ought to have been Osgyth's. The offer and acceptance were sealed by the handshake, and Wystan was slightly buoyed by the realisation that he was going to be valued far more than by his sire, as long as the oxen did not wander like a trickling stream. That part still left a niggling worry, but he would find out soon enough.

Osgyth closed the door behind him, but not immediately. She stared after the young man with the broad shoulders and determined stride for a few moments.

Wystan felt suddenly more of a man and no longer just the youngest brother, the family 'spare'. It was like being admitted into the tithing, which all lads felt made them grown up, until they were grown up enough to realise that they had not been. He smiled to himself, and, still in a reverie of his own, raised a hand in vague acknowledgement to the man leaving the house next door and just closing the door of his home behind him, though nothing but a puzzled frown came in return.

Chapter Ten

The mill at Ripple was set back a little from the breadth of the Severn, concealed from the landward side by willow trees pollarded so many times they had formed into gnarled and twisted figures like ancient old men, and with its leat creating a little island between mill and the powerful river, though in the winter the islet was often lost beneath the water. Now, though, there were geese upon it, vying with the swans already building nests of straw and twig, claiming it as their own, and only the still boggy ground at the riverside showed the river's encroachments the previous month. The miller's family lived on part of the upper floor of the mill, adjacent to where the great stone querns crushed the grain, since it gave them protection in times of flood, and a set of steep stairs led up to the door. However, at ground level there were double doors standing open, revealing a man and youth moving sacks of flour. Both of them were sturdy, and broad in the shoulder, with the hair of old men, made pale with the dust from the flour, and both face and hands were likewise coated. The visitors were not noticed until Catchpoll hailed the miller.

'Gives a man a dry throat, all that dust, eh?' His tone was friendly enough, and the miller turned to respond.

'That it do, right enough.' The man now saw not only that there were three men before his mill, but that one wore good raiment and had the unmistakeable demeanour of a lord.

'And what name do you have?' Bradecote was less convivial, thinking that playing the lordly role and letting Catchpoll seem the understanding one was a good start.

'I am Godebrand, my lord, though all about knows me as "Dustig" for the reason you can see.' He spread his arms and then clapped his hands together, so that the dust came off him and played about him in a cloud. Catchpoll hid a smile. He would guess most of the millers of the shire answered to 'Dusty', at least to their friends rather than their mothers.

'We are seeking the killer of your priest, Father Edmund.' Bradecote wondered how the man would react to "your priest" and saw that he did indeed flinch a little and his convivial manner fell away.

'A man were hanged for that.' The miller was no longer open and approachable, but very careful.

'Aye, "for it" but were not the one as did it.' Walkelin spoke up, and it took Bradecote a little by surprise, for he sounded almost as Catchpoll would.

'I did not even see the hangin', bein' as we was workin' and does that wet or dry.'

'We do not need any witness to the hangin', not now. What we wants is to find out why a man beat a priest into a bloody mess.' Catchpoll did not actually say 'kill him'.

'You see, that is not somethin' as a man would do just 'acos the penance he got were a bit weighty. There would need to be a good reason – a very good reason.' Catchpoll was now watching the miller as a cat does a mouse, and his voice dropped a little. 'And I ain't sayin' as we would disagree with that reason, either.'

Bradecote threw him a warning look, for whatever else, the Law could not ignore a killing, but Catchpoll did not see it, or chose not to see it.

'Has the lad work to do upstairs?' Catchpoll jerked his head towards the upper floor.

'Aye. You go and prepare the next sacks of grain, son.' The miller looked at the youth, who sensed something was not right and looked questioningly.

'You sure, Father?'

'Aye. There's a good lad.'

There was silence as the son turned and went to climb up the internal ladder-stair to the querns.

'You have a daughter, a young daughter.' Bradecote stressed the age.

'And no word will I let 'er have with you, not even if you was the King of England.' The miller's hands went to his hips and his chest was thrust out. It was aggressive, but also protective.

'We are not here to speak with her. We know enough of Father Edmund's wrongdoings not to need to do so.' Bradecote could almost feel the man's admission of guilt exuding from every pore. 'Tell us what happened, exactly as it happened.'

The belligerent look slipped from Dustig the Miller like a

dropped cloak. His shoulders sagged a little, but he held his head up proudly enough.

'What I did I would do again, my lord. That's truth. I cared not that 'e were a priest, in fact it made it worse. Not been right, our Berthe, all over the winter, and like a ghost she is now, 'ceptin' she is the one as is haunted. I thought she were sick of body, and Mother Agnes comes often enough but will never say what ails the girl. Few days past I saw her, my little girl, step into the leat, not fall. She wanted the water to end everythin' and she is but nine years old.' The man's voice had pain in it, a father's agony. 'Imagine that. I pulled 'er out, and the wife came at my cries and when Berthe were all dried and kept close and crooned over until she stopped weepin' and slept, I found out why. That was why I went to the church, knowin' Father Ambrosius was rowed over the other side and that animal would be alone. I wanted to kill 'im, I do not deny it. I beat 'im till he fell senseless and then I kicked 'im for good measure. I wanted to smear 'im over the flagstones, I did, until none would say there were ever a man there, for what I kicked were not fit to be called a man, let alone a priest.'

'But you stopped?' Bradecote raised an eyebrow. 'Why?'

'My wife came in and begged me. She said as Berthe needed a father more than ever right now and if I killed the priest she would 'ave none, nor could the lad take on the mill alone. I told 'er I thought it were too late and he were dead already. We came away, over the churchyard wall so as not to go through the village proper, and came back to the mill. We did not know of Thorgar, and mighty sorry I am that the lad is dead, but once it were done, I could do nothin' to get 'im back, and there be a family to feed.'

'So you beat the priest but you did not stab him.'

'Stab 'im, my lord? No. What need have I of a knife when I has these?' The miller held out his big hands and muscled forearms. Lifting sacks of grain and flour gave a man strength. 'And he were dead, as I saw it. Why say you he were stabbed?'

'Because he was, and that killed him. I accept you might achieve the aim with your bare hands, but a woman is not as strong, and might be as vengeful. Did she play a part?' Bradecote pressed him.

'My wife did nothin' but keep me from dealin' further blows, my lord. I swear my oath on it. I did not kill the priest and nor did my wife.'

'But we have to ask, for if you did not, who did?'

'I did.'

The lord Sheriff's men spun round at the woman's voice, which was very calm. Agnes the Healer stood straight, arms folded, the bony elbows sticking out at an angle.

'This ends now. It 'as gone on too long and cost too much.' Her voice commanded.

'You said you did not kill him, when we asked before.' Bradecote was not going to accept this admission without consideration.

'Then there was no likelihood of another needless death.'

The miller was staring at her, open-mouthed

'How did you kill 'im?' Catchpoll was as wary.

'I stabbed 'im with an awl. You asked me if I came to pray in the church on my return from Naunton and I said no. Well I did, and I came in and saw the mess on the floor and found 'e breathed, sad to say. So I went to the treewright's workshop, took an awl and ended 'im.'

'Then what did you do?' Bradecote sounded merely interested, but hung upon her answer.

'I put the awl back on the bench, my lord, so none would know.'

The representatives of the Law let out a collective breath. Since it was Gwydion who placed the awl back in the workshop, whoever killed Father Edmund, it was not Agnes the Healer.

All four men stared at the healing woman for some moments in silence, the miller astounded that she had killed a man, and the three shrieval officers stunned that she had confessed to something which they knew she did not do. There was only one possible explanation for her act of altruism.

'You would give yourself up to death to protect another?' Bradecote looked at the woman with a mixture of respect and astonishment.

'I did it, my lord. I killed Father Edmund.' She stood a little straighter, almost proudly, and her voice was steady.

'You can stand there and say that till dusk, woman, but it ain't true, and we knows it.' Catchpoll did not sound disappointed that the killer was not yet found out, but weary of tangles that led nowhere.

'And I did not kill the man, my lord, though I would face the Justices and say why I tried, but for the shame on my girl from makin' it known what was done, and I doubts she could bear it. Whatever the law says, what 'e got were deserved.' The miller, whose mind had swiftly run through emotions from fear and desperation to shock and disbelief, pulled himself together.

'I left 'im for dead, yes, but if'n there was breath still in the bastard, it was not me as killed 'im.'

Bradecote was trying to assimilate everything and make sensible decisions.

'I believe you. Now, neither of you is to speak of this to anyone. If the priest was stabbed by someone other than an avenger of little girls in the parish, they think they are safe. They are not.' He looked severely at Agnes the Healer. 'And offering yourself up as a sacrifice is no help to Ripple, because we know of one other possible reason that Father Edmund was killed, and if that is the reason, as I think, it means a killer is in Ripple whose motive was not righteous revenge, but simple greed.'

'But priests takes a vow of poverty and none would steal from our church. It would be – wrong.' The miller, a man who minutes before had admitted to wanting to kill a man, was all outraged decency.

'He was given something for safekeeping. It is now safe and beyond their grasp, but his killer may well be seeking more – we shall see.' Bradecote turned and began to walk back towards the village houses. Catchpoll and Walkelin followed.

Once beyond even the keenest of hearing, Bradecote shortened his naturally long stride, so that his companions could walk alongside him, and then he voiced the most important question.

'Since we now have the miller's admission he attacked the priest, I simply do not think another avenger finished it. I think that all of this has been about Thorgar and the treasure.'

'Aye, my lord. And do we take the miller for the attack?'

Catchpoll's voice clearly wanted a negative answer.

'No. As he said, he did not kill the man, and – no. Justice would not be served, and the Law would be at fault. It would have been different if the assault had been the end of it, and the priest had brought complaint, but taking a damaged child's father, a family breadwinner and the village's miller, for an act any father would do, is not just or fair. Upon my decision, we leave it.' Bradecote sighed, and felt a great burden lifted. When they hunted the killer now, for all that the victim deserved no tears shed over him, they could do so knowing they did what was right and also just.

'Aye.' Catchpoll said no more. The line of investigation was closed, and immaterial henceforth.

The feeling of relief that flooded through the the trio of law officers that they were no longer seeking a man who had done what they themselves would have felt justified in doing in the same situation, was tempered by the fact that they now faced going back several steps in the trail of whoever killed Father Edmund, and the trail would be the colder for it.

'Were we foolish to set aside the treasure as a reason to kill the priest?' Bradecote felt he had to ask the question.

'No, my lord, not once we knew what the bastard did, and the manner of the death. The beatin' came first and the man were red-mist mad with anger. That was not from greed. Nor were we wrong, since the beatin' was for just that reason. What we has to get our 'eads round now is that time after the miller and his wife left the church. We do not know if the priest were senseless for a few minutes or an hour. Did the killer come at that time by chance or plan?'

'The miller went to the church 'acos it were about the time of the Office, surely, for 'e did not mention goin' elsewhere. The killer surely thought the same, but mayhap saw the miller go in, and the wife after, so waited.' Walkelin, whose mind seemed to store details so neatly, was mentally sifting the treasure 'wheat' from the vengeance 'chaff'. 'And it were to the killer's advantage that the treewright were sick and the lad abandoned the bench to prove 'is courage to Mildred.'

'Yes, very true, Walkelin. I would love to say that it narrows our search to any who at least knew Pryderi was sore of head and sick of stomach, and not fit to work, but it could just be that the killer decided to watch the priest and would have confronted him in the priests' house had there been no opportunity at the church and father or son had been working.' Bradecote set self-blame aside and looked cheered.

'All very well, my lord, but we cannot just follow this trail *earslings*, starting at the death and endin' back at a man, since it would offer us many who could, not just one as did.' Catchpoll pulled a thinking face.

'Go on.'

'We starts at the beginnin' as well. Thorgar ploughs up this treasure that all of Ripple has sat about their winter fires talkin' over for generations till it has grown into a king's treasure. Thorgar keeps quiet about it and gives it, at least in part, to the priest for safekeepin', which shows sense. But someone did know, or found out. They might 'ave confronted Thorgar, but he were big enough to defend hisself and not reveal where it lay. The priest were neither big nor strong. If they found out about the ploughin' up and watched Thorgar, and saw 'im with the priest more 'n usual, they might well decide to threaten the weaker man, or even guess the treasure had been given "sanctuary" with the priests.'

'And the priest would 'ave to be killed after, in case Thorgar found out.' Walkelin was following this carefully, and then stepping ahead. 'The miller need not risk the priest speakin' out, since that would also bring the evils to light. Other than anger, there was no need to kill 'im.'

'And the killer must be a man, since a woman could not go to threaten the priest with violence and demand the hiding place, and when they entered the church, the killer could not know they would find the priest beaten more than half to death. He might have gone first to the priests' house, knowing one was away and the other at the church for None. We saw the house showed signs that someone had been hunting for something, and I do not think that was Father Ambrosius, who sought and found the chalice, or Father Edmund—' Bradecote suddenly realised they had all three been avoiding giving the man his name as if erasing him from existence, 'finding it gone and then looking elsewhere in the chamber. That would be foolish.' He frowned, thinking it through. 'And the priest must have been at least part in his senses so that the killer could demand the treasure's location. Only if he refused, would he then be silenced.'

'But the priest was never described as at all brave, my lord, so would 'ave given up the treasure. He must have known that the chalice was gone with Father Ambrosius, and denied it bein' in his possession 'acos it were true.' Walkelin was methodical. 'So the killer either did not believe 'im or went and killed 'im anyway so they could collect or keep lookin' for the treasure.'

'That would fit, but even if we take the killer, unless we discover the missing part of the treasure, I cannot see Ripple being at peace.' Bradecote approved of Walkelin's theory.

'Small chance is there of us findin' it, for Thorgar could 'ave buried it under a particular tree root or – anywheres. So we need not grab spades and dig up the parish.' Catchpoll gave a small smile. 'But if we thinks about the killer comin' to know of the treasure it might give us fewer names.'

'Fair enough, Catchpoll,' conceded Bradecote. 'If Thorgar, as has proved right, feared the treasure would lead to envy and trouble, and took the chalice to the priest, and let us remember he might have been just as happy giving it to Father Ambrosius, if not more so, then it would be strange for him to then tell someone else. The only obvious person would be his mother, and sense says if he revealed its existence he would say it was safe with the priest. I would swear she knows nothing, or she would have spoken of it to us, because it would be the one unusual thing that happened shortly before both deaths.'

'Osgyth, the sister, my lord?' Walkelin had had least contact with Osgyth.

'No fool, that girl, and what the lord Bradecote said about the mother be as true for the daughter. She would tell us.' Catchpoll was confident of his answer.

'So none was told, but one saw. Either that was when the treasure came up out of the earth, or when Thorgar took it to the priests.' Walkelin was persistent, as eager as a hound upon a scent.

'And that man kept the knowledge to hisself and bided his

time. We can at least discount the miller and the shepherd, whose lives are not spent close with the other folk of Ripple, nor an outsider from elsewhere in the parish.' Catchpoll sucked his teeth. 'Someone will be wary now, and watchin' us, my lord, so we has to be as watchful back.'

They walked on in silence, each thinking of all the interactions they had had with the men of Ripple in the last few days. They were almost passing the church when they heard yelling. It was not cries of anger but distress, and all three began to run towards the sound, Catchpoll soon a little to the rear. He was swearing, though in his head as he needed all his breath for the running.

There was a gathering of people before the house next door to that of Thorgar's family, the home not of Wilf the Worrier but of Oldmother Agatha. A lad, whom Walkelin instantly recognised as his ferryman, was being comforted by a woman. Another youth was sat upon the doorstep, head in hands. Bradecote barged unceremoniously through the crowd.

'What has happened?' He already guessed at a death, but it might simply be a natural one.

The youth on the step looked up.

'We found 'er on the floor. Must 'ave tripped over the cat and . . .' He shook his head.

With Walkelin and Catchpoll at his back, Bradecote stepped into the gloomy chamber. A man was about to turn over what looked like a crumpled bundle of clothes.

'Wait!' It was a command, and the man stopped, and looked up.

'She was my mother. I cannot leave 'er on the floor,' Ulf Shortfinger's voice shook a little.

'Let us see first. Catchpoll.'

'Aye, my lord. Stand back, friend, and let me see. Someone bring a light over.'

Walkelin, not shocked into immobility like so many of the villagers, found a rushlight and lit it, bringing it close to the body.

'It was your sons who found her?' Bradecote asked Ulf, in part to distract him.

'They did, my lord, and came runnin' for me. I suppose her bad leg gave way, or else she just dropped dead, bein' old and frail.'

The youth from the step now came back into the room, his face a ghostly pale in the light. He avoided looking at the body.

'Or she tripped over the cat,' he offered again, stifling what he considered an unmanly sniff.

'And was the cat 'ere? Did it run out past you when you came in?' Catchpoll, moving the grey hair from the nape of the neck with the delicacy of a lover's touch, asked the obvious question.

'Er, no.'

'Sure?'

'The cat weren't inside, but—' The lad now sounded confused.

'Them as cannot see knows their own place without need for eyes, unless something is out of place, like the cat, I agree.' Catchpoll was speaking to the youth, but he was focused upon the old woman's body. 'So you thinks a near-blind old woman,

in a dark chamber, fell over a black cat, which makes sense –
but it was not there.' He grunted. 'She ended on the floor, but
it weren't no accidental fall. There's marks at the throat. So
even if the cat had been in the chamber, it did not cause your
oldmother's death. Some bastard did for 'er, and . . .' Catchpoll
grimaced, and Walkelin wondered if it was his knees playing up.

There was a gasp from those gathering at the doorway.

'Who would kill Oldmother Agatha? She 'ad nothin' to
steal and was a good old soul.' This came from a voice in the
doorway, and was met with mutterings of agreement.

'She might have banged 'er neck when she fell, though,'
came a voice from the back, hopeful rather than confident.

Catchpoll ignored this. The old woman had not so much
tumbled forward as crumpled at the knees, and the marks, with
a long bruise, showed an applied force, and he remembered
what Selewine's small son had reported seeing.

'Who saw her alive last?' Bradecote wanted information and
then for the crowd to disperse and leave the Law to its task.

'We left this morn, early, and worked Oldmother's garden
for a while, then went to our own.' The younger grandson who
had been comforted, spoke up.

'And I came and put a fresh dressin' on that leg.' Agnes
the Healer, for whom the crowd had parted, stepped into the
chamber and crossed herself. 'Poor old soul. Been dead long?' It
was a question posed in professional curiosity, and very calmly.
Catchpoll marvelled at the woman's ability to enfold herself in
her craft when only a short time earlier she had offered her life
to judicial death.

'When did you come, and did anyone see you?' Bradecote,

thinking fast, realised that the healer could not simply be excluded from among the suspects.

'We was in this garden and waved at Mother Agnes as she left, my lord,' offered the younger lad.

'But the door is at the front and the garden at the back, so how did you see her?' Bradecote asked.

'I called out thanks as I saw Mother Agnes pass between this 'ouse and the next, and she waved back.'

'I did, my lord, and went to visit little Baldred next door, who 'as been sickly these last few days, and a worry to his poor, grievin' mother.'

'Thorgar's mother?' Everything had to be exact.

'Aye, my lord.'

'And I can tell you that is true, my lord.' It was the voice of Osgyth, who came to the doorway, pushing aside other curious folk. Father Ambrosius was beside her, and whilst the young woman remained outside, he came in, knelt beside the body and began to pray.

'What do you think, Catchpoll? Has she been dead many hours?'

'No, my lord. She be not yet full death-cold, and if she died in the forenoon I would expect that and first signs of stiffenin'.'

'Did anyone else come here, or was seen at the door?' Bradecote had to almost shout now that the villagers were talking amongst themselves, divided between those who wanted it to be an accident after all, and those now fearing some unknown murderer in their midst.

'I passed the door after noontide, my lord,' volunteered Selewine the Reeve, looking a little flustered, having been fetched from a favoured fishing spot, and bearing three small bream in the shallow basket under his arm as if some bizarre offering to the dead. 'I had been next door, discussin' the future with Winflæd – Thorgar's mother.' He added the last part because Bradecote had clearly not recognised the name. 'Osgyth 'ere will tell you it was so.'

'The reeve came, and spoke with Mother,' the girl confirmed, 'and it must 'ave been just after noontide. Been busy, we has, with all the visitors today, what with Mother Agnes tendin' to Baldred, then 'im,' – she jerked her head in a less than courteous way towards the reeve – 'and then the man who is offerin' to guide the plough for the rest of the spring, and to give us the aid of good strong muscle in field and garden.' This was said in a triumphant manner, and she smiled, knowing it would both perplex and annoy the reeve. 'Very welcome, that offer is.'

'Who made it? There is no ploughman not needed elsewhere, and I will not—' Selewine blustered.

'Did you see anyone, Master Reeve, when you arrived or when you left?' Bradecote interrupted, not having any interest in who guided the Ripple plough, but a lot in what Selewine might say.

'No.' The reeve replied immediately, but then paused and frowned, his dark brows forming a single, heavy line as he thought. 'Though wait, there was a man going up out of the village toward the Old Road.'

'Did you recognise him?'

'I—' Selewine stopped, and frowned, 'I thought he reminded me of someone, from years back, but no, I did not recognise him. I cannot believe anyone in Ripple did this, my lord. I cannot.'

This clearly sat well with those still listening. A murderous stranger, passing through and then gone far away, was less worrying than a neighbour they had known all their lives turning upon their own community.

'What did he look like?'

'Ordinary enough, and I only saw the man for a moment. He wore a grey woollen cap and stooped a little.'

This immediately had those within earshot mentally surveying all the men they recognised from neighbouring settlements.

'What about Siward the Chapman? Used to come through regular enough and stooped a bit,' a gruff voice suggested.

'Died three springs back, as I was told, in Tewkesbury,' came a wheezy response.

'No, more like 'twere that wanderer as comes for alms from the church once or twice a season.'

'It is unlikely that this killing was committed by a stranger.' Bradecote's voice cut through the mumblings and chatter. 'No stranger would have knowledge of what was found by Thorgar, and left by him with Father Edmund. He turned up with the ploughshare a silver chalice and other things that were buried long ago.'

'The Priest's Treasure!'

Bradecote could almost feel the change in the crowd, with fear replaced by a tingle of excitement. An old woman they all knew well had been killed, and they might be at risk, but the idea of unspecified riches coursed through them like a flash flood after a drought. He understood what Father Ambrosius had said about it being a dangerous thing.

'But what would that 'ave to do with Oldmother?' The older youth looked confused, and both undersheriff and underserjeant thought the question valid.

'Father Edmund were seen at this door, the mornin' of 'is killin', and with the cat under an arm and a small sack. No doubt the killer, knowin' of the findin', thought that it contained the silver.' Catchpoll gave the explanation.

'That would be a fool thing to think,' snorted Agnes the Healer. 'No reason could there be for 'im to want to give it to an old woman whose needs were for no more 'n company and lovin' kin, which she possessed.' She nodded at Ulf and his sons, acknowledging they had done all they could for her.

'The chalice has been returned to the lord Bishop, as the "descendent" of the bishop who gave it to Ripple and also replaced its loss. What else there was is not of great value. None of it was worth a death, and now it appears there have been three deaths because of it. There will be a fourth, when we take up whoever killed Father Edmund and Ulf Shortfinger's mother.' Bradecote was speculating on what had been found, but sense said that the village would not have had much to hide beyond a little coin, not much used in the rural community even now, and some pieces of simple jewellery, passed down the generations to be kin-treasured.

'And they belong to the lord King, unless it is proven that kin can identify them,' Walkelin added, which made both his superiors glance swiftly at him. 'Any gold or silver that was hidden with the intent to later take up, but never was, is his.'

The muttering now sounded disgruntled. Bradecote overheard a male voice complain that King Stephen had lots of gold and silver and a little more would be meaningless to him.

'Ask yourselves if this treasure is worth what it has cost Ripple, and ask who might put it above friend, neighbour, even kinfolk. Such a man is not worth protecting, deserves no oath swearers, and if any have information, they must bring it to us, and us alone. Gossip now puts lives at risk.' Bradecote thought he might as well exploit any distrust or fear that would bubble up when the first amazement over the treasure passed. 'Now go to your homes and, this evening, drop the bar to the door.'

A woman gasped and crossed herself. The crowd did not just drift away but parted into little family groups like water droplets on a waxed cloth.

'My lord, what about us?' It was Ulf Shortfinger.

'We would speak a little with your sons, and then you may take your mother's body to your home or to the church, as you and Father Ambrosius decide.'

'Will you take who did it, my lord?' It was a plea rather than an angry demand. The immediacy of grief had fallen like a great, toppling boulder upon Ulf Shortfinger and crushed him. Anger was for later.

'I am confident that we will, but I cannot promise it. We will strive our best, that I can promise.'

'No more could I ask, my lord. Now, you asks all you need of my boys, and then let 'em go home to their mother.' His face crumpled a little, and his voice thickened. 'A mother is always a comfort.'

Chapter Eleven

The two youths were soon dismissed home. They could give little information beyond the fact that when they had left their oldmother that morning she had been in good spirits, but since it was already known that she was still alive when visited by Agnes the Healer, that was no advance. When they returned in the afternoon to light the fire and be company to the old, nigh-on bedridden woman, she was as she was found, dead in a crumpled heap upon the floor. The cat had been present in the chamber when they left it in the morning, and had caught a mouse, but was not there on their return. This meant that the healer was the last person known to have seen Oldmother Agatha alive. The thought that worried Bradecote was that she thus had opportunity to have killed her, and whilst they had 'proved' she had not killed Father Edmund, what if she had given the falsehood about putting back the awl just so that it showed her innocence? It was a dangerous game to confess to a murder and hope that the confession would be dismissed, but Agnes the Healer was a woman who clearly did not suffer fools nor was a fool herself. He did not want to suspect her again but . . . It was only then that he realised she was still in the room and tidying it. She was tidying it.

'Stop.' Bradecote's command was urgent, and everyone instinctively stopped what they were doing. He looked directly at the healing woman. 'What have you done? I mean here and now.'

'Nought but set the stool upright, and back where it should be, and arrange the bedclothes. Liked everything just so, she did, and I respects that.' Agnes the Healer sounded affronted.

'You came in often. You can tell us even better 'n the lads what is out of place.' Catchpoll did not sound challenging at all, in fact emollient, and Bradecote wondered if only he was thinking twice about the woman's innocence.

Agnes straightened her back and stood very still, except for the movement of her head as she surveyed the chamber. It was as though she was measuring every distance between objects, noting every cobweb in the rafters, every ash mark on the hearthstone. When she spoke again it was a pronouncement, as clear and definitive as Holy Writ.

'I changed the bandage on 'er leg most days, and kept some in a basket, covered so as that cat did not sit upon 'em as a soft bed. And when I came this forenoon, the cat lay curled next to 'er where she might sometimes reach out and stroke it. I pushed it off when I needed to turn back the blanket and it hissed at me. I hissed back. When I left, it came back to its chosen spot on the bed. What happened later would scare it away, for sure. Agatha kept a stick on the bed, by 'er right side, in case she 'ad need to get up. It was across the end of the bed when you came in.'

'Which fits with the marks, my lord, across the front o' the throat, not a squeezin' by fingers. Broke the windpipe, by my judgement,' Catchpoll concurred.

'I agrees, my lord.' Agnes nodded, becoming in a moment part of the investigating team rather than one who might be investigated. 'Agatha were best part blind and a bit deaf, but she knew the folk as came in regular just by their footfall, mayhap even their smell. She would speak to me afore I spoke to 'er, most days. Whoever came in and killed 'er, she was surprised enough to ask who was there, or at least why they was there. I reckon half the village thinks she just lay there all day and was aware of nothin'. It would come as a shock to one such to be called out to, if they thought to look about the place without 'er knowin'. You'll be thinkin' the killer believed the treasure to be left here, but I swears nothin' was in this chamber when I left it that was not here a month back, other than a few new cobwebs.'

'I see. Is anything else out of place?' Bradecote still wanted to know whether Catchpoll regarded the healer as a suspect.

'Oh yes, my lord.' The woman ticked off things on her long, thin fingers. 'The pissin' pot under the bed is now almost at the bottom end, not near the top. The cookin' pot, which ain't seen pottage in nigh on six months, has the lip pointin' the wrong way to what it was, the besom has been moved and no doubt used to sweep under the bed. Someone looked and looked again, and no doubt found as they had killed Oldmother Agatha, whose time were near but ought not to 'ave been now, for nothin' at all.'

'I might as well retire,' murmured Catchpoll, appreciatively.

'Thank you.' Bradecote turned to Ulf Shortfinger, who was knelt praying with Father Ambrosius. 'We will all leave you now.' There was just a small stress on 'all', and the healer pursed her lips, nodded, and left before the shrieval trio, who went straight to the priests' house. Father Ambrosius, who rightly excluded himself, would be some time with Ulf and the body. Bradecote did not speak until they reached the priests' house.

'Why did someone think Oldmother Agatha had the treasure anyway?' Walkelin had been puzzling at this. 'It would be an odd place for the priest to take it if he possessed it. If there had been somethin' new and unusual the grandsons would be likely to have noticed, and for sure Mother Agnes would with 'er windhover eyes. It would be puttin' it where it would be sure to be found.'

'That means thinking it through as we would, Walkelin, and we do not know that the killer did that. You heard what Agnes said about the killer not expecting to be challenged when they entered. That fits with not considering how difficult it would be to conceal something, and just imagining that an old woman confined to her bed would not know if a neighbour came calling and hid the treasure while they gossiped.' Bradecote frowned in concentration. 'The folk of Ripple will be barring their doors now, so we begin once more in the morning. We asked before if any had seen the priest on the morning of his death and had no answer bar the child's offering, but if even those who did not know the worst of him did not like him, it might be that they would not want to point a finger of potential guilt at a neighbour. They will not feel the same now that an aged and defenceless member of their community has been killed.'

'Aye, done us a favour has that.' Catchpoll nodded. 'And we discounts Ulf Shortfinger and all the family, for the way they was rings true, and the only men as would not need to explain bein' there would be them. Neither need nor wish could there be to kill.'

'True enough, though one of them might have seen the priest with the cat, and another watching him. It still leaves us with plenty to do on the morrow. It has to be one of no more than fifteen or sixteen, even including striplings, but since the treasure was never in the oldmother's home, whoever killed her is still seeking it, and everyone is at some risk.' This worried the undersheriff. 'Catchpoll, Selewine the Reeve really did not want you to believe his son, which makes me wonder, in view of this death.'

'Aye, my lord, we needs to find out exactly where Master Reeve was all day today, and after noontide the day the priest were killed. I did not detect any great panic in 'is voice when he spoke of the priest and cat, but that need not be a proof. It is work for the morrow, once latches is lifted.'

'And Thorgar? It was the reeve as made the decision.' Walkelin did not think the ploughman was forgotten, but this new death put his more to the edge of their investigation.

'He could not have known that Thorgar would find the priest. That was chance.' Bradecote was firm on that. 'But it would be to his advantage if the whole matter were seen as over and done with swiftly and tidily.'

'Would that be murder, then, my lord. Getting a man you knows to be innocent strung up for your crime?' Walkelin was curious.

'Morally, I cannot see it as anything else, but in terms of the King's laws, I simply do not know, Walkelin. I am not a Justice in Eyre.'

'Nor me, my lord, but I 'as seen the Justices at work these twenty years and more, and I thinks they would see a man usin' the Law as a weapon, and if that makes them as fair angry as it does me, they would see it as much murder as if the man used a knife.'

'True enough, Catchpoll. What I can say is it would remove one obstacle to his wedding Osgyth.'

'I thinks the biggest obstacle to that, my lord, is, and will ever be, Osgyth 'erself.' Catchpoll permitted himself a small smile.

'He was very keen to see us looking for someone outside the village.' Bradecote was collating all the circumstantial evidence in his head. 'I was interested in his reaction, and he was quick to create a diversion. Yes, the reeve is now one we watch closely, and into whose recent actions we delve into deeply, for I do not think we have so much that he would be bound to admit his guilt, or his oath swearers desert him.' He sighed.

'Once we has food in our bellies and a night's sleep, my lord, we can ferret out more.' Catchpoll was philosophical.

'Let us hope so, Catchpoll.'

* * *

Selewine the Reeve was grim-faced as he knocked upon the door. He had not planned to return for several days, but the death of Oldmother Agatha changed things. The village was in uproar and folk were frightened. This household would be no different, and they lacked any protection. He could offer that, and it would be the tipping point that would have Osgyth say yes. He had seen Osgyth in a huddle with the other young women of the village, no doubt exchanging opinions on the killing, which would give him the chance to speak with Winflæd alone. It did not surprise him that the door was not answered swiftly.

'Oh, it is you Selewine.' Winflæd did not look very eager to let him in.

'Come on, Win, you ain't afraid of me, and it's about your safety I am come to see you.' The expression on his face softened slightly, but was still solemn.

Winflæd took a pace back and opened the door. He stepped within. The child Baldred was curled up on the bed, and the younger two were prodding woodlice, watching them curl into little armoured balls, strangely like their bigger brother.

'What ails the boy?' Selewine asked, jerking his head towards the bed. 'Not catchin', is it?'

'No. I think the loss of 'is brother struck a cruel blow, especially since Baldred were the one as always walked at the oxen's side and helped in their care. Made the bond stronger.' Winflæd looked at her son, and the worry was clear on her face.

As long as no risk of contagion existed, Selewine was no

199

longer very interested in Baldred.

He did not ask permission to sit, but took a stool and did so anyway, with a touch of having the right to do it. Winflæd sat slowly and eased herself back against the plank that made hers a chair.

'Look, Win, I am no fool. I knows that Osgyth would not choose me, but she is young and full of dreams. We both of us knows dreams disappear in the cold of dawn, and reality alone stays. What I said this mornin' is even more important now. Oldmother Agatha has been killed, and the lord Undersheriff says as it is to do with The Priest's Treasure, and your Thorgar brought it up with the ploughshare. None of us is safe, not while there be someone seekin' it, and especially not you, as Thorgar's family. Remember what fallin' out were caused years back when a single bronze pin were found in the north field? Of itself it were worth but a pair of silver pennies, but for weeks everyone watched close every time a neighbour bent down within reach of another's strip of earth, and my father had almost to step in and break up fights. That were but one pin, and now we knows The Treasure itself 'as been found. The lord Undersheriff can announce that the silver chalice is rightly back with the lord Bishop and that whatever small items is left belong to King Stephen and must be handed over, but who in Ripple believes there be but a few silver pennies or a brooch? Everyone knows the hoard contained everything the folk of the parish, not just Ripple itself, thought the Danes would steal, every silver penny, gown pin, ring or torc. To a king it would be but nothing, and nothing is what the King will see, mark my words, but to any of us . . . Such wealth makes good neighbours into enemies. Thorgar brought up The Treasure, and kept quiet about it, but someone found out, and that led to both Father Edmund's death and, by a twist of *wyrd*, his own. Now Oldmother Agatha is dead. Do you want Osgyth, or your boys to be next? You cannot protect them, nor yourself. I can. If you were a few years younger and not crippled, I would be content with you, Win, for you were a comely woman once, but Osgyth has to be told the realities and set dreams aside.'

Winflæd was actually several years younger than Selewine, but painfully aware that her disability made her an object of pity to some neighbours and avoided as one who had been God-cursed by others. She already felt guilt that Osgyth bore so much of the household duties, and now she would be asked to accept a man she despised because her mother was crippled and aged beyond her years.

'I cannot force her to accept you, Selewine, and it would be easier if you did not always treat her as you do, knowing it angers her.'

'As for that, she likes to show spirit, and it is all in jest.' He brushed the idea way with a gesture of his hand. 'And you can make her see reason. She is a dutiful daughter, when all be said, and will not see the family starve in the longer term, nor face violence in the shorter. Send 'er to me tomorrow with the answer.'

Selewine got up and left, well pleased with himself, and in a dutiful mood decided that as the village reeve, he would rise early next morning and knock upon the door of the few households without a man, to check all was well. Winflæd, however, rocked in her chair and wept, watched by the pale-faced boy who curled even tighter upon the bed and whimpered.

Walkelin awoke before his superiors, and not just because he did not have the benefit of a proper bed. Father Ambrosius, upon his return from comforting the living and praying for the dead, would not hear of sleeping in his own cot, and insisted that Serjeant Catchpoll took it, while the other remained for the use of the lord Undersheriff. He had therefore taken his blanket and slept the other side of the hearth to Walkelin. The small black cat, which had been proved innocent of any involvement in Oldmother Agatha's death, had slipped in with him when he had returned, and curled up between him and the hearth, and drifted into slumber with a low, consistent purring. Father Ambrosius regarded the hardship engendered by this charitable act as good for his soul, even if not for the quality of his slumbers. However, the priest had in fact fallen asleep quite swiftly, and had been found to be a snorer. It was not so loud as to rouse the other two, but Walkelin, already tracing strands of thought through his head, found it intrusive. When he finally slept, his dreams were troubled, and he awoke feeling jaded. He sat up, easing his neck and shoulders. Those with proper beds were not yet stirring, and he decided it was best not to shake shoulders.

Bradecote and Catchpoll actually roused when Father Ambrosius went to his first private prayers of the day, kneeling before the cross on the bed end wall of the house.

The prayers were murmured, but enough to bring both serjeant and undersheriff to consciousness.

Walkelin, his thoughts filed, stood up, casting the rough blanket from him. He poked the last embers of the fire with his foot, but they steadfastly refused to show any greater signs of life.

Catchpoll, stifling his morning grumble in view of the priest's prayers, got up a little stiffly from the cot, and pulled his boots onto feet that had grown cold in the night. He came to stand on the edge of the hearthstone, hoping it might hold some residual heat that would pass through the soles of his boots.

'Serjeant, I was thinkin' afore I slept.' Walkelin spoke barely above a whisper so as not to disturb the prayers.

'Glad to hear it, unless it were about that Eluned of yours back in Worcester. Them thoughts is best kept to yourself.' Catchpoll rubbed his hands together, chafing them.

'No, though that would be nice.' Walkelin blushed and smiled, though the smile faded. 'We said yesterday that the killer has to be someone of Ripple, but we really means in Ripple. We knows . . .' he remembered Father Ambrosius saying he was part of Selewine's kindred, and decided not to name the reeve, just in case, 'our most likely man, but would it not be wrong to discount the treewright and his son? They 'ad been in the village a week when the priest were killed, and lodge with Tofi, so who is to say that old tales was not told to them as they sat about the fire? They could have come to know of the silver and of the priest lookin' after it. We just thought that when the priest yelled at Tofi's door, in

Welsh, 'e were complainin' about Pryderi not bein' at work and ale-sodden, but that need not have been in Welsh. Why did 'e use Welsh that others could not understand? It niggles me like a sore tooth, do that.'

'To show off, mayhap?' Catchpoll did not offer this up with confidence. 'You is right that we must not discount the pair of 'em, though.'

'Discount who?' Bradecote, who had been sat upon his bed, pulling on his own boots and gathering his thoughts, drew close. He had not fully heard all that had been spoken.

'Pryderi and his son, my lord,' answered Walkelin. He repeated his reasoning.

'Ah. Well, you go and speak with them, Walkelin, as soon as they go to their work.' Bradecote went to the door and opened it to the burgeoning light of an early spring morn, and the innocence of birdsong. The air was cold but smelt fresh, especially after the staleness of a chamber with four men and a hearth fire.

'And I was wonderin' how we is to speak with each family when they is all in the fields again, my lord. Does we ask each where their cott stands in the village?' Catchpoll could foresee some confusion.

'I thought of that before I slept, Catchpoll. All I need is a stick.'

'A walking staff, my lord?' Walkelin looked puzzled.

'No, Walkelin, just a good, pointed end of a thin branch, strong enough for me to draw in the earth with it. I will draw in where the oak stands, and the church, and this house, and then Oldmother Agatha's. Each household can point to where they live, and I draw a square on the earth. That way we literally build a picture.'

'Now, I would never have thought of that.' Father Ambrosius crossed himself and rose to his feet, then turned to look at them. The black hair about his tonsure stuck out at very strange angles, and made him even more heron-like than usual.

'Father, we would not ask you to break the seal of the Confession, but you are almost the only man in Ripple we know to have nothing to do with the killing of Oldmother Agatha. You know these people, so if anything strikes you as odd in their behaviour, be extra eyes and ears for us and tell us, please.' Bradecote spoke earnestly. 'It need not be that they are the killer, but perhaps they are afraid because they have a suspicion and dare not speak with us. Encourage them to do so, because while it is only known to them they are at risk. A man who would attack a defenceless old woman will harm anyone he fears will give him away, even if he is mistaken.'

'Oh dear, yes. It still seems beyond belief that any of my parishioners could have done such a thing, but it must be so.'

'Thank you.' There was a pause. 'What sort of man is Selewine? I ask because he is the reeve and might also be more likely to know all the undercurrents in the village, but might he be so close to everyone that he would be reluctant to give us information?' Bradecote thought this might glean more than a more direct question, and felt rather than heard Catchpoll's slight sigh of relief.

'As I told your underserjeant here, I am by way of kindred. My father was his father's younger brother, so he is my *sweor*, though I am a few years older than he is, for he and Tofi came late as sons, after daughters and babes that died. He and Tofi are both like their father, very aware of the status of reeve, even if Tofi does not hold the position. I have even heard him call himself "Reevesbrother". Such foolishness. They set much store by the position and the power in the village, but then they have rarely gone further than Tewkesbury and think Ripple far more important than it is in the shire. They value power more than true friendship, I think, and are not even close as brothers, alas. I do not think you need worry that Selewine will conceal knowledge if he has information that would see one of his neighbours hang. After all, he showed no compunction with poor Thorgar.'

'Yes, that makes sense. Thank you, Father.' Bradecote was now wondering even more whether Selewine might offer up another to pay a blood debt that he himself owed, and whether that might lead them to incontrovertible proof of his guilt.

Walkelin almost sauntered through the churchyard, as casual as though he had been given leave of absence for the day and was wondering what to do. However, the treewright and his son were not in their temporary workshop, so his feigned insouciance was wasted. The only persons in view were industriously digging a grave in the far north-west corner of the churchyard and were already only visible from the chest upwards. Walkelin smiled to himself. That would not be the grave for the respected oldmother. Father Ambrosius could not refuse to bury his brother priest within consecrated ground, but he was ensuring that he was as far from the sanctity of the east end as possible. No crime had been proven, nor even charged, but it made a statement that all Ripple would understand, and applaud. Walkelin entered the church, the door's creak amplified by the acoustics of the space, but the voices he could hear did not alter and evidently had not heard him. He went forward towards the chancel and from the corner of his eye noticed the stretcher with a blanket cast over it just inside and to the left side at the back of the church. There was a shrouded body on trestles in the chancel, and for a moment Walkelin wondered whether the priest, however disgraced, still took precedence over the blameless parishioner. The voices, with the distinct cadences of Welsh clear even before he could make out words, came from the north porticus, a small chamber like a stunted transept. Pryderi was up a ladder held in place by his son, and driving home pegs into a half-lap joint where the rotten end of a tie beam had been replaced.

'*Bore da*,' called Walkelin, in a friendly tone.

The '*bore da*' that came as the reply was an automatic 'good morning' from men concentrating on their task and not thinking about who was addressing them. Walkelin, whose understanding of Welsh was improving, thanks to his wife, still had a very limited vocabulary in which terms of endearment predominated, which made continuing in the language impossible. He held up his hand as a phrase he did not understand was spoken, and excused himself, and then Pryderi looked down properly.

'Oh, 'tis you, Underserjeant. Sorry, I thought – where did you learn "good morning"?'

'My wife is Welsh.'

'Got good taste, then.' Pryderi sounded just a little more friendly and perhaps willing to speak.

'I thought you was not workin' inside until after the burial.' Walkelin did not specify which of the two burials that were now needed.

'Father Ambrosius said as we could, and the old soul's son did not mind, for we is so behind with our work. She lies peaceful enough before the altar and will not hear us. We said a prayer for 'er too, when we began today.'

'So the priest is the one back—' Walkelin jerked a thumb towards the west end of the church.

'Oh yes. Father Ambrosius said some prayers over him yestereve, as we was told, and then 'ad the body moved and the oldmother lies altar-ward. As soon as them outside can dig a grave deep enough, the priest will be buried with due ceremony and no mourners. Whole village will come for the next one.'

'Can you come down to answer a question?'

This time Pryderi paused before speaking.

'What more could we say? This is not our village and we know none, beyond Tofi's family, and not even everyone by sight.'

'We wants to know why you did not mention that Father Edmund was Welsh.' Walkelin did not split hairs and say 'half-Welsh', in part to find out whether the treewright considered the man Welsh enough to count as a countryman.

'Nobody asked. That is why, and we did not think of him as Welsh, see, just able to carp and complain and threaten in the tongue. Nasty, that's what 'e was, if you wants to know the truth of it.'

'The truth is always what we wants, Master Treewright, and it is folk not tellin' us all of it makes our task the harder.' Walkelin let complaint enter his voice. 'It is what leads to more folk dyin', too.' He folded his arms, in a gesture he copied from his superiors. 'So, come down and tell me what made the priest "nasty".'

'Well, see now.' The treewright frowned, even as he descended. 'I would not trust the man, not from the first day we arrived. Wanted to feel powerful, which is not the way I thinks a good priest should be, and wanting to use folk to his own ends. Found fault, 'e did, even with the choice of oak we felled, and the man knew no more of trees than a *baban* at the breast. Just wanted to niggle and make us feel small. Then 'e kept on about the speed we worked, as though the lord Bishop pays us by each single hour we labours. What is important to the lord Bishop is that the work is done well and to the glory of God, not done swift just to be cheap, and so I told Father Edmund.'

'The priest also complained the mornin' of the day he died. Did he know you was ale-sodden?'

'I cannot see how, and besides he were not shouting at me but our Gwydion.'

'Your son? Why?'

'For speaking with the maid Mildred the day before.' Gwydion himself spoke up. 'She came by the workshop to say her *mam* was making dumplings for the pottage just 'acos I said I liked them so much. I was in 'ere at the time.'

'She needed to come and tell you this? Was it important?' Walkelin felt it was more an excuse than a reason. Gwydion blushed, and so Walkelin put two and two together. 'Was it more the maid wanted time to speak with you without father or mother listenin'? Was that when she set you the test of manhood?'

Gwydion just nodded.

'But the maid was not chastised.' It was an assertion, for Walkelin realised that otherwise Tofi would have heard the priest berate her in English.

'No, which were unfair. And what business was it of the priest, anyways?' Gwydion now sounded aggrieved.

'You did not say that was what you spoke of.' Pryderi glowered at his son. 'You said it was just the pottage.'

Walkelin was not entirely surprised at the youth's deception. He would expect his father to object to any entanglement with a village beauty. Parents rarely thought a lad old enough to start thinking of maids at the stage when maids began to fill the dreams.

'That itself is no crime, Master Treewright. Killin' the priest is. Tell me once again, Gwydion, what you did that afternoon.' Walkelin's mind was already drawing from memory what the lad had said the first time, for comparison.

'Mid-afternoon I had finished making the oak pegs for the joints, and the priest came and said as he would report

210

my *tad* to the lord Bishop if he missed another day's work, and then I went up the hill yonder, where the *ysbrydion* is meant to appear among the trees, and I went to the place Mildred 'ad described, so I could tell the answer to the question as proved I went there, and then I came back, and the ploughman was already hanged for killing Father Edmund and all was upset.'

'So why did you go back to the workshop and not back to the pottage and dumplings? I would 'ave thought you would tidy up afore you went ghost huntin'.' The question had arisen suddenly in Walkelin's mind. He felt the original reason might not be entirely true. 'Why did you really come back to the church and offer to assist the women who laid out the body?'

'Never seen a dead man afore,' admitted Gwydion, with a mixture of embarrassment and bravado. 'Leastways, not one dead by violence. I wanted to see, and to see if I am man enough not to be sick to the stomach from it. I went in and asked if they needed aid to lift the body, and to fetch the trestles.'

Walkelin could understand that feeling. It rang true enough, though it was also true that if Gwydion had any involvement with the killing it would have been useful to see if any incriminating evidence were left behind, and he had indeed found the awl. He looked hard at Gwydion. His serjeanting intuition, whilst not nearly as honed as Serjeant Catchpoll's, told him that the youth was no killer as it had with serjeant and undersheriff. He asked a final question.

'And how did you feel?'

'Not bad right there and then, not doing things, but after – I felt a bit sick. I saw the man alive a few hours afore and there 'e was, just cold flesh.' Gwydion looked at the ground.

'First time I saw a body that did not die natural, I felt like that too,' admitted Walkelin, with a small smile. 'No less of a man did it make me.' Gwydion was perhaps no more than ten years his junior, but Walkelin realised he had just been quite paternal. Was marriage making him feel more mature?

'The underserjeant speaks true, Gwydion *bach*.' Pryderi sighed. He acknowledged to himself that part of him did not like to think of his son as even nearly full grown. Then he addressed the underserjeant. 'The lord Undersheriff spoke of a treasure, last eve. We knew, and know, nothin' of that. We are 'ere in Ripple to repair the church, and that is all we have done. Whoever killed that poor oldmother, and the priest, they were Ripple folk, not us. That is the truth and I would swear oath upon it, Underserjeant.'

'I believe you, Master Treewright. *Diolch yn fawr.*' Walkelin nodded, signalling that the interview was ended, and left the church, genuflecting towards the altar, and completely ignoring the shrouded body on the elm board by the west door.

Chapter Twelve

Bradecote, having availed himself of a good stick from the hedge on the north side of the field, first approached Selewine the Reeve, and spoke to him. This alone drew everyone's attention, and heads were raised and backs straightened as though a rabbit warren was suddenly aware of stoats on the hunt. The reeve's beckoning hand drew them close enough for the lord Undersheriff to address them, but first Bradecote took the stick and drew rough squares in the earth, a cross marking the church. Serjeant Catchpoll stood a little back and observed in silence.

'I want each household to come forward, one at a time, and show me where their home stands in relation to the church, the priests' house, and Oldmother Agatha's. I will mark it in. I need to know if anyone, young or old, saw Father Edmund on the morning of his death, with or without a black cat under his arm, and near to her door.'

There was a murmur of mild surprise, then silence. Nobody stepped forward eagerly. Bradecote scowled.

'This is not a mere wish. You will all come forward. You,

Master Reeve, you and your sons will be last. And your brother Tofi will be first, with his family. The quicker you obey, the quicker you can return to your labours.' He sounded every inch the implacable lord. 'Ulf Shortfinger, you and yours will be second, so everyone get in line behind Ulf . . .'

Some glanced at the reeve, wondering. Tofi snatched his woollen cap from his head and stepped forward, followed by his wife and children, though Mildred was not present. Bradecote knew the location of Tofi's house, but it was good to make it all obvious and the same. He had him point to where his home stood, and he drew the square with his stick.

'I saw nothin' of Father Edmund after he left our door, complainin' at the Welsh, my lord. Honest.'

'And your family? Where is your daughter Mildred?'

'Not workin' the field today, my lord. Ask the wife why.' He frowned a little.

'She be unwell, my lord.' Tofi's wife dipped in an obeisance, her skirts dragging in the muddy earth. 'The morn Pryderi were the worse for ale,' she glanced at Tofi briefly, including him by implication but not by name, 'we worked indoors, for it were just too wet to do much, not early on. We went in the garden a mite later. I never saw the priest after he went from our door, and the children was about my skirts. They could 'ave seen no more'n me.'

The children, looking nervous at being mentioned before this stern lord, nodded quickly in confirmation of this.

Household by household, Bradecote placed each family on his plan. Some would clearly not have had line of sight to the oldmother's door. One woman said she had seen the priest collect his bread from the communal village oven, but he was definitely not carrying a black cat when he did so. She could not say whether he covered the loaf in anything when he left. It gave greater weight to the possibility that he had been carrying bread when he went to Oldmother Agatha's door, but if he had taken the cat from within the priests' house, it was odd that he had not left the bread there.

Walkelin arrived quietly, and watched the people as Catchpoll had taught him. Eventually Bradecote called forward Selewine and his sons, though he knew the location of their home. Selewine shook his head, and said he had gone out, despite the rain that morning, and checked the footbridge over the Ripple Brook, since it had been reported to him the day before that one of the planks was loose and the increased flow with the rain might have washed it clean away.

'You did not say this before, Master Reeve.' Bradecote looked disapproving.

'I were not asked if I were indoors all mornin', my lord.' Selewine looked a little hurt.

'And your sons?' Bradecote looked at the boys. They stood together, the older one behind the younger, his hand on the smaller boy's shoulder. Bradecote thought he saw a squeezing of that shoulder. Both just shook their heads. 'I see. Lying to the Law is a serious matter. You,' he pointed at the smaller child, 'told Serjeant Catchpoll here that you had seen the priest, Father Edmund, at the door of Oldmother Agatha on the day he died, and that he held her cat.' Bradecote omitted the bag. 'Why is this memory now gone from you?'

Hugh Bradecote was not a man who liked to use his

authority to frighten people. It was a thing used sparingly, and he was far more likely to make efforts to be approachable when dealing with children. Just at this moment, however, his voice exuded command, even threat. The child twisted from his brother's grip, and stepped forward, though his face crumpled, and his voice was breathy with a sob.

'I did see, lord. I did see, and it were not a dream.'

'Good. Now tell me, did you see anyone else at that time?' Bradecote's voice softened to a more normal tone.

'Only 'im,' the child pointed to the man Wilf the Worrier, 'carryin' a pail to the midden. Nothin' different to most days.'

The child, Catchpoll realised, remembered that he had been asked if had seen anything odd that morning. A man with a midden pail was not odd. All three of the sheriff's men were surprised at the answer.

''Tis true enough, my lord, but I did not look towards Oldmother Agatha's, nor saw Father Edmund at all. I would 'ave said.' Wilf the Worrier clasped his hands together in a gesture that was almost pleading, and rushed his admission.

Bradecote was about to ask another question when the high-pitched shouting was heard.

A female figure ran across the field towards them, holding up skirts to aid speed, and seeming to skip over the furrows. As she drew near, Bradecote recognised it was Mildred, and her face was white, and her eyes doe-wide.

'Please, come quick. 'Tis Mother Agnes.' She was gasping, as much from shock as from running, and all the coquettish poise was gone, leaving not the woman but the girl. 'I think she's dead.'

* * *

Having given strict command to the reeve that all but Mildred remain in the field, Bradecote led the way back to the cluster of village homes at the run. Whilst Walkelin was the youngest of the trio, Bradecote had the longest legs, and reached the healer's cott before his companions, trailing behind him. Agnes the Healer made her pristine home look unnaturally untidy, for she was sprawled upon the floor, her arms flung out in front of her and her head on one side as if she were listening for mice among the rushes. She was barefoot, a thick shawl lay flung carelessly on the ground behind her, and a linen nightcap was tied under her chin. This was now stained at the back and a small pool of sticky blood was forming, with her plait of brown hair preventing its spread.

Bradecote, dry-mouthed, knelt at her side and leant down close. The light was not good, but when he laid a hand upon her back it rose and fell gently. She was not dead.

'God be praised,' he muttered, devoutly.

The light diminished further as Walkelin stood in the doorway until pushed in fully by a breathless Catchpoll. Mildred, who had run the distance twice, stopped short of the door, unsure whether she would be commanded to enter, and unwilling to do so otherwise. She had seen someone who was dead before, since few reached her age without losing some family member, young or old, but never by violence.

'She lives. Walkelin, see if you can find bandaging cloths among her preparations, and anything that you recognise as being for wounds. Catchpoll, you have more experience than I do. Her head bleeds a lot, but is the skull broken?'

'I am no physician, my lord, and used to the dead, not the

livin',' Catchpoll got awkwardly down on his knees and felt the back of the head, ignoring the blood on his fingers. 'Nothin' says to me the skull is broke, my lord. If we – and she – is lucky, she will waken at some point, and we 'as to hope as she remembers who came to the door early. Often as not, though, them as is left like this cannot recall anythin'. Best we get her onto the bed.'

With Catchpoll taking her shoulders and Bradecote her feet, the two men lifted the woman, who was not heavy, onto the bed, putting her on her side so the wound was accessible. Walkelin, who had been smelling various bottles, some of which had made his eyes water, brought a small pot, bandages, and a pad made from the cleanest cloth he could find. At Catchpoll's instruction, he held it very firmly against the wound to staunch the bleeding.

'I thinks the pot is a paste of selfheal. Smells like it to me, leastwise.' He spoke, but did not take his eyes from his task. The cloth was reddening, but did not reach a sodden state.

Bradecote turned to Mildred, beckoning her inside. She obeyed, but nervously.

'Why did you seek Mother Agnes?' It was meant to be an easy question to begin the conversation, but the girl reddened instantly, and looked to the floor. There was a pause, then she murmured her response.

'Mother Agnes makes things as is good for the gripes of women.'

It was Bradecote's turn to be embarrassed. He almost rushed into the next question.

'Was the door open when you arrived?'

'No, my lord. It were shut, but not fully. I knocked and called out, but there were no answer, so I pushed the door a little and saw 'er on the floor and all the blood and—' Mildred bit her lip and stifled a sob.

'And did you see anyone as you came to the house, anyone at all?' Bradecote did not expect any useful revelation and was not surprised that Mildred simply shook her head.

'Thank you. Now, you go to your mother, but you are not to say anything of what you have seen or heard here. Do not say that Mother Agnes is alive. Understand?'

'Aye, my lord.' In truth, she did not understand at all, other than it was a command from the lord Undersheriff and must be obeyed.

'Wise, my lord,' commented Catchpoll, after she had gone. 'We don't want whoever did it comin' back to finish her off.'

'What concerns me, Catchpoll, is that last night we did not actually say that no treasure could have been brought to Oldmother Agatha. The killer might still think it true, and Agnes the Healer spoke up, saying the idea was foolish, which he might have seen as a lie to cover her having discovered it and taken it. He knows it was not in the priests' house, nor the oldmother's, and the healer admitted she had been in the house that day. We ought to have kept her safe.'

'Well, if you thinks she would have accepted Walkelin sleepin' by the fireside I thinks you is in need of somethin' for addled brains, my lord. She would have sent 'im away with a tongue-lashin', for sure.' Catchpoll wanted to stamp firmly on the undersheriff's tendency for self-blame, for it only got in the way.

'Possibly, but we ought to have made the attempt. Has the bleeding stopped, Walkelin?'

'Nearly, my lord. Shall I put the ointment on and bind it up?'

'I think so, though I know as little of healing as you do.'

It was probably a good job that Agnes the Healer was unconscious, for she would have had found little to commend in Walkelin's neatness of bandaging, but it was at least effective. Had the situation not been so serious, Bradecote would have laughed at the result.

'She would have had no qualms about answering her door, even early, for her skills would be needed at all hours.' Bradecote stared at the pale face, severe even in immobility.

'And our warnin' might have made her a mite cautious about invitin' someone in, but they would 'ave been kept on the doorstep anyways, since she would need to dress. She would tell 'em to wait but not put the bar down again, 'specially if her mind was already workin' out what she needed to take with 'er.' Catchpoll was also staring at Agnes the Healer, but in his head was playing out the scene as it must have unfolded. 'My guess is the man stepped in almost as soon as the door closed. She has not untied the strings of the nightcap, and she would have placed the shawl on the bed if she had removed it 'erself. Also, she lay facin' a bit to the door, but mostly as if turned away from it, so the blow landed as she looked round at the intrusion.'

'Yes, that makes good sense, Catchpoll. The girl Mildred thought she was dead. Do you think the man who hit her really left thinking he had silenced her forever? I mean, we are thinking he was searching for treasure in her home, but should we also consider that he thought she might know something that would mark him as the oldmother's killer?'

'If it were a simple thing, my lord, she would 'ave come to us last eve, straight away.' Walkelin was conscientiously trying to set the pot of ointment back as he had found it. 'So it must 'ave been a thing she might recall late. And, my lord, these pots is still in a straight line and I does not think anyone but me has moved one, other than Mistress Agnes 'erself.'

'Aye, look about you, my lord, as she did in Oldmother Agatha's. This is not "tidy" by 'er standards. The bedcover thrown back we could take as just gettin' out o' bed to answer the knock at the door, but the chest at the bed end is not quite closed, so if we lifts the lid,' Catchpoll suited the action to the word, 'we can see things not neatly folded but disordered, like someone rooted about among 'em as a pig roots for beechmast.'

'So the treasure was sought, but we should not discount that her remembering something was not also involved. After all, there are few if any in Ripple as observant or astute. Walkelin, whilst it would be useful to have you with us when speaking with everyone, family by family, we have to ensure nobody enters other than Father Ambrosius or us, especially not the reeve, or, being fair, Wilf the Worrier, since some possible suspicion lies upon him now. It will also be useful if we have someone at the bedside in case she wakes and can tell us who hit her.'

'Understood, my lord.'

'Anything she recalls may aid us, even if not a full picture. You have a good head for setting things in order, and will make the most of anything we learn.'

'Let us just pray she wakes, first, my lord,' cautioned

Catchpoll. 'You cannot always tell with them as is left senseless.'

'Oh, I have been praying since we got here, Catchpoll.' Bradecote was very earnest.

'If'n she wakes and recalls nothin', does I tell what we know? It might begin to bring some memory back.' Walkelin was thinking ahead.

'Aye, you do that.' Catchpoll nodded. 'Sometimes there is nothin', not for hours afore the injury, and it never returns. Other times bits come back gradual like, in no order, and not even the most important.'

'Wait. Could it even be that she was attacked late yesterday and has lain all night as we found her? She might have been ready for her bed and—'

'If that had been so, my lord, she would be chilled to the bone, and although not bed-warm, she was cool but not overnight-cold.' Catchpoll shook his head. 'Also, anyone comin' out late would 'ave had to give a good reason to their family, whereas in the morn, well, everyone does their tasks, be it fetchin' water from the well or takin' a pail to the midden. Bein' abroad a mite earlier than usual would not be odd.'

'But in that case the assailant took a great risk of being seen by others, Catchpoll.'

'Not if it were timed right, my lord. It would just need to be early enough for there to be few folk to avoid, and the healer still abed, but not so early as to be questioned.'

'Well, we will not catch whoever did this standing here. You and I, Catchpoll, will go and ask if anyone saw or heard another abroad unusually early this morning.'

'And does we say direct that the healer is dead, my lord?'

'If we say she has been discovered, "left for dead", we might avoid that specific question, and if asked we can say she is like to die, for she is – if not this day, then one day.' A small smile played about Bradecote's mouth. 'The Law should not lie, but it need not reveal everything it knows, eh, Catchpoll?'

'Oh aye, my lord. Many things is best kept privy.'

'If, by some miracle, the healer wakes and is sure who hit her, Walkelin, send if you can to us by anyone you see about the village, but do not leave her.'

'I will keep 'er safe, my lord.' Walkelin looked resolute.

In fact, those labouring in the Great Field had taken Mildred's first cry that Agnes the Healer was dead as a certain fact, and did not think to question it, which made it much easier for Bradecote and Catchpoll. First of all, the pair gathered in the villagers like sheepdogs bringing in the flock for penning, though one man held back, and was allowed to do so. Wystan was not of any Ripple home. He was also in charge of the plough oxen for the first time, though Selewine had stressed he was on probation and would likely not be good enough, and he rather liked the idea he could continue without anyone paying him any attention, just in case his furrows were not quite straight, or his headland turns not tight enough. He was permitted the aid of one of Ulf's sons to guide the beasts. Then Bradecote stood before them all, arms folded and expression very serious. He asked if anyone had been out early that morning, though no reason for this was given.

'I was out early, my lord,' volunteered Selewine the Reeve, before anyone else could speak. 'I thought it my duty, as the reeve, to check upon the households without the protection of a man beneath the roof.'

'Did you visit all of them, Master Reeve?' Bradecote enquired, ensuring he did not sound too interested in the answer. Was the man volunteering information so that he looked innocent and helpful?

'Selewine came and knocked upon my door afore I had twisted my plait.' Widow Reed held up her hand as she spoke. 'Fair scared me, it did, that great fist upon my door and 'im bellowin' to ask if I stayed safe and well.'

'So you did not cross any threshold?' Bradecote looked at the reeve again.

'Too early it were, my lord, and folk just risin'.'

'I ask again. Did you visit everyone, and did they give an answer?'

'Aye, my lord, but that were just the Widow Reed and Mother Agnes. I did and they did. Mind you, Mother Agnes did not thank me, just threw a patten, from the sounds of it, at the door. Cantankerous she be, though, so no surprise were it to me.'

'I see. And did you see anyone else as you made your early rounds of the village?'

'I saw only Wilf, my lord, as I were goin' over first to the Widow Reed's.' Selewine the Reeve looked very serious. 'But in fairness, everyone know Wilf sleeps light and wakens early, and 'e were only off to settin' spade to earth in 'is garden afore field work.'

'Mayhap 'e 'as somethin' buried in the garden.' It was a youthful voice, and accompanied by a snigger. Clearly the speaker did not think Wilf the Worrier a man likely to have secured the treasure and hidden it again.

'No, I tell you, that ain't true,' Wilf the Worrier blurted out, his face at first paling then reddening.

''Twere but a jest, Wilf,' came a woman's voice, soothingly.

Catchpoll, however, did not look at all soothing. His eyes were narrowed to a gimlet gaze and his lips drawn into the thinnest and most disquieting of smiles.

'Not just vegetables lies in the earth, eh, Wilf. Even things as were lost can be found there.'

'I does not 'ave the treasure.' Wilf's voice rose almost to a squeak. 'I swears it.'

'O' course you doesn't. You—' The soothing voice began, but was interrupted.

'Not treasure of silver, no,' conceded Catchpoll, very slowly, his eyes not wavering. 'But some things is worth more 'n silver.'

'Gold?' This was a child's voice.

'No, young 'un. A good mother, a good father – a good wife.' The last was given weight.

'My wife left me, and went to Worcester, last autumn.' Wilf the Worrier's cheeks were white, and his breathing as fast as if he had run. His voice was urgent, almost desperate.

'You see, that is a thing as worries me, and I am not one as worries without cause.' Catchpoll let his words fall slowly. This was almost too easy. 'I knows Worcester as you all knows this field, where is the better ground and where the least productive, where it is the stoniest. I knows the folk of Worcester, and them as comes to live there, and no woman called Eadild of Ripple plies a trade or tends a cooking pot within the walls.'

'She went off to be with 'er sister, Leofcwen.' A woman's voice came from the rear of the gathering.

'And the trade that Leofcwen plied was the oldest, and she died three years past.' Catchpoll revealed this without mirth.

This news, of itself ideal for gossiping women to mull over for days, changed the atmosphere. Those about Wilf the Worrier stepped back a little, if not physically then in spirit. A seed of doubt was planted in the collective village mind.

'Then she must 'ave moved on, findin' her gone.' Wilf tried to give the suggestion an affirmative tone, and failed.

'Catchpoll, this is not for now,' muttered Bradecote, casting the serjeant an angry look.

'Things come to the surface when they is ready, my lord.' Catchpoll was still watching Wilf the Worrier.

'So we now have witnesses that saw you outside on the morning of the priest's death, when he went to Oldmother Agatha's, and also this morning, which is likely when Agnes the Healer was attacked. It looks – suspicious. Did you see anyone, on either occasion?' Bradecote decided this was the only way to get back to the matter in hand.

'Not the first one, my lord, and this morn only Selewine, who saw me as I saw 'im.' The man sounded on the verge of panic, as if he were a drowning man come up for air.

'But what of Eadild?' The woman spoke up again and Bradecote gave up.

'When we dig up your garden, Wilf, where will we find your wife's remains?' Bradecote sounded bored, not excited.

There was a collective gasp at the bald question, and Wilf the Worrier's eyes widened and then his eyeballs rolled up into his head and he fell in a dead faint upon the earth.

Whilst Catchpoll, and now Bradecote, were sure the man had killed his wife, all that linked him to the other deaths and attack was being seen outdoors, not near the homes of either woman.

'If'n he killed Eadild, a wolf in sheep's clothin' is Wilf, and like as not killed again. Yet, of all men in this village, he would be the last I would name as violent.' This, from Selewine the Reeve, was met with mutterings of agreement, though another male voice added 'after Thorgar, that is.' Selewine scowled at that. Bradecote thought it one attempt too far to divert their thoughts elsewhere.

'We will look deeply into this, but I say to all of you, still be careful. There is no connection of itself between the death of Eadild and the other deaths, and it may yet be another who has killed these last days.' Bradecote could not simply tell everyone to avoid their reeve, but felt he would be remiss if he did not put everyone on their guard.

Catchpoll, having motioned to the reeve to assist him, pulled the inanimate form of Wilf the Worrier into a sitting position, and tapped his face, not entirely gently, until he groaned and raised his head.

'Now then, you can get up slow, and come with me.' Catchpoll did not sound threatening, just very calm.

Wilf the Worrier struggled groggily to his feet, focusing gradually. He swallowed hard and looked about him at his neighbours. What he saw was that these people were suddenly as cold as strangers to him. He shuddered as Catchpoll took his elbow and led him back towards the village. It was a troubled undersheriff who followed him. That there should be two murderers in the small community of Ripple might be unlikely, but if Eadild was, as he expected, to be found beneath the earth of the man's garden plot, that death was differentiated by time and motive. He still felt it was a dangerous distraction, though he understood that it was not so long ago as might reasonably be left as simply for the judgement of God, and out of the hands of the Law.

Wilf the Worrier's home was far from homely. It was not dirty, nor particularly untidy, but had an air of lacking a woman's attentions. Bradecote closed the door behind him as he entered the dim chamber. The man, still pale, was thrust onto a stool, and Bradecote, arms folded across his chest, regarded him dispassionately.

'We will find your wife, even if it means digging up every spadeful of the garden behind your cott. Tell me, since we know when she disappeared, why it was that you killed her, and how.'

Wilf the Worrier stared at the undersheriff as if he were speaking Foreign. Catchpoll made a growling noise in his throat, but did not touch him. After a few moments, Wilf heaved a great sigh, and unburdened himself. As he did so, he seemed to grow, sloughing off a weight upon his soul.

'I loved Eadild. I did. She grew restless, though, always pursin' her lips when I warned of problems, always complainin' that I only saw the worst that might be. Well, I was right often enough.' He gave a twisted smile. 'The night she died she threw a beaker at me and said she had borne enough. She was goin' to Worcester and would live with Leofcwen. I thought it mere words, but she took her second shift, better gown and cap, and began to pack them into her shawl. I-I don't rightly know what happened. I cannot remember it now, just that I knew she could not leave me. I would not let her. I grabbed her and shook 'er and she slapped my face. Odd it is that some nights I wakes feelin' the burnin' of my cheek as if it is red still.' He was speaking more to himself than to the sheriff's officers. 'Then I grabbed 'er by the throat, for she were shoutin' at me and – then she went all limp. I realised she were dead and so I went out in the dark and buried her in the garden, next to the cabbages. None but me digs the garden.' Wilf the Worrier looked less worried, and now 'saw' the lord undersheriff before him.

'My lord, I did not want to kill my wife, but I did. God forgive me, I did. But the death of Father Edmund and poor Oldmother Agatha and Mother Agnes, those deaths are not at my door. What need would I have for treasure? You was right, Serjeant, I buried mine.' His eyes misted, and then he bent his head and wept.

Neither Bradecote nor Catchpoll doubted he spoke the truth.

'There is nothing you can do for Eadild, but you can do something for your village, and those who need justice now. If you saw anything that has bearing on recent events, tell us.' Bradecote spoke firmly enough to get through the man's emotional outburst, but not harshly.

'My lord, I can only say as I saw Selewine the Reeve this morn as I took my spade. I raised it a little in greetin', though no response did I get. Not that it would surprise me, for Selewine more 'n often ignores me. I warned 'im last year, when he turned up a silver penny, aye, and it would be in the very strip that went then over to Thorgar, that all his burrowin' in the earth like a little black mole would do is bring up death. Not that any more came to 'is fingers, but now I am proved right. Mind you, Selewine must be sick to 'is stomach that The Treasure came up to another, not his mighty reeve-ness, just for the fame of it. Well, you can keep that sort of fame.' Wilf almost snorted. He clearly felt both vindicated in his view and affronted that his prognostication had been ignored. Just for a moment his own spiral towards death was forgotten.

'So Selewine had held that land until the Court Leet. That is interesting.' Bradecote frowned. It was customary for villages to reassign the field strips every few years so that no one person only had poor land, nor only the best. When he had made it known to all the village that Thorgar had ploughed up treasure, Selewine had not commented at all, and Bradecote's reading of the man certainly agreed with Wilf the Worrier's that Selewine's pride, if not desire for self-aggrandisement, would have raised an exclamation. It was another hint that pointed the finger of guilt towards the man. The undersheriff, lost in his own thoughts for a moment, realised Wilf was watching him, awaiting his next pronouncement. It was nothing to do with Selewine, however.

'You will get your spade and dig again, so that your wife gets a Christian burial.'

'But after all these months in the ground . . .' The man's eyes grew wide and fearful.

'We all has to face the results of our deeds. You put the woman in the ground so you can fetch 'er up again.' Whilst he would not say it before the murdering husband, Catchpoll knew that it would not be the most pleasant of sights, and he did not relish it, but nor would he avoid it. 'You just—' Catchpoll was interrupted by a loud thumping on the door and a female voice screeching for admittance.

'Oh, what now?' Bradecote sounded peeved and went and opened the door himself. Osgyth almost fell over the threshold.

''Tis Baldred. Gone, 'e is.'

Chapter Thirteen

Osgyth wrung her hands together.

'He is dead?' Bradecote was stunned.

'No, gone. Gone from the bed. Disappeared. Mother fears the grief be so bad he might throw hisself into the river.' She began to sob loudly.

'He was sick. He might feel better today and have just wanted some air.' It sounded foolish even to Bradecote's own ears, but his was a mind in confusion. There were but three of them to deal with the deaths, and Walkelin was guarding Agnes the Healer and now someone would need to guard Wilf the Worrier, not, realistically, from absconding, but more likely from doing himself an injury, and there was a missing child, but still a killer to be found.

'When did he go missing?'

'Mother is not sure, but she fell asleep, since sleep 'as been poor these last days, and when she woke up Baldred were gone. My little brother Odda went back to fetch a sack to put about his shoulders, middle forenoon, since the cold got into the bones of 'im, and Mother were awake then, but Odda says she were sleepy.'

'So perhaps a couple of hours have passed. He could be well hidden by now.' Bradecote did not suggest 'drowned'.

Another figure appeared at Osgyth's shoulder. It was Wystan the wheelwright's son.

'My lord, I need to speak with you.' He sounded sincere.

'Why? We have many—' Bradecote was cut short, which was unusual.

'I looked when you drew the village on the earth, and now I sees proof which way round they is, I am sure.'

'Of what?'

'I saw a man at a door, my lord, a door I thought his own, after I left Osgyth and 'er mother, yesterday afore dark, offerin' to work their land. But the man were the reeve, and the door were that of the oldmother as were found dead a mite after.'

'Then we need to speak to Selewine the Reeve, even before we help find your brother, Osgyth. Osgyth?' Bradecote's brows drew together. The girl had gone from sobbing to silence and her hand was across her mouth, her eyes fixed in a blank stare. She swallowed and managed the words in a whisper.

'Tis Selewine as said 'e would lead the search for Baldred, since as reeve it were his duty to be foremost in the search, and I was to get everyone else. Already gone after Baldred, he is.'

Bradecote felt a chill run through him. He asked one question, slowly.

'Osgyth, was your brother Baldred always with Thorgar and the ox team when ploughing?'

'Aye, my lord, for 'e walked by their heads, and encouraged 'em with a twitch if needed.'

Bradecote made a decision.

'Wystan. You are to remain here, and see that Wilf does not harm himself or try and leave.'

'I will not—' Wilf began, but was silenced with a single 'Quiet'. Bradecote stared at the wheelwright's son. 'Understood?'

'Yes, my lord.' Wystan nodded.

'Osgyth, go and ring the church bell. Keep ringing it. That will bring everyone to the church. Catchpoll, we need to get Walkelin, and we search most diligently.'

'And as we searches we prays, my lord.' Catchpoll looked very grim.

'We do.'

'For what, my lord?' Osgyth could not help herself.

'That we find your brother before Selewine the Reeve does.'

Baldred had made his decision. He felt a little dizzy on rising from the bed, having not eaten more than a token spoonful of pottage since his brother's death, and barely leaving its confines. Osgyth and his mother saw his 'sickness' as an extreme physical sign of grief, and he did grieve, but far greater than his grief was his guilt. It was his fault that his brother was dead and buried as a criminal, beyond sacred ground, his fault Oldmother Agatha was dead, Oldmother Agatha who used to give the youngest children of the village the scrapings from her boiling of autumn fruits with honey to make a preserve. Just remembering it made his mouth water. It was his fault also that Father Edmund was dead, and although the priest had been rather scary, he was a priest, so God would look very harshly upon anyone who had caused his violent death. Thus Baldred felt he was likely to be damned even in the life to come. He could not remain and see his mother's grief, nor confess to her or kindly Father Ambrosius. The only answer was to be like a leper, and leave all he loved behind. Going 'far away' to him meant Gloucester, a big place he had heard of but never seen, down the River Severn, and getting there would be accomplished most easily and swiftly by taking the little ferrying craft and letting the flow take him. How he would land when he reached Gloucester he had no idea, nor how he could get the boat brought back to Ripple, but if he was already condemned for bringing about deaths, how could it matter if he was also condemned as a thief. Baldred trembled, and wiped his eyes. He wished time would roll back and all be as it was but a few short days before.

Leaving the house without being seen had been a problem he could not solve, since there was but the single chamber for the family, and his mother did not leave the house very much. Imprisoned within his own guilt-grief, however, Baldred had not considered the effect of nights with little sleep, and that sorrow-haunted, upon his mother, though he saw that she drooped more than usual. After Master Reeve had come and spoken about Osgyth she had slept even less, and eventually this morning, deep slumber claimed her. It was then he knew the opportunity had to be taken.

Once he felt steadier, he went to the door and opened it cautiously. The daylight dazzled him for a moment, then he checked that he was not observed and slipped behind the cott, over the hurdle fence that kept the sheep from the garden and into the cover of the hedge line, which he could use to give cover down towards the river. He would never see his brothers and sister again, nor his mother, nor Ripple itself. He felt the weight of this severing, and it was with swimming eyes and a running nose that he worked his way along the bank to the upturned boat. He was then faced with a problem, for he had to turn it over and launch it into the river and he was not a big boy. He tried to heave at it and failed. Then he remembered the coracle that Tofi and Selewine the Reeve used for fishing. This was far lighter, and when he had located it half hidden and tied to some scrubby willow, he was able to tip it over and push it to the bank. He had seen men use a coracle before, and balancing as you stepped in seemed the hardest part, but fortunately, as he thought, there was a shallow beach and he could do so while only getting one foot wet. He climbed in, balancing carefully, sat down, took the paddle and pushed himself away from the beach using the paddle as a punt pole.

At first very little happened, for there was so little water beneath the coracle it barely managed gentle drifting. As he tried to imitate the figure of eight action he had seen used by the men he wobbled rather too much for safety, but it did seem to direct him further out into the river. He had wanted the current to take him downstream, but once the Severn found the little round craft, it bullied it and took it almost playfully as a cat might with a poor mouse. Baldred, despite thinking God was going to damn him, prayed. It did no good. He was aware that he had no control and was at the mercy of the great river. The current's pace was no faster than Baldred's own if he trotted along the bank, but it never flagged. It was relentless. It occurred to Baldred that his idea of going to Gloucester would not work if he could not manoeuvre the coracle to a quayside or close enough for someone to throw him a rope. If he did not succeed, the Severn would take him to its very mouth and out into The Sea, where he would assuredly be eaten by a huge fish. He tried the paddle again and felt the force of the water. He put more effort into his stroke and leant forward, for his arms were a bit short to angle the paddle correctly. He heard a man's voice, shouting, a little way behind him and half turned, losing his balance and tipping forward. The cold water enveloped him as he fell in, drawing him into its chill embrace. He could not swim.

So this was his *wyrd*, to drown and be lost forever, unshriven and condemned by Heaven. His limbs flailed about him and he spluttered as he swallowed the cold water. He went under.

And then a strong hand grabbed him.

Walkelin sighed. The task was important, he understood that, but he was bored within a few minutes of his superiors leaving him, and since he was bored, time dragged its feet as if shackled at the ankles. Watching a woman sleep, other than perhaps a lover or a new wife, was not a thing to inspire a man, and if Agnes the Healer was insensible rather than sleeping, it looked the same to Walkelin. He had sat down upon a stool to wait, his elbows on his knees and his face cupped in his hands, but after a disturbed night's sleep, it very soon encouraged him to close his eyes and drift, which was a dereliction of duty, so he stood up, stretched, and tried to truly look at the home about him, imagining what he would learn if he had never seen the occupant. He took in the whole, including the odours of herbs and wild plants, which was technically cheating, but he excused them, with a smile to himself, as 'sights for the nose'. He would have said, upon that overview, that it was a home without children in it, for keeping everything precise, with not the smallest stitched ball rolled into a corner, or whittled animal lying half-concealed where it had been forgotten upon a new game coming to mind, was difficult for the most house-proud of women. It was a woman's home too, unless perhaps that of Roger the Healer of Worcester, who had the same obsessive neatness in his workshop. A man, in Walkelin's view, was somehow untidier by nature, so it was unfair of wives to complain at them. He had been a little surprised how quickly his own Eluned had begun to chide him, just as his mother would, about his best cotte left casually dropped upon the end of the bed, not folded away in the small chest, or the shavings from his whittling not being gathered to add to the kindling for the fire. He sighed. Thinking of Eluned was not his duty either. He refocused. The number of pots and pestles and all manner of dried plants hanging from hooks that had been driven into the crossbeam of a truss, equally apart, declared this to be the home of a healer. Were all healers so ordered in their lives, he wondered? The craft did not make one rich in a village, for the small chest, which contained raiment, was not full when he lifted the lid, and nor was everything folded properly. It had not been taken out, shaken and dumped back in, but hands had rummaged among the garments and there was a carelessness to the whole. If there had been anything other than clothing and lavender stalks to keep out the moth, it would have been discovered.

Agnes the Healer made a low moaning sound, and moved her fingers. When she had seemed less deeply unconscious Walkelin had moved her onto her back, but slightly propped up. One hand had been placed over the other upon her spare bosom, which would have been fitting if she were no longer breathing. She did not open her eyes, but spoke.

'I is not dead yet.' The assertion was made in a dry, whispery voice, but it strengthened a little when she took a deeper breath and her eyelids fluttered open. What she saw was Walkelin's concerned face looming over her.

'Ah, 'tis you.' She initially seemed to accept this without question,

'It is, mistress. How, er, do you feel?'

'Silly question. My 'ead aches like someone took a club to it.' She frowned. 'Why is that?'

Walkelin's heart sank.

'You was found on the floor, blood everywhere, mistress, and as if you had risen from your bed to answer the door and someone clouted you on the back of the head.'

'I was?'

'Yes. What is the last thing you remembers?'

'I went to bed last eve.'

'And you know what 'appened yesterday?'

'I am not completely addled of brain, Underserjeant. Someone killed Oldmother Agatha.' The healer frowned, and winced, for even the puckering of a brow seemed a great effort and painful. 'Was it meant to be me, next?'

'It seems so, mistress. They looked about, lookin' for somethin', so . . .'

'If they moved my potions I will take the besom to 'em, when I is up and doin' again.' Her hand went gingerly to the bandage about her head.

'Mistress, unless you gets better very swift, I hopes as we will 'ave taken that man to Worcester and the Justices in Eyre. He will face more 'n a besom thrashin'.' Walkelin looked serious, and Agnes the Healer, who saw folk rather than just looked at them, thought, in a slightly hazy way, that it was not natural to him.

There was a knocking at the door, and when Walkelin went and asked who was there, Father Ambrosius answered. The priest was let in.

'I have been saying the service over Father Edmund, and only just heard about – Oh!' As he entered, Father Ambrosius saw Agnes the Healer in bed but clearly not dead, as he had been informed.

'Heaven be praised!' It was a heartfelt declaration, and he raised his arms in a gesture that was thankful and yet also seemed to be welcoming a soul, one he had thought departed, back to earthly living.

'Indeed, Father, but no miracle. The lord Undersheriff did not want it to be known the attack upon Mistress Agnes did not succeed in killin' 'er, in case the man tried again.'

'Ah yes, I understand.' The priest beamed at Agnes, his joy in no way diminished. 'Shall I pray with you?'

'Aye, Father, but first I would ask you to bring me a little of what is in the bottle at the far end of my bench. Last year's bramble wine is that, and a thumb's breadth in a beaker will do me good.' Agnes the Healer, who spent her life healing others, had no intention of allowing herself to linger in ill-health or injury.

Father Ambrosius hurried to fulfil the request, and when Agnes had sipped it, she ran her tongue over her thin lips.

'There was knockin' at the door about sunrise. That comes back to me now. I gets so many knocks at all hours I thought it just another memory, but it was this day.'

'And it must 'ave been someone you knew, Mistress.' Walkelin wanted to prod the memory back into full functioning.

'True enough, but who I cannot say, leastwise not now. I were asleep, the sound of fist on door woke me and I went and asked who needed me.'

'You said it were first light, so you must 'ave opened the door to know that.'

'Yes, but – I am sorry, but no face can I see. It were a man, though, for I can tell when men knock at my door, not women. Sounds different. From the moment I lifted the latch all seems gone.' Agnes looked aggrieved, as if her assailant had stolen the memories. 'Pox be upon them.'

It was not a huge help, since Walkelin knew that the killer being a woman was already discounted.

'Forgiveness is the Christian path,' murmured Father Ambrosius, chiding in the most gentle manner.

'And one I will tread when good and ready, Father, when my poor skull is not throbbin', and I knows who did it.'

Agnes' answer was swift. Outrage was vying with the pain and beginning to win, and Walkelin hoped that this would itself encourage remembering. However, it first took her to the reason she had been attacked.

'What need would I have for treasure? None, and all the parish knows it. So why would a man come and try to end me for somethin' I would not possess?' Her mind had latched onto the only plausible reason why anyone would search through her belongings.

It was the priest, rather than Walkelin, who had the answer for her.

'Alas, when a soul gives in to the sin of greed, it is often the case that they cannot see that it does not also consume everyone else. They then become jealous also. Thus does Satan ensnare the unwary.' The good priest sighed and shook his head.

The 'Hmmph' response from Agnes the Healer made Walkelin think that if Satan tried to 'ensnare' her, he would not only fail but get a stiff telling off.

'Mistress, it could also be that the man thought you found it in Oldmother Agatha's home and took it away because you thinks it ought to go to Thorgar's kin.' The thought struck Walkelin and he voiced it immediately.

'Well, I do think that, but no right has I to interfere. I am the village healer, not the lord Undersheriff.' She winced. 'I doesn't want any more words, just a good rest. You say some prayers, Father, and then you can both leave me be.'

'I am sorry, but my orders were to stay here and let none in, except of course Father Ambrosius, in case whoever did it comes back.'

'But the village believes her dead, my son.' Father Ambrosius looked confused.

This made Agnes give a snort, which she regretted as it made her head spin. 'They'll find out soon enough that is not so and—'

Father Ambrosius had held up his hand, and she stopped.

'The church bell is ringing, ringing without ceasing. What calamity has befallen us now?' He looked distressed, and went to the door, but as he opened it, he found the lord Undersheriff on the doorstep.

'What has happened, my lord?'

'Baldred has gone missing. It looks as if he has run away, and the village is to turn out to find him. His mother fears he has gone to the river.'

'Oh! His poor mother!' The priest clasped his bony fingers together.

'What is even more of a concern is that Selewine the Reeve has gone first to seek him, and we now have a strong belief that it was he who killed Father Edmund, Oldmother Agatha and tried to kill Mistress Agnes here. If he has not found the secular parts of Thorgar's hoard find, he may well think that the boy would know.' Bradecote raised his voice a little. 'Walkelin, you come with us. Father, it is now far less likely that Mistress Agnes is at risk, if the reeve is focused upon the boy, and still thinks her dead, but I would ask you to remain here, bar the door and—'

'But I should be with Winflæd in her distress.' The priest sounded torn. Bradecote noted that he did not seem completely surprised at the revelation about the reeve, his kinsman.

'Then go, Father. You, Underserjeant, can aid me to get up and to the door, and you can all go away. I will bar the door to all, with pleasure since it will give me peace, and go slow back to my bed. I am not so weak as I cannot do that.' Agnes the Healer sounded decisive, though she was glad of Walkelin's arm and was very tottery to her door. 'Good luck to your search. Now go away.'

She shut the door behind them, and they heard the bar drop and a muttering as she shuffled back to her bed.

'My lord, we does not know the land hereabouts. I suggest we take my young ferryman, Ulf's son, to guide us at least to where children tend to go and play near the riverbank.'

'A good thought, but you will have to be swift to find him, for all the village is being called by the church bell and Serjeant Catchpoll is set to send them in different directions so they do not all search the same places.'

'I will go to his mother.' Father Ambrosius raised a hand in a blessing of their action and hurried away. Bradecote and Walkelin ran to the church, where most of the villagers were now gathered, looking frightened and confused. There was too much upheaval for quiet village folk used to nothing more than a fox taking someone's best layer. Catchpoll was dividing them into groups and had sent one party towards the hill with its ancient banks and ditches.

Walkelin scanned the huddle of villagers for his ferryman, and wove his way through the crowd to tap him on the shoulder.

'You are to come with us and show us the places you would go, if you was but Baldred's age and wanted to hide.' Walkelin realised he did not know the youth's name, and asked it.

'I am Merewin.'

'Then show us the way, as soon as Serjeant Catchpoll has decided the directions of the other parties. We seek not just Baldred, but Selewine the Reeve, who is ahead of us all in the search.'

'Well, with luck 'e will find Baldred, Underserjeant.'

'No, that would be a bad thing.' Walkelin did not explain further, but took Merewin by the arm and drew him apart from the others and presented him to the lord Bradecote.

'I would prefer to take our horses, since Selewine has a head start on us. Merewin, you can get up behind Underserjeant Walkelin. Both of you go and bring our mounts and I will stay to speak with Serjeant Catchpoll. Meet us here as soon as you can.'

'At once, my lord.' Walkelin and his guide set off at the run. Bradecote went to Catchpoll, but said nothing as the serjeant finished deploying the villagers. When they had all dispersed he asked the important question.

'What are our chances, do you think, Catchpoll?'

'About even, my lord, no more 'n that, since Selewine knows this land and is ahead of us.'

'Walkelin has got us his young ferryman, so I hope his knowledge will even things up a little, though they must come swiftly with the horses.'

'Aye, my lord.'

Selewine the Reeve tried to think clearly, but it was increasingly difficult. His justifiable aim of recovering 'The Priest's Treasure', which was assuredly his by right, since he had worked its resting place for most of the last five years, and was the head of the village to boot, had seemed so simple but had thus far proved impossible to achieve, and had resulted in deaths which had not been planned, though they had become unavoidable. A small voice of conscience, almost smothered by his growing obsession with the silver, murmured that if anyone he approached and pressured to reveal the whereabouts of the treasure had then to be silenced forever, the trail of corpses could not but lengthen.

'The Priest's Treasure' had fascinated Selewine since he was a child, when he had first heard the story around the hearth fire of a winter's evening. It gave him a sense of pride that Ripple, the village of which his father was reeve, was so special, and had such a history. When his son Osberht had told him about Thorgar turning it up with the blade of the plough from earth he, Selewine, had planted and tended over several years, he had been outraged. It felt like theft.

The priest, barely returning to consciousness, even after being shaken, had denied ever having any of it except the chalice, which he no longer had in his possession, and had done so even as he begged to be allowed to live, which was why he had been believed, though he could not be left alive to tell of it. Selewine's first thought thereafter was that Thorgar had kept all but the church treasure in his home, but if he had done that his mother would know of it, and Win knew nothing. She had never been a woman of guile, and he had seen no attempt at concealment. It was then that the odd incident of Father Edmund taking that wretched cat back to Oldmother Agatha had grown into a clear indication that he had quietly hidden it where none would seek it, in Oldmother Agatha's home. It was devious, and the priest had ever been a bit weasel-like. It had seemed obvious, right up until the old woman's home had nothing of value in it and she had spoken to him by name. That had made him jump, for he could not imagine how she might be able to know it was him when her eyes were so milky and her ears often needed a cupped hand to even make out what her grandsons said to her. He certainly could not trust her to keep quiet about his intrusion. It followed that if his treasure was not there, then it must have been moved, and Agnes the Healer was the one who went in and out each day, and was the sort of woman who always nagged, niggled and enjoyed doing both. He recalled how she had treated him no better than a servant when both his first and second wives had been ailing, telling him to do this and fetch that, and be swift about it. And after all that they still died. No, Mother Agnes liked to meddle, and stealing The Treasure just to spite him would be in character. Catching her off guard and felling her with one sweet blow from a stout stick with a hefty root-ball end, had given him satisfaction, even if the ensuing search had been fruitless. He had been so sure each time and yet his treasure eluded him still. He had even wondered if it was his *wyrd* that he should not have it at all, and then, when he saw Osgyth too distracted by worry even to snap at him, he knew the answer had been in Thorgar's house all along. Baldred the Ox Leader! Why had he not thought of it? Or at least asked Osberht who had told him of it? Of course, the lad Baldred would have been with his brother when the treasure was ploughed out of the earth, and it followed that brother told brother where it was secreted, even if with the injunction to 'tell nobody'. He had been distracted from one person to the next, as though taking stepping stones across a brook, when he could have leapt over it in one jump!

Where would the child go? Winflæd had sobbed of him drowning himself in the river because of his grief for his brother, but Selewine could not imagine the boy doing that unless . . . If he had run away to hide and be found and fussed over afterwards, he might have gone in any direction, but what if the boy blamed himself? Then he would run away for ever. The river as an end was a possibility, but more likely he would 'exile' himself and head to where he would not be found but could find shelter and work. That meant he was heading up to Worcester or down, not to Tewkesbury, where Ripple folk went often enough for him to be seen, but Gloucester or even eventually Bristow. So north or south? Selewine stood still for a moment, for this was an important decision. A swan flew overhead. It happened to be flying south and it was a water bird. It felt a sign and so he went not in the direction of the road but the river and determined to follow it southward. If Baldred was on foot he would have to detour to cross the Avon by the ferry, so would he try and take a boat? The boat the villagers used to cross over would be too heavy for him to manage, but . . . Selewine smiled to himself. He had fished for years from the coracle he and Tofi shared, but now it might well be that what he wanted to catch was already in it.

Merewin had never been on a horse before and clung tightly to Walkelin as they trotted from the ox stable to the churchyard. He watched the lord Bradecote mount the big, steel grey horse, which he considered rather terrifying, and Catchpoll, hissing as his knee objected to him hopping to give himself the impetus to mount the third horse.

'Now Merewin, you say where we go. Think as if you were Baldred, trying to hide, or even run away. Where would you go?' Bradecote was brisk.

'Them's two different things, my lord.' Merewin was flustered, not least at being addressed by anyone as important as the lord Undersheriff. 'There's places the village little'uns has used from our oldfathers' time, but those are for avoidin' tasks we doesn't want, or playin' games. If Baldred does not want to return, then the river is the answer, and a craft to take 'im downstream, even mayhap all the way to The Sea.' This last was said in a voice that held awe. 'The Sea', unseen, but spoken of by the shipmen that plied the Severn, was a thing so vast and unknown it was almost nightmarish, aided by the tales of serpents and storms that grew in the telling.

'So we have to decide which we think he has done.' Bradecote frowned.

'My lord, we knows Baldred has pined since Thorgar died, more 'n would be usual, even for a brother. Thing is, guilt would make it worse, and if Baldred feels all the deaths are his fault, then returnin' is not an option.' Walkelin was now wondering whether the boy had indeed put an end to himself rather than run away for good.

'This is true and fits better than just running off to return and be fussed over. He has seen how the loss of Thorgar has affected his mother. He would not increase her distress lightly. We look to the river. Whether that is for a craft, or just signs of Baldred, remains to be seen. We also need to consider whether

Selewine will have come to the same conclusion.'

'Best we assume yes, my lord.' Catchpoll looked grim.

'Then take us along the riverbank, at the places most likely, Merewin.' Bradecote beckoned Walkelin to lead the way, and under Merewin's direction they headed to the Severn bank, a little upstream of the village. Merewin dismounted and went to the reeds.

'My lord,' his voice was urgent and excited. 'There is usually a coracle kept ashore 'ere. It belonged to Selewine and Tofi's father and they fish from it. It is gone.'

'Well done, Merewin. A coracle is light enough for a lad to turn over and push to the water.'

'But if it was Selewine's, my lord, it would also be a place he would look.' Catchpoll pulled a face.

'And if he found it missing—'

'He would go to the village ferry boat, my lord, south o' the mill.' Merewin, feeling very much part of the chase, was eager.

The lord Sheriff's men encouraged their mounts and cantered along the riverside to where Walkelin had been ferried across the river. The little ferry craft was not upturned on the bank.

'If any are to use it to cross, they tells folk,' declared Merewin.

'Well, we knows that Selewine is on the way down-river, and after the lad. My lord, our problem is we are bank-bound.' Catchpoll did not look happy.

'But a horse can go faster than a man in a small rowing boat, Catchpoll, and—'

'Seek you a child?' A boat came round the slight bend of the river, being rowed upstream by a crew of sturdy men. The captain, a man with but one eye, hailed them with his hands cupped to his mouth.

'We do,' cried Bradecote in reply.

'Then I am to tell you the lad was plucked from the river by a boat going down to Gloucester, and is safe in Tewkesbury. I told his father the same when we passed him rowing downstream, so no need is there for further search. No doubt the father will bring him home by eventide.'

'Thank you.' Bradecote did not think they had time to waste explaining that they now needed to move with even greater urgency. He turned to Merewin.

'You have been most useful, but now we ride to Tewkesbury at speed. Your task is to return to Ripple and tell everyone you can find that they need not keep searching, and go also to Baldred's mother and tell her that Baldred is in Tewkesbury.'

'Yes, my lord.' Merewin slipped, a little relieved, from Snægl's back. He did not like the idea of riding at speed.

'And thank you.' Bradecote nodded his thanks and dismissal, and Merewin began to run back towards the village.

'You kick that beast of yours so hard your heels meet in the middle, if necessary, Walkelin, for if you do not keep up, we will leave you behind.' Bradecote was very serious. 'We ride to the Avon ferry and hope Selewine has not yet persuaded whoever holds Baldred in Tewkesbury that he has the right to take him,' He touched heel to flank of his own horse and it set off eagerly.

Chapter Fourteen

Swein Olafsson, whose craft it was and who had spotted the coracle, its capsize, and the drowning boy, looked at the shivering scrap of frightened life before him, and folded his arms.

'Bit young to fish alone, lad. I am guessing you took that coracle without permission, and there will be a mighty search once you are missed. Where are you from?'

Baldred did not reply, and just stared wide-eyed at the big riverman, with his tow-fair hair, muscled arms and piercing blue eyes that bored into him. Swein did not press for an answer, but had two empty sacks brought to rub some warmth into the child, and a cloak to wrap him in thereafter. Going back upriver was not an option, for he needed the tidal flow and the river's natural pace to get him and his goods to Gloucester without delay, but he could come alongside briefly in Tewkesbury, at the confluence of the Avon with the Severn, and set his 'catch' ashore there. By his guess, the boy had not come very far downriver, and kin would naturally search that way once the coracle had been missed. In time, there would be a reunion, and a mixture of admonition and relieved tears. Foolishness and daring were at their peak in the young, and a parent's role was to ensure that was kept in check enough for age to bring a little sense. Had it been his son, he would set a hand to his rump the once as he reminded him thieves were hanged and he was getting off lightly, offer to teach him how to wield a paddle better, and then hug the breath out of him.

Just before they reached Tewkesbury another vessel passed them, heading up the Severn, and Swein hailed it, and told them to tell any seeking a missing boy that he was safe and would be landed in Tewkesbury. That would be enough to allay worst fears and have kin swiftly in the town to find him. Then he ordered the steersman to bring the vessel alongside the Tewkesbury quayside.

As they threw a line ashore to tie up, another craft was in the process of unloading, and the quay busy. Swein ignored those with bent backs and loads across their shoulders and hailed a bearded man in a red, woollen cap, who was directing operations from the far end of the quay. The man turned and walked towards them, raising a hand in acknowledgement, but frowned also.

'Not expectin' you, Swein. Thought you was for Gloucester this downriver.'

'And I am, but I picked up a small cargo best set ashore as soon as may be.' Swein took Baldred, dwarfed by the riverman behind him, by the shoulders and pushed him a little forward. 'Found the boy in the water, drowning, and an upturned coracle. Must be from somewhere upstream, but not far by my reckoning. Not an experienced riverman, this one. I passed word to Hereward One-Eye, on his way upriver, to let any he sees searching the banks that the *barn* is well and will be found in Tewkesbury.'

'Fair enough, but what am I to do with 'im meantime?'

'Feed him, and give him a bed if none come for him before nightfall. He does not look as if he slept or ate for a while. I doubt you will need look after the lad for long.' Swein clearly thought his act of charity was complete.

'I doesn't know who . . . wait now. Yes, just the person. You give the child to me, and set that coracle ashore, and I will take 'im to Oldmother Holeway. She will keep 'im and fuss over 'im until kin come seekin' the lad.'

'Then I am for Gloucester, and mayhap a cargo down to Bristow. Do not look for me until a week is past.' Swein gave orders to let go fore and aft, and the steersman guided the craft gently out into the flow of the river.

The man in the red, woollen cap looked down at the child. Perhaps it was the recent brush with death which made the grey eyes look so haunted. He judged he could leave the unloading safely enough for as long as it would take him to get the boy to Oldmother Holeway, and it was not such fair weather as would find her out washing.

'Come with me, lad, and we will see you safe and warm.' He set a hand to the child's shoulder and felt the flinch at the contact. For a moment he wondered whether the child had run from a heavy-handed father, but it was no business of his, and if the old woman made it hers, then more the fool her.

* * *

Oldmother Holeway was a woman about whom all Tewkesbury had an opinion. An independent soul, long widowed, she had no time for fools or for gossip and little for the clergy or authority, but nothing was too much effort if it helped a child. Her own sons were gone from Tewkesbury, one as a man-at-arms in the service of Earl Robert of Gloucester, another gone from plying the Severn as a steersman to the bigger challenge of the Bristow Channel trade, and a third had married a girl she described as 'too mild and mousey', a tailor's daughter from Gloucester, and moved there to take up her father's craft and eventually business. If she regretted the lack of grandchildren in Tewkesbury to play about her skirts, she never spoke of it, and got on with living, mending clothes for pennies from those who could not afford new but wanted the repairs to be near invisible, for none plied a better needle in the town, and doing extra washing for folk in the summer months. Whilst she charged for these things, she was free with her advice, whether it was sought or not, which meant that she was revered, feared or loathed, but always respected.

Her cott was the last dwelling on the east side of the street that headed north to the crossing of the Avon to Mythe and up the hill towards Worcester, and stood barely a hundred paces from the junction where the markets were held. It was more modest in scale than its neighbour, or the new burgage plots on the west side that gave onto the channel that brought the Avon's waters to the abbey mill. Burgeoning wealth surrounded it, but did not touch it.

Baldred, cold, hungry, miserable and confused, did not register where he was led, until a door was opened and he looked up at an old lady with weathered skin, bright, twinkly brown eyes and a slightly hooked nose, whose challenging expression softened as she beheld the damp little boy set before her.

'One of the Severn boats picked this little sailor up out o' the river, Oldmother, from an upturned coracle. No name do we 'ave from the boy, and we thought of you afore the monks.'

'Good thing too. What he needs is warmth and food and motherin', not prayin' over in a tongue 'e cannot understand. Name and kin will come later. Just you make sure any who asks is directed to me.' She beamed at the boy and held out a hand whose finger joints were gnarled and arthritic.

The townsman smiled inwardly. He had guessed that any mention of otherwise taking the boy to the Benedictines would be sure to make the cantankerous old widow take him in without a thought. He pushed the child forward, and left for the riverside, firm in the belief that he had done a Christian deed that would offset a few minor sins.

'Now then, you come on in and let Oldmother find you a good, wool blanket and wrap you up better than those rivermen will 'ave done, by the looks of things, and a drop of mulled mead will do no harm either. Poor little soul, what made you leave hearthside and kin I wonder?' The old woman took the child's hand. She could see that though the boy was damp and cold his garments were not tattered, and he had been cared for, even if now he looked wraith-white and had dark rings beneath haunted eyes. She did not expect an answer and did not press for one, for that was a confidence that had to be won with kindness. She did as she had said and brought a blanket, poked her small hearth fire into a better glow, and left the poker in it to heat. She brought the beaker with a little mead in it, and then sat upon her stool and took up the blanket, opening it wide and invitingly, and smiled at Baldred.

'Come to Oldmother.'

It was a soft command he could not resist, and he came to be enfolded and pulled into the old woman's warm hold. Her voice soothed and cosseted, and he relaxed. The mulled mead was not to his taste, and he choked over it, but the afterglow warmed him from within, and that and his exhaustion eased him into a better sleep than he had enjoyed for days.

'Poor lamb.' The old woman smiled, and held him rather than attempt to lift him to the bed.

Selewine was confident that Baldred would be easy to find. He might even be still on the quayside, if nobody knew what to do with him, and he would have no reason to fear his village reeve, other than being cautious and respectful. He would accept returning to Ripple without question, and none would question Selewine's right to take him back to his worrying kinfolk. It had been his original intention to force Baldred to give up the location of Thorgar's hiding place for the silver and then drown the boy, so that he might say he had been unable to find him, but since folk in Tewkesbury would be able to say he had been there with the child, he would have to adapt that plan. He would say he had discovered the boy, and begun to row upstream to bring him home, which would be a tiring endeavour, even though it was little more than three miles down the Severn, but Baldred, fearing he was in great trouble for running away, was not thinking clearly and had stood up in the boat too early as they came towards the shore and then lost his footing, fallen in and drowned in the Severn, despite his own best endeavours. It would be annoying, since he would have to get wet, and it would mean a damp and cold return to Ripple, and carrying the weight of the body, but he would be thanked for trying his best and for at least bringing Baldred home. He might even be treated as a hero. He would then wait a couple of days before locating his prize, after the lord Sheriff's men had gone away. If they had not conclusively found Father Edmund's killer, why they had Wilf the Worrier, who had murdered his wife and owed a life for it, so, by Selewine's reckoning, they might as well put the blame for the other deaths on him. It was what he would do in their situation.

What Selewine had not at first considered was what he might thereafter do with the silver. So convinced was he in his own mind that it was his by right, he regretted that he might not flaunt it openly before his neighbours. However, not only would it raise new suspicions, it would also create jealousy and the risk that he himself might be robbed of it. He realised, sadly, that he would have to keep it hidden and known only to himself, and then use it little by little, piece by piece. If he took a gilt to market in Tewkesbury, he could claim the pig sold for more than expected and buy himself a cap of stoat fur for next winter. He had seen several of the wealthiest burgesses in Tewkesbury with fur hats. That would mark him out as more important than the other villagers. Over time he would use up his hoard and find reasons why he had extra coin to spend.

He felt happier when he thought of it as deceiving those who did not give him the respect he deserved. It was thus in a very positive mood that he shipped the oars and tied up the little boat in Tewkesbury, and as if to prove good fortune now shone upon him, a bearded man in a red cap strode towards him and actually asked if he was searching for a small, wet boy. This was so easy.

The child smelt of the river, but yet also retained that child-smell that Oldmother Holeway had almost forgotten. Her left arm was going to sleep, but she did not want to move it and wake the boy. Her mind drifted, just for a little while, back to when she had rocked her sons to sleep after some bad dream in the night-time. It was so long ago, that happiest of times. She was in the half-awake and half-asleep state where time does not exist, when her door was opened and a big, fair-haired man whose hair was receding from the front, filled the doorway.

'I am come to collect the child.' He sounded important, or rather, to Oldmother Holeway, self-important.

'Are you indeed. And just who might you be, Master Dunghill Cock?' There was something about the man she did not like, on top of resenting that he had come into her home without so much as a knock and request to enter.

Walkelin was sore of heel and hard of breath by the time they rode into Tewkesbury. Bradecote was focused on riding straight to the quay, but Catchpoll, whose serjeanting senses seemed to hear things others dismissed as 'nothing', pulled up short.

'My lord, listen.'

The first house to the left, a small and rather insignificant one, had the door half open, and there was an argument coming from within.

'Not our prob—' Bradecote began, thinking Catchpoll was simply alert to any domestic disturbance, but a determined female voice cried out very clearly.

'I doesn't care who you say you is, get out.'

'That be no man and wife fight,' Catchpoll growled, and dismounted.

'No.' Bradecote followed suit, and Walkelin was told to lead both animals to the abbey and return immediately.

Catchpoll sidled in through the half-open door, followed by Bradecote. An old woman was stood a pace back from the hearth, with Baldred in front of her, held back close to her skirts with a bony hand. Selewine the Reeve was level with the hearth and facing her.

'Afternoon, Oldmother,' Catchpoll nodded affably, 'We is come to relieve you of your unwanted guest.'

Selewine's head turned so fast it clicked.

'And who might you be?' Oldmother Holeway challenged the shrieval pair, though neither was looking at her, but rather at Selewine the Reeve. The way they did so meant that Selewine cast any thought of feigning innocence aside. His eyes did not move, but his hand did, and swiftly. There was a scrape of steel and he lunged, grabbing Baldred, waving the knife at the old woman's face, and then turned to face Bradecote and Catchpoll, with the knife held pricking-close to the little boy's white throat.

'That'll be far enough.' He sounded calm, even confident.

After all, he had a hostage.

'No good will come of another death, Selewine. Let the boy go.' Bradecote matched the calm tone.

'"Another death"? So is this – this man, a murderer?' Oldmother Holeway looked more disgusted than frightened. 'And he comes over my threshold and spins lies, not that I believed a word. Hmm.'

'Quiet, you old witch.' Selewine did not look at her.

'Well, you ain't the first to call me that, but I am a good Christian woman, for all that that fat priest of the parish grumbles about me.' Oldmother Holeway did not look chastened. She turned her gaze upon Catchpoll and made a shrewd guess. 'You'll be the Worcestershire serjeant and,' she looked Bradecote up and down, 'the lord Sheriff?'

'Undersheriff, Oldmother.' Bradecote would have smiled at her matter-of-factness had the situation not been as serious.

'There's a rope for you in Worcester, Selewine, and you will meet it, but there is still a choice.' Catchpoll's voice was silky soft, and the more threatening for it. 'You can let the boy go, come in quiet, and walk to the noose, or you uses that knife and they will need to carry you to it, and you will be beggin' them to get there faster.' There was nothing at all in the laws that mentioned the mistreatment of the condemned, but the murder of small children by a man in cold blood was a crime that had those who witnessed the hanging angered if the condemned looked hale and hearty. In such cases it was not unheard of for the closest kin of the victim to be given time with the chained killer in the cells, with the proviso that that might not end the life. A guard was left just to make sure they did not go too far. If the man was lucky, it would be the father, who would use his fists and beat him. If he was unlucky, it was the mother. As a young serjeanting-apprentice, Catchpoll had seen a woman, a quiet soul who would not raise her voice to any, shred the back of the man who had raped and killed her little girl, using the comb she had used on her hair, with all the tines sharpened till they acted like a bear's claws. She had screamed curses as she did so and for so long she lost her voice. Catchpoll was convinced that Hell was like that cell that night.

'I will not go to Worcester.' Selewine shook his head. 'You will not risk the boy's life.'

'Why did you kill them?' It was Bradecote's question, for he did not think it likely Selewine would leave Tewkesbury alive, whether they managed to prevent him killing Baldred or not, and it was better to have the confession at least to present before William de Beauchamp.

'It was mine by right, The Priest's Treasure. On my land for years, and I am reeve. When I learnt it was found, from my Osberht, I knew I must act. Then I heard that Father Ambrosius was gone across the river and saw Thorgar leaving the village on a morning too wet for field work, and I knew it was my time. When Father Edmund went to the church in the afternoon, I slipped into the priests' house and searched it, but there was nothin', not a single piece of it. I went to find Father Edmund in the church, and feared some other had word of it and beat 'im for it, but he said the chalice were gone and he knew nothin' of the rest. I believed that, but he would have told of The Treasure and everyone would know, so I ended 'im.'

'And Oldmother Agatha? She was no threat.'

'But she recognised me, even though I spoke not a word. I thought the bag of silver went there with the cat, but it were not there, nor with Agnes, as thinks she is more important than any man in Ripple. Turns out 'twere this one 'ere,' and his knife pricked just enough for Baldred to whimper, 'who knows where it is. Now, I has finished speakin'. You just step right back against the far wall, and me and the boy will leave. If you doesn't do as I say, I will slit his throat, and you would not want to tell 'is mother you made that happen.'

'If you harm the child, Selewine—' Bradecote began.

'The serjeant can keep 'is empty threats and you will be wantin' to string me up for the priest and the old woman anyways, so that makes no difference. So move. There is no other way.' Selewine exuded confidence. After all, he had the knife at the child's throat, and nobody would risk him executing his threat.

At this moment Walkelin arrived, slightly out of breath and fearing he had missed any excitement. His entry was a surprise, and drew Selewine's focus a little from the two sheriff's men. Both began to move, but were not fast enough. What all the men had done was completely forget the old woman, which any inhabitant of Tewkesbury would have told them was a mistake. In that instant, Oldmother Holeway was not a frightened old woman or a comforting grandmother, but an avenging angel armed not with a heavenly sword but a serviceable poker. Her aged bones did not normally permit fluidity in bending, but in this moment she bent, snatched up the poker and wielded it with all her power at the side of

Selewine's head, without so much as a pause. It felled him on the spot, the knife loosening from his hold and falling to the floor as he crumpled at the knees and tipped back to fall with his head cracking on the hearthstone.

'There's always another way.' She then ignored the fallen man and stared at Bradecote. 'No man stands in my home, at my fireside, and threatens a poor mite, and then gets away with it.'

Catchpoll knelt by Selewine. The blow might have been enough to kill him, for the skull was clearly dented and the wound clear, but it was the hearthstone that had certainly been the end of him. His eyes stared to the rafters, and saw nothing.

'He is dead?' Bradecote did not really expect the reeve to have breath in him.

'He is, my lord.' Catchpoll sounded slightly regretful, for it had been a death too swift for one who had committed two murders, attempted a third and intended a fourth.

'Well, 'twas God gave me the strength, assuredly, me bein' but a poor, feeble old woman, in fear of 'er life and a poor child's,' declared Oldmother Holeway, still looking at the undersheriff, and so far from feeble or afraid that it was almost laughable. 'Would the Law say as I could not defend myself?'

Bradecote held the stare. She had not been afraid for herself, but she had acted to save Baldred, and whilst it was a pity Selewine would not face trial and hang, the child's life was more important.

'No, Oldmother, it would not. But this is Tewkesbury, and not our jurisdiction but the lord Sheriff of Gloucester's, so if any ask, the Reeve of Ripple was killed by us as he tried to escape with the child as hostage. You understand this?'

'Aye, my lord. I does.' She nodded acceptance and perhaps, just perhaps, grudging thanks for preventing any repercussions.

Baldred, who had remained standing stock-still even after the cold steel of the blade had been removed from his pale throat, now trembled, his eyes wide and staring, and then he began to sob. Oldmother Holeway, abandoning both poker and belligerent defiance, gathered him to her and stroked his head, murmuring soothing words, but the child was not calmed. Bradecote let him weep for a little while, and then spoke.

'Why did you run away, Baldred?' He asked, gently.

Baldred twisted in the old woman's tender hold and looked, not at Bradecote, who was too important a person to address, but at Catchpoll, who was dusting off his knees. Catchpoll was power Baldred could understand.

"Tis my fault, Thorgar is dead, all my fault. I killed my brother by disobeyin' 'im. He said as I must not tell anyone of the treasure, but I did, I did. I was not goin' to, but Osberht kept sayin' as I were a *nithing*, and Father and Thorgar just ox followers, and he would be the reeve one day after his father and . . . and I told of the silver, and the cup, and Thorgar givin' it to Father Edmund, because I's not a *nithing*. Is I?' He ended unsure, wondering if in part the fate of his brother had been a judgement for pride.

'No, lad.' Catchpoll's face was very serious, and Baldred looked fearful, despite the answer. Catchpoll, reluctantly, adopted Bradecote's way with children and crouched back down, groaning a little as his knees objected to the posture. Walkelin, being helpful, thrust Oldmother Holeway's single stool forward so that Catchpoll could at least take the weight off them. He received a look that mingled thanks and annoyance. 'You listen to me, for I have more years than you could even count, and I am the lord Sheriff's Serjeant of the Shire.' Catchpoll intentionally gave himself the grandest title that came to his mind. 'First of all, you did not kill your brother. What killed him was *wyrd*, the malice of Selewine here, and a bit the foolishness of folk as forget to think like people and just think like foolish sheep. As for bein' important, well you remember we all needs food, and without a ploughman to guide the oxen and the plough there is no sowin' and no harvest. So a ploughman is just as important as a reeve, or even a serjeant. What is more, whatever you do, the thing is to try and be the best at it. You aim to be the best ploughman you can be, just as Underserjeant Walkelin here,' he nodded towards Walkelin, 'aims to be the best serjeant, and the lord Bradecote the best undersheriff of a shire.' Both Walkelin and Bradecote noted that by omitting himself he was effectively saying he was already the best serjeant. 'Now, this Osberht is Selewine's son, yes?' Catchpoll wanted it made absolutely clear. He did not want to discover there was some other lad of the same name in the village.

'Aye. Two years older than me, and a bit more, and very proud. He is always laughin' at me and my little brothers, and prods us with sticks, saying we is stupid oxen.' Baldred's sense of grievance was strong. 'And oxen is not stupid.'

'We will speak with Osberht, never you fear. But first we will take you home to your mother and sister, who are worried witless. They need you more 'n ever now Thorgar is gone.' Catchpoll slapped his hands to his knees in a gesture, which might look as if a conclusion to his oration, but was actually to add support as he stood, grimacing as he did so. He looked at the old woman. 'You heard none of that.'

She gave him stare for stare, and a slow smile grew. 'Old 'uns is deaf, and I possess many years, Serjeant, so I can be as deaf as needed with ease. I also possess good wits, which most do not. My question to you is what cause you would 'ave me give for that,' she pointed at Selewine's body, 'comin' in and seekin' the child's death?'

'The tale you should tell to Tewkesbury, Oldmother, is that he came seeking the child so that he might stand in good stead with the boy's sister, who he wanted to wed, and we found him here and confronted him over his killing of the priest and old woman. He took the child hostage simply to avoid being taken for those killings.' Bradecote thought that close enough to the truth to work well, and had already decided that the best thing Ripple could do was never talk of treasure again.

'Fair enough. The boy needs 'is mother most, and I wants the body off my hearthstone so I can scrub it. You'll be goin', my lord, yes?'

'We will, once Underserjeant Walkelin fetches our horses.' Bradecote turned to Walkelin.

'I want you to go to the quay and tell whoever seems in charge there that the Ripple ferry and the coracle are to be put in the next boat going upriver, and set ashore where the boat normally lies, at the lord Sheriff's command. The rivermen will all know the place. Then collect the horses and meet us back here.'

'Yes, my lord.' There was just a hint of feeling hard done by in Walkelin's voice, for he had only just come from leaving the horses at the abbey stables and was going to feel a fool going straight back to collect them again, but left immediately. There was a slightly awkward silence, for everything that was needful had been said. Then Oldmother Holeway remembered Baldred had not eaten, and busied about finding him a rind of cheese and a hunk of reasonably fresh bread, which she pressed upon him and encouraged him to eat, cajoling him when he looked reluctant, for he was at the stage where he was ravenously hungry and yet felt sick at the thought of eating. She eventually persuaded him by dint of saying how upset his poor mother would be if he fainted from sheer hunger on her doorstep. He was finishing the crust when Walkelin knocked and announced that all was arranged at the quay, and that the horses were ready outside.

'Remember what I said about what happened, Oldmother, and . . . ' Bradecote paused for a moment, 'the Law thanks you.'

'Never thought I would hear those words, and no mistake. Pity they cannot be known by them as thinks themselves so high and mighty in this town.' The old woman gave a twisted smile and an obeisance, which was far less grudging than she usually showed to any in authority.

Bradecote took Baldred and set him upon the big grey horse, climbing into the saddle behind him, and Walkelin and Catchpoll dragged Selewine's body from the hearth and outside to sling over Snægl's back and tie in place, and then Walkelin threw Serjeant Catchpoll up into the saddle and was given a hand to climb up behind. They wanted to be back in Ripple before eventide, but they would not be travelling at speed.

Chapter Fifteen

Wystan the Wheelwright's son was a young man who took his duty seriously, but waiting as guard over Wilf the Worrier felt more like idleness and a dereliction, when Osgyth's little brother was missing. Without even thinking, what Wystan had taken on out of kindness and friendship with Thorgar had transformed overnight into a desire to do whatever he could to ease Osgyth's burden, though he realised that telling her so would not be wise.

Wilf just sat and looked as though he had stopped everything but breathing.

After what seemed an age, there was a knock at the door, and Father Ambrosius came in. Wilf got up so suddenly he staggered, and Wystan rose also, in alarm, but Wilf cast himself down at the priest's feet and begged to make confession. Father Ambrosius looked down upon him and smiled sadly.

'Of course, my son.'

Wystan could not remain, he knew that, but he made the priest promise not to leave until one of the lord Sheriff's men returned, and to tell them why he, Wystan, had left his post, and that he was going to find Osgyth and help her look for Baldred. Hearing the touch of eagerness in the young man's voice, Father Ambrosius hid a small smile and promised faithfully to remain.

Eventually it was Walkelin who came, and with the news that caused the priest to raise his hands in jubilation and give praise to Heaven, though it was tempered by the explanation of what had happened, and Selewine's death.

'That his life would end soon, by the Law, was inevitable, but this, with no chance to confess and repent, is sad news.'

Next door, there were more tears than hallelujahs. When Bradecote opened the door, Baldred just stood on the threshold and stared at his mother.

'My baby! Oh, my Baldred!' cried Winflæd, standing and holding out her good hand. The twins, huddled together for comfort, began to cry, and then Winflæd began to sob in great gasps, her fallen face distorting the more.

'I had hoped all the searching parties would have been stood down and returned, mistress, but Osgyth is not here. Do you know which direction she took?' Bradecote had to repeat the question to get an answer.

He rode, for the light was still good enough and he could both see further and be seen. He found one group still calling Baldred's name and sent them home rejoicing, if tired, and then found Osgyth and Wystan in the reed beds some way north of the mill. She looked very cold. Her cheeks were pinched, her nose scarlet, and when she came to dry land her feet were white. When she looked up at him and he smiled, she gave a soft gasp and simply fell to the ground in a faint.

'Osgyth!' Wystan stumbled in the muddy ground as he rushed to her side.

'It will be a mixture of the cold and the shock,' remarked Bradecote calmly, dismounting and removing his cloak from about his shoulders. 'Here, wrap her in this, and then let us waken her and get her up onto my horse.' His boots squelched in the mud. 'Do not forget her shoes.'

The pair patted her hands and cheeks in a restrained and self-conscious manner, and Bradecote was struck by the thought that Agnes the Healer would have shaken her head at their ineptitude. However, the girl did stir, and between them they got her up behind Bradecote and persuaded her to hold on. He did not think that she would manage at anything faster than a walking pace, so they returned her home so slowly that by the time they got there she was asking questions and urging him to go faster, without any thought of sounding deferential or even respectful. He smiled at that. When they reached the door, Wystan held her at the waist as she slid down from the big grey, to which she did not object, and Bradecote trotted off to stable his mount before returning to ask the important question that remained to be asked.

Bradecote let the sister make much of the prodigal's return, but when the tears and exclamations quietened a little, he spoke.

'Baldred has told us he saw the silver Thorgar dug up in the field, and revealed to Osberht, when goaded, that Father Edmund had it for safekeeping. But we know that Father Edmund only had the cup.'

'It came out that way and I did not want to make it seem I was not sure. Osberht would not have believed me.'

'But you know where the other part of the hoard has been hidden?' Bradecote made the question one that expected a positive answer, and posed it gently.

'Yes, my lord.'

'So where will it be found, Baldred?'

'In the ox stall. He hid it in a cloth hung on the wall behind the harness. Nobody ever goes in with them, only us.'

Bradecote said nothing for a moment. The silver that had brought death and injury had been within feet of them every time they attended their horses.

'Well I never.' The voice was Agnes the Healer's, and she had entered quietly. A bandage showed about her brow from beneath her coif, but she looked strong enough. 'I decided I was in no greater danger 'ere than at home, and more use,' she explained. 'And the mists are cleared a bit more from my poor head too. Selewine it were as came to my door this morn, and Selewine as tried to do away with me.'

'He is dead.' Bradecote said, simply.

'And no loss,' was her response. 'Now, what can I do for Baldred?'

Whilst Bradecote took Baldred back to his mother, Catchpoll went to knock upon Tofi's door. He could not remember whether Tofi's wife had been one of the searchers, but some folk had to remain and look after the younger children of the village, and he was in luck. The door was opened with some caution, for as far as the woman knew, there was still a murderer in Ripple. Catchpoll saw the subtle change in her face when she saw it was him. He was more used to the reverse in Worcester.

'Serjeant? What news?' She sounded tired, but there was compassion in her voice. She felt for Winflæd in her distress, her own mind reaching out and touching, then recoiling from, the known depths of fear and panic that she had felt as a mother when a child was lost, even for a short time.

'Baldred is found, and is back safe with his mother.'

'God be praised!'

'Your husband's brother, Selewine, is dead, however, and it was he who killed the priest and Oldmother Agatha, and tried to kill your healer and Baldred also.'

'Selewine?' The woman crossed herself, not thinking of his soul, but that he had lived right next door and might have harmed Mildred or even her younger siblings.

'It means his boys are orphaned.' Catchpoll kept it to that, in part to see how she reacted.

'I have Frewin here with mine.' She looked him straight in the eye. 'I do not know what Tofi will say, but in this I will prevail. Frewin can stay with us. He is kin and a sweet child, gentle as his poor mother was, and never seemed happy once she was gone. Not surprising, when you look at Selewine, or his half-brother Osberht, who is his father's image by Selewine's intent. A hard lad, and I would not take him, not him, for he has bullied not just his little brother but the other younger ones of the village. He thinks himself near a man, since he comes to the tithing by year's end, and went with Alsi Longshanks and Tofi, in the search.

'Do you want me to tell Frewin?' Catchpoll accepted the woman's reasoning and did not think it foolish. It was good enough of her to take the younger child; another mouth to feed, clothe and raise, though kinship would play a part. It would be that, he guessed, that she would use first with Tofi.

'No, I will do it. It will upset 'im a little, because he cannot imagine any other life than the one that ends now, but he will not grieve much, bless 'im.'

Catchpoll simply nodded, and then thanked her, though she raised her hand to halt him and shook her head.

''Tis what any would do.' She was wrong, but it showed her character. Catchpoll felt she deserved better than Tofi as a husband. It did leave the issue of Osberht, but that was solved, unexpectedly, by Father Ambrosius, who volunteered to look after the lad for a while, since he was kindred.

It could not be said that the men Catchpoll detailed next morning to go up to the Old Road and disinter Thorgar's body from its dishonourable grave looked happy. He made sure Tofi was one of them, since it was known that he had 'encouraged' his brother to act and hang the man, though Catchpoll had no doubt this had been simply to pressure the reeve, and the others were those who had made up the original burial party. They would know how deep to dig, and when to dig gently so as not to damage the body further, for the sake of their own stomachs rather than the good of the deceased ploughman.

'But Thorgar's been in the ground the better part of a week,' complained one man, looking a little green.

'Well, you be thankful you is not Wilf the Worrier, for

Eadild was put underground last autumn.' Catchpoll had no sympathy. He had already decided he would oversee Wilf's digging, and leave Thorgar to Walkelin's supervision, since Walkelin was not so hardy of stomach.

At the thought of this, two of the men crossed themselves, and no further complaint was made. He sent them with spades and shovels, a length of cloth, a plank provided by Pryderi, and a handcart. Walkelin led the way, looking sombre but not worried, since he had been told he was not going to find anything worse than he had seen in his time as serjeanting-apprentice.

The grave, with the noose still pinned to it with withy pegs, was not a full-depth grave, having been dug in some haste towards the end of a day, and without ceremony. It was little more than three feet deep, and the men were cautious after three spade spit depths, feeling the division between the natural compacted soil and the disturbed earth that had been thrown back over Thorgar and not yet settled. When they felt they were deep enough to be close to touching the body they halted and looked at Walkelin.

'Now what?'

'You put 'im in, so you get 'im out.' Walkelin, trying his best to sound like Serjeant Catchpoll, schooled his features into a mixture of grim and unconcerned.

'What if we digs too deep with our spades?' The least happy man whined.

'A spade cannot feel. Get down on your knees and dig by hand, and in that position you can pray for Thorgar the better as you goes.' In truth, Walkelin felt for the ploughman he had never met. He was an innocent victim in all this, yet had been sent unshriven to an unconsecrated grave. Now he was to be restored, if not like a Lazarus, then at least to a grave where he would choose to be, and with many godly brothers who would pray for his soul.

'We will feel the skin.' The man was horrified.

'You felt it but a few days past, and it won't be much changed. Now get on with it, since the lord Undersheriff will be accompanying the body to Tewkesbury and will not want to spend all forenoon waitin'.' Mentioning the lord Bradecote ought to speed things up, Walkelin thought, and he was right.

Very carefully, and initially working down where the arms were judged to be, the men began to scoop away the earth. Cotte and then the hands came to light, the skin greyish-pale and dirty, but not the nightmare the men had conjured up for themselves. Nobody wanted to uncover the face, but eventually Tofi, feeling that, as at least acting-reeve, he should show courage, gently wiped away the earth as if drying soil tears. The eyes had been closed, so Thorgar did not stare at them, but they stared at him, remembering that he had said his death was upon their souls.

'Will Thorgar haunt us?' whispered one man, crossing himself.

'Not the sort of man to do that, not Thorgar. Forgivin', that is what he were.' It was more an expressed hope than a strong belief, but it gave the diggers a little impetus to take up the body carefully and lay it on the plank. Walkelin shrouded it with the cloth and then it was placed on the handcart.

'Tofi. You go to Thorgar's family and tell Osgyth we is ready. You will find the lord Bradecote there also. We will await him.

Tofi obeyed the command without a word, and Walkelin, who had expected some demur, wondered if his air of authority was more impressive than he thought.

Wilf the Worrier's garden was not so large a space that Catchpoll could not have eventually studied it enough to make a good guess as to where the body would be found, but Wilf was almost eager to show the place. Catchpoll looked carefully at the earth before spade was set to it, in case the knowledge would ever prove of use in the future. There were cabbages planted close by, but upon close inspection the earth was slightly domed for the length of the grave location, and there seemed a few more small stones. That made sense, since the underlying land was gravelly. The cabbages did not seem to have suffered from what lay beside them.

The digging up of Eadild was done without conversation, though Wilf the Worrier was repeating the *Nunc Dimittis* over and over under his breath as he dug as though the prayer would protect him from seeing what was to come. Catchpoll instructed him to dig wider than the grave cut, which took longer but would enable the board, made by Pryderi chopping the legs off the table from Wilf's home, to be slid under the remains. The bed coverlet would keep all but Catchpoll and Wilf from seeing the body, and the sexton and his lad, who had been very busy these last few days, had begun digging a grave in the churchyard at first light so that the committal could take place immediately.

Serjeant Catchpoll had a fair idea what he would encounter, but Wilf gasped and then wept when the corpse was revealed. The shape was Eadild's, the clothing was Eadild's, but the skin was dirty grey where it remained at all on cheek and chin, and the lips had receded a little to show the teeth in a macabre grimace, though she did not stare up at him, for the eyes were but voids. There was nothing that reminded Wilf of her person other than the plait of hair that curled from under her coif and lay upon her breast.

'I deserve what is comin' Serjeant,' confessed Wilf, between sobs. 'God will be merciful to my wife, and I can but pray that my remorse is known. Father Ambrosius says as where it is true and deep, God may yet not send a soul into the Eternal Fire.'

'Well, let us take your wife to a decent grave in holy ground as a mark of that remorse. You lift the foot end and I will take the head end.' Catchpoll grunted as he bent to lift the tabletop, but the body was not heavy, and the two men made their way slowly from the garden patch to the churchyard, and the sexton went to fetch Father Ambrosius. It had been agreed that after the burial, Wilf would remain in the church with the priest. Catchpoll stood at the graveside for the words to be said over the woman, and then went to Thorgar's house to report to the lord Undersheriff.

When Tofi arrived with news of Thorgar, his mother covered her face and hugged her remaining sons close. Osgyth, grim-faced and controlling her emotions, insisted that she would follow her brother to the monks.

'I promised I would see justice for my brother. This is the

end of it, my lord. My first steps was to Worcester, and my last shall be to Tewkesbury.'

'I have no right to prevent you, and would not if I did, Osgyth.' Bradecote gave her what was her due. 'You have done as much, if not more, than any brother could have asked of you.'

The lord Sheriff's men rode at the walk behind the handcart that was pushed to Tewkesbury, while the men who had dug the grave took it in turns to do the pushing. It was a little over four miles, and took till noontide, but luckily for them it was downhill for much of the way to Mythe and the ferry crossing, and the ferryman, who removed his cap as a mark of respect as he took the cart across the river, would not take payment for it, or Osgyth.

'A good man, Thorgar. Nothin' I can do for 'im but this, and I is glad to do it.'

The solemn cortège was viewed with mild curiosity by those of Tewkesbury who saw it pass and who crossed themselves piously. When it reached the gate of the abbey, Brother Porter bade them wait, and sent a young novice to inform Father Abbot and the Master of Novices of the arrival.

Abbot Roger came with measured tread, and an expression that was both sorrowful but also welcoming. Osgyth, presented to him, dipped low, but was surprised when he stepped closer and offered his hand as she rose back up.

'My daughter, I can see that you grieve, and understand that grief, but let your heart rejoice, for your brother is completing the instruction he had from God to come and join us here in this House. He had hopes of singing in the choir with his brethren, but it is the will of God that he sings rather with the angels in Heaven. His earthly remains will be laid alongside those of our community who have already left this imperfect world and journey to Glory, and we will hold him in our prayers as if he had been with us from novitiate to final profession of vows. I can tell you, truthfully, that I have rarely met a man whose being was lit by the Holy Spirit as much as your brother. Tell this also to your mother.'

'I will, Father. I promise.' Osgyth, whose eyes were wet, managed a whispered response.

'Then will you trust him to us now, and return home with hope instead of misery?'

'Yes, Father, and I will try.'

'Good,' Abbot Roger looked then at Bradecote, who had dismounted at the gate and was holding his own horse.

'My lord, the innocence of Thorgar, whom you bring home to us, is obviously proven. That is no surprise to me, but I am glad, nonetheless. I prayed for your endeavours.'

'Thank you, Father. It is proven, and the man who killed the priest and an old woman in his greed, and tried to kill another and a child, is himself dead. It was the village reeve, Selewine.'

'Pity it is that a man can be dragged so deep in sin by Satan.' The churchman sighed. 'We will pray in Christian charity for his soul also, for he is one for whom many, many prayers are needed.'

Tofi, who had opened his mouth, thinking to announce his kinship and hope of elevation to his brother's position, thought the better of it, hearing these words.

'And the silver that proved the temptation, my lord? Is it still sought?'

'No, Father. It is found and will not cause further sin. Ripple seeks it no more.'

'That is good. I would have you give my respects to the lord Sheriff, and I will give thanks that all has been resolved.' Abbot Roger bowed his head, and then directed two Brothers, who had appeared from the infirmary with a stretcher, to take Thorgar's body to the mortuary chapel.

The Ripple party set off back the way they had come, though Osgyth was persuaded to ride up behind Serjeant Catchpoll on the return journey, for now that nothing more could be done, the strain of the last days began to take its toll, and she looked suddenly more the girl and less the woman. As they reached the last houses of Tewkesbury, Bradecote glanced to the right as a door opened. An old woman with twinkling brown eyes and hooked nose, and carrying a basket, bent her knees and head, just a little, and Bradecote acknowledged Oldmother Holeway with a small smile and the hint of a nod.

It was towards the latter end of the afternoon when they reached Ripple at last, and the men dispersed to their homes. Bradecote was mulling over something, and also wanted to speak to the whole village, which would either mean them leaving their labours early or the shrieval trio riding back to Worcester in the dark with very little moon to guide them, which he did not want to do, so he decided that they would stay in Ripple one last night. He apologised to Father Ambrosius for the inconvenience caused, but the priest just smiled and shook his head.

'I am happy enough, my lord, though I do fear Osberht will still be a resentful presence. Little Frewin will do well with Tofi's wife to mother him, and he is in his poor mother's mould, not Selewine's. Osberht's mother was more mettlesome, and Osberht has had his father's influence far longer. I think he will resent his uncle being reeve, even though he knows he is too young by many years for the role. He needs a little time and patience, and perhaps being shown that kindness and charity are not weakness. Then I will take him to Tewkesbury, not to the Brothers, but to see if one of the craftsmen will take him as an apprentice. There is a saddler, a good but firm man, whose apprentice died at Candlemas as I recall, and he would be glad of a replacement. Tofi is inheriting enough to give a little, even if it is just to get the boy off his hands and away from Ripple. My new house companion, the little black cat, does not approve of Osberht, nor he her, alas. I hope she does not scratch him.'

Bradecote had come to a decision, and it was one which sat well with both his subordinates when he revealed it. They arose with Father Ambrosius at his first prayers, and Walkelin was sent to knock upon every door, before they headed to their labours in field or mill, telling them to gather before the oak where Thorgar had been hanged. The tree, barely a week after its unfurling leaves had dripped tearfully over Thorgar's hanging, now wore its fresh green mantle with pride, the youthful leaves susurrating in the morning breeze, making it even more alive. It had been 'The Village Oak' for centuries, had been a strong tree before any treasure of greater value than its acorn-children had been buried in the parish. Looking at it, Bradecote was struck by the thought that it would be unfortunate if it was now renamed 'The Hanging Tree'. A stronger gust made it rustle its agreement. He sat astride his big, steel grey horse to address the village before the Law departed. Walkelin had Wilf the Worrier, hands bound, tied at the end of a length of rope, which a few murmured would be the rope he dangled from in Worcester, though in fact it was just a length of rope that Catchpoll had nigh on insisted upon so that he would be led from the village in a way they would all remember.

'Once up on the Old Road, we can put Wilf the Worrier up behind Walkelin, since otherwise we would take twice as long to reach Worcester, and the man will be no bother. Always best to leave a memory of power, one that says that the Law does not tolerate bein' broken and finds them as does it. Makes folk think a little afore they does somethin' that brings us back, and I prefers my own wife's pottage and my own bed of a night.'

Catchpoll was right about Wilf the Worrier. The man was no problem to bring in. He had made a long confession to Father Ambrosius, and seemed eased by it. In fact, he seemed without worry, which struck Bradecote as odd until he thought about it and realised that the man's life had been one of expecting the worst and worrying about the possibilities, and now there was just one certainty and no new things to worry over. In a strange way, Wilf the Prisoner was a free man.

Surveying the faces before him, Bradecote saw the 'flock' of Ripple, though now he could identify many by name, and also those who were no sheep at all, such as the maid Osgyth with young Wystan just behind her shoulder, very slightly protective, Agnes the Healer, arms folded to show she would listen, but grudgingly, and Dustig the Miller, with his family called from the mill. This was just a small community where the seasons passed and regulated their lives by sun, rain and frost and antagonisms between neighbours were no greater than grumbles and the occasional hunched shoulder. The majority of these simple-living people were easily led, but not fools. They made decisions, important decisions, about whom they wed, when they sowed and when they harvested their garden produce, but the scope of their lives never needed them to think beyond such things, and, when faced with questions outside their experience, they did not know how to find answers and would agree with anyone who voiced an opinion with conviction. It was, again, something which set himself, Catchpoll and Walkelin apart from the majority, for they spent much of their time seeking answers and making decisions that affected life and death very literally.

Just under a week ago these people had listened to their reeve, a murderer, and collectively condemned an innocent man of whom they knew no ill. Realisation of that was visible on some faces, combining regret and guilt. What they needed now was an end to the fear, confusion and distrust of the last few days, and indeed an absolution. For the latter they would have Father Ambrosius, who had been right to worry over the effect of 'The Treasure', but for the rest it was up to him, the lord Undersheriff, to return them to their safe and mundane world. He spoke authoritatively.

'What has happened cannot be undone, but some of the damage can be lessened. Thorgar, a godly and innocent man, has gone at the last to the monks of Tewkesbury as he was called by God to do, and will be prayed for as they do for all the Brothers now departed. The lord Bishop will decide who will be reeve, but since it has run from father to son for some generations it is most likely that Tofi, who will act as reeve in the meantime, will be confirmed in Selewine's place. To him I advise learning from his brother's mistakes in the way he led the community, and to listen to Father Ambrosius. Ulf Shortfinger's loss is great, but the family will not face hardship because of it. Thorgar's family have lost the man of the house, and would face a difficult future but for the kindness of Wystan, so treat him as one of you, not an outsider.' Bradecote paused for a moment and let that sink in.

'It was also Thorgar's plan that when he left his family to join the Benedictines the part of the hoard that was not the Church's would go to his mother. The Law, which he did not know, says that all treasure that is buried to be retrieved and not then collected by those who buried it, belongs to the King, unless it is proven to belong to kin of whoever owned it. The chalice went rightly to the lord Bishop, as successor to the bishop who gave it to the parish, and the King could claim all the rest. However, the King's Justice was not served when Thorgar was hanged, and therefore it is my ruling, as his representative, that the items of silver that were adornment should be presented to the lord Sheriff for King Stephen, but the silver pennies should go to Thorgar's mother, Winflæd, as compensation, *wergild*. It is not a great deal, but will buy geese and fowl, or other livestock, which is probably what Thorgar expected. This is not her gain, for her loss far exceeds it, and nobody will begrudge it.' His eyes fixed on Tofi first, and then ran over the others. There were nods, and even a hesitant cry of ''Tis right'.

Bradecote made no mention of Father Edmund. He was forgotten by all but those who could not forget, at least not yet. Time, their mothers, and perhaps Agnes the Healer's balm of gentle good sense, would help that particular healing.

'That is all I have to say. It is spring, and planting time. Return to that, and do not let these events taint Ripple.' As a valediction, Bradecote did not think it inspiring, but it was enough. He felt the collective breath taken by the crowd as he released them from listening, and, glancing at Catchpoll and Walkelin, turned his horse about and set it walking out of the village.

The Ripple folk did not move or speak, as they watched the three riders, with Wilf the Worrier trailing behind, head towards the Old Road, and only when they were lost to sight did Tofi call them to take up their bags of seed and their tools, and head to the field.

Sarah Hawkswood describes herself as a 'wordsmith' who is only really happy when writing. She read Modern History at Oxford and first published a non-fiction book on the Royal Marines in the First World War before moving on to mediaeval mysteries set in Worcestershire. She also writes Regency romances under the name Sophia Holloway.

@bradecote
bradecoteandcatchpoll.com